Damn Yankee

OTHER BOOKS BY
Troy D. Nooe

THE FRANKIE MCKELLER SERIES:
MURDER IN MYRTLE BEACH

The Ocean Forest

Long-Legged Rosie

Damn Yankee

MURDER IN MYRTLE BEACH

BY **Troy D. Nooe**

A **FRANKIE MCKELLER MYSTERY**

Last Call Press
Myrtle Beach, SC

Copyright © 2012 by Troy D. Nooe
Cover painting by Joe Burleson
Book design by Luci Mott
Originally Published by Ingalls Publishing Group, Inc

ISBN-13: 978-0692581902
ISBN-10: 0692581901

Library of Congress Cataloging-in-Publication Data
(from Ingalls Publishing Group, Inc. edition)

Nooe, Troy D.
Damn yankee : murder in Myrtle Beach / by Troy D. Nooe.
p. cm.
"A Frankie McKeller Mystery."
ISBN 978-1-932158-97-7
1. Private investigators--Fiction. 2. World War, 1939-1945--Veterans--Fiction. 3. Murder--Investigation--Fiction. 4. Myrtle Beach (S.C.)--Fiction. I. Title.
PS3614.O64D36 2012
813'.6--dc22
2012006559

Acknowledgments

I WOULD LIKE TO THANK all of the people who helped to launch The Frankie McKeller Mystery Series with their encouragement, enthusiasm and unwavering support. None of this would be possible without the many selfless people who went out of their way to help insure the success of my little project.

It would be impossible to name all of the wonderful people who were in my corner when I needed them, both old friends and new. That said, I would like to give a special thanks to Dad for all of his advice and first line editing skills. To Laura, for taking care of the technical web stuff I was too dense to figure out. To Swavek for giving me the platform to spread the word. To Rob, Dino and Holland for all their help dotting the i's and getting the details right. To Mike Kennedy for keeping me mobile.

To Audrey, Melissa, Robin, Nancy, John, Tom, Kristen, Debbie, Rick, Rudy, Eric, Cheeseburger Bill, Dierdre, Steve, Natalie, Billy, Damon, Mike, Dusty and Rachel, Mack, Stacy, Carey, Paul, Ron, Jamie, Elena and Momma Gargano for seeing this through from inception to the next leg of our journey and for believing in what I was trying to do.

To my entire family for not kicking me out of the clan years ago.

To my great friends at Fosters Cafe and The Marriott Grand Dunes for going above and beyond with their never ending support.

To my kids, Emily, Gregory and Andrew for putting up with your weird old father.

To Tom and the staff of Litchfield Books for giving me a running start.

To Bob and Barbara Ingalls, Judy Geary and all the great people at The Ingalls Publishing Group for helping me bring my vision to life.

To the terrific people of Myrtle Beach for embracing my little idea and taking Frankie into your homes.

To everyone who I'm sure I forgot to mention.

And Rich.

Dedicated to my Aunt Betty Jean Zimmerman.
You bought me my first real book.
It was a Hardy Boys Mystery and I still
remember the plot to this day.
See what you started?

Damn Yankee

Chapter One

THEY have a saying in the South. A Yankee is someone who comes down from the North to visit. A Damn Yankee is one that comes down and stays.

That would be me.

A strange turn of events landed me in Myrtle Beach, South Carolina, a long haul from my hometown of Baltimore. I'm not complaining. I lucked into a job as the house dick at the Ocean Forest Hotel and, all things considered, it's not a bad gig. I still hate my job, but it could be worse. It's easy work and a steady paycheck, two things I wasn't used to up North.

These days I'm not much more than a glorified bouncer, looking after the hotel's big-shot guests, providing some semblance of security, checking valuables into the hotel safe. Other than that, I spend most of my days wandering through the hotel corridors making sure everything is on the up and up, throwing out the occasional riff-raff that drifts in. It's not exactly brain surgery but it beats following cheating husbands to sleazy motels, which is what I did as a private dick back in Baltimore.

The pay's not all that great but the job comes with plenty of perks. First off, I get to live for free in one of the finest hotels on the east coast. They give me full use of the hotel's 1946 Studebaker Starlight Coup and I also get to feed from the hotel kitchen, grabbing a juicy steak whenever it strikes my fancy. Plus, I have an open tab at the hotel bar. That last benefit the hotel management is seriously reconsidering but I plan on milking it for as long as I can.

Things were going pretty smooth for me. I had settled into my new life, wallowing in the lap of luxury. My career move proved to be far from taxing and I developed a routine of going through the motions, and trying to make it look like I was doing enough to justify my weekly wages. Everything seemed to be going along just fine.

Then Ellen Highsmith entered the picture. Of course, that day she was advertising herself as Eleanor Highsmith.

I was standing at the front desk when she came strutting through the door like a peacock in heat, all feathers and fluff. A bellboy brought up the rear, overloaded with her three large suitcases. She was quite a sight, the widow Highsmith.

She stood a whopping four foot three with pale complexion and a slight, scrawny frame. Her dress was a red velvet number that looked like it might have been quite fashionable before, the war but it showed signs of wear and was dull and faded, crushed and thin in spots. It hung loose off her shoulders like it had been made for a woman with more girth to her.

Over her shoulders draped a fox fur wrap, bright orange, unlike the hide of any fox I had ever laid eyes on. Like the rest of her, it looked weathered and worn, matted down in places and missing patches of fur in others.

Her face was narrow with deep-set eyes, under a rhinestone-studded bonnet with two large feathers sticking from it, one frayed, the other bent and disheveled. Despite it all, there was a handsome and distinguished look to her, something proud and determined in her features and carriage. I judged her to be in her early fifties, but guessed she might have been younger but aged prematurely, the way life does to some through hard times and difficult struggles.

"Young man," she said to the desk clerk as she approached. "I am Mrs. Eleanor Highsmith of the Greenville Highsmiths. My husband was the late Frederick Highsmith."

"Yes ma'am," the clerk answered as though he had any idea

what she was talking about.

"I believe you are holding a reservation for me."

The clerk went about searching through the reservation book while I continued to study the old dame. There was something forced in her accent, southern as it was, nothing like the South Carolina aristocrats I was used to dealing with at the hotel. Hers was thick and boisterous with careful enunciation to every syllable, like the Queen of England's might be if she were raised in the hills of the Carolinas.

"Yes, Mrs. Highsmith, I have your reservation and everything is in order. I will have your luggage sent directly up to your room."

"Please do. In the meantime, I wonder if there might be somewhere I could relax with a cup of tea? It has been an exhausting journey."

"Of course, madam, the Brookgreen Lounge is right down the stairs or we have a full service restaurant just over by the terrace."

"Young man, do I look like the sort of woman to consort in a *lounge*?"

"No, of course not, ma'am."

"I would like an escort arranged to take me to the restaurant. I would also like to speak with the manager at his earliest convenience. I will need to speak with the hotel's head of security as well."

"That would be me," I chimed in.

Eleanor cocked her head to the side slightly, a look of surprise in her eyes. "You are the manager?"

"No ma'am. That would be Mr. Buntemeyer. I'm the house detective here at the Ocean Forest. I'm in charge of all security issues."

She held out her hand for me to shake. "It's so nice to meet you, Mr. McKeller."

"Likewise," I said even though I was wondering how she knew my name.

I volunteered to take her to the restaurant and we made our way across the lobby, her spouting various pleasantries as we walked. Once in the restaurant, she picked a suitable table and we settled in, sitting across from each other, waiting on our tea to arrive. There was something about the old gal that wasn't adding up but I figured I'd play along.

"What was it you wanted to speak with me about?"

"First and foremost, I want assurances my family jewelry will be adequately protected," she explained, reaching into the front of her dress and pulling out the necklace hanging from her thin, wrinkled throat.

The necklace was large and bulky, tarnished metallic links knotted together in a cluster. Dangling from it was a two inch oval surrounded by dull gold leaves, the center a glass ornament that might have resembled something close to a diamond when it was new but now looked more like weather-beaten paste. I'm no jewelry expert, but I'm guessing it wouldn't have brought more than a few bucks in a two-bit pawn shop. Two and two was adding up to five but I continued to play along.

"That's very lovely," I remarked as she tucked it away. "I can assure you it will be perfectly secure in the hotel safe."

"I also have concerns about my family's welfare during my stay."

"What concerns might they be?"

Eleanor smiled. "Mr. McKeller, I come from a very wealthy and influential family. There are those who could see our visit as an opportunity to try and take advantage of our position in society for their own gains."

"Yes, of course, I see what you mean." I had absolutely no idea what she was going on about.

"Myrtle Beach is a bit more … rural … than we are accustomed to. I'm sure that a town like this has a few more unsavory types than we get where I come from. I don't mean to belittle your fine town. I'm sure it's quite delightful, but it's just that you know how Greenville is."

Not only did I not know how Greenville was, I didn't even know where it was. "You mentioned you were traveling with family."

"I'm afraid I wasn't very clear. I am traveling alone. I'm here for a visit with my daughter."

"Your daughter lives in Myrtle Beach?"

Eleanor's face tightened up some and the smile seemed to drift away for a moment before bouncing back brighter than ever. "Heavens no, she has been here on an extended stay, visiting with friends."

"Is she expecting you?"

Eleanor paused for a second, gathering her thoughts before answering. "I feel certain I must have mentioned it to her the last time we spoke but the truth is I don't recall. I've become quite scatter brained as late."

"That's not a problem. If you could just tell me who she's staying with, we'll call over and let her know you're in town."

"In my haste to get here, I'm afraid I may have forgotten to bring along the address or telephone number."

"Can you call home to get it?"

"The house has been locked up and the servants were given leave until I return. There's no one there to answer the call."

"Mrs. Highsmith, I don't know how you expect me—"

She cut me off with a high pitched chuckle. "I do so hate to be a bother, Mr. McKeller. I can understand how my absent mindedness can be a burden on those around me, but you can't expect me to come all this way and not see my only daughter."

"No, of course not, Mrs. Highsmith. I just don't know how I'm supposed to find her without an address or a number."

Eleanor's grin got bigger and friendlier. There was a devious look in her eye. "You are a detective, aren't you?"

This dame had to be crazy.

I couldn't get a read on her. Her appearance sent one message while her words and demeanor sent another. The bottom line was she was likable enough and, no matter how nuts she might be, I didn't mind helping her out if I could. After all, she was a guest at the hotel and at the Ocean Forest the staff's job was to see to a guest's every need. Like it or not, I was staff.

"At least tell me you know your daughter's name?"

The small woman laughed about as hard as a small woman can. "Of course I do, silly."

Chapter Two

THERE is a side to the big hotels that few people ever get to see. Hidden from the grand lobbies and luxurious ballrooms, away from the comfortable accommodations and fine dining areas, there's a network of corridors and offices, the guts, if you will. This is where everything comes together to make the guest's stay as pleasant as possible.

These places aren't much to look at, mostly white walls and tiled floors—the places that house the cooks, housekeepers, laundry staff and banquet crew. These places are all about hard work and sweat and they're what make a place like the Ocean Forest Hotel run smoothly. They're the reason people pay top dollar for three days and two nights in a place they can be pampered and catered to. This is where my office was.

By office, I mean the former broom closet they managed to wedge a desk and a filing cabinet into. The desk was bare except for a telephone, and I used the filing cabinet to house a phone book and a bottle of whiskey. On the wall behind where I sat hung the certificate I received for graduating from a six-week course at the Staley School of Private Investigation. It gave the place an official look about it.

This is where I was, working away on the Highsmith problem.

The daughter's name was Patricia. She was nineteen-years-old and, as far as I could tell, she'd left home for Myrtle Beach a few months before. Eleanor couldn't have been any more vague on the details.

She knew her daughter had friends at the beach, and she figured she was staying with them, but she couldn't produce any names as her memory wasn't what it used to be. There was a boy in the picture as well.

From the tone Eleanor used when she talked about him, I gathered she wasn't a big fan. Not exactly front page news, as parents are seldom fans of the guys their daughters hook up with.

The boy in question went by the name Timothy Vincent. He was a few years older than Patricia and Eleanor believed he lived in or around Myrtle Beach. That was about all she gave me to go on.

I'd spent the better part of an hour calling around to the various hotels, motels and boarding houses in the area. There weren't a lot of them and none were on the scale of the Ocean Forest but I didn't know where else to begin. I'd asked about a Patricia Highsmith and or Timothy Vincent, if anyone by either name had ever stayed in their establishments. Neither was registered anywhere in town and nobody recalled ever having them as guests.

I had all but given up and was ready to pack it in when Buntemeyer decided to make an appearance. It was rare my boss stopped by my office, and I was sure having both of us in the cramped room was some sort of fire code violation.

Buntemeyer was bigger than me, strapping in a not so scrapping kind of way but nowhere near as intimidating as he tried to be. He had an odd round beard that curled around his chin and hid the lower half of his face. His eyes were wide and intense, darting about as he spoke, and he was a man consumed with many things at once, a consequence of being charged with running the finest hotel between Atlantic City and Miami Beach.

"I just spoke with Mrs. Highsmith," he said, omitting the usual polite greetings normal people begin a conversation with. "She's very impressed with you, McKeller."

"Yeah, well, she made an impression on me too."

"I understand you agreed to do her a little favor."

"About that—"

"I think that's top rate, McKeller. That's exactly the kind of thing we like to see from our people here at the Ocean Forest, above and beyond."

"The thing is, I'm not really sure I'm going to be able to help her out."

The satisfaction plastered across his face turned sour. "Nonsense. There is no request that can't be accommodated at the Ocean Forest."

"It's just that she didn't give me much to work with."

"She wants you to look up her daughter, McKeller. It's not like she's asking you to split the atom."

"If I had a clue where to start it would be a good thing."

"We're talking about a young girl in a town of under twelve hundred people. How hard can that be? You're the detective, get out there and start detecting."

He made it sound so easy when he said it like that. It reminded me of my instructors at the Staley School.

"You know anything about this Highsmith broad?"

"I know that she's a guest at our hotel and not a broad," he snapped back. "What else do I need to know?"

"Does she seem a little fishy to you?"

"I have found that when working with South Carolina's wealthier families they can sometimes be a bit eccentric, if that's what you mean. I suspect that Mrs. Highsmith is somewhat stuck in her ways and maybe a little high strung but that's to be expected from a woman in her position."

"So, you don't know anything about her?"

"I know she is a Highsmith, of the Greenville Highsmiths. I know she was married to the late Frederick Highsmith and I know she wired payment for three days stay in advance. What else is there to know?"

"Have you ever heard of this Highsmith clan before?"

"Well … no but I have never been to Greenville."

"Neither have I."

"That's neither here nor there. The important thing is we do whatever we must to keep all of our guests happy. Speaking of which, I'm going to need you to be on your toes this week. We have the SCC PAA coming in for their convention."

The sick what?"

"I told you all about this, S.C.C.P.A.A., the South Carolina Certified Public Accountants Association. We're going to have over a hundred accountants from all over the state. I'm going to need for you to be on top of any and all matters where they're concerned."

"Oh yeah, I almost forgot. The egg heads are coming."

Buntemeyer cleared his throat. "We'll have none of that talk. The SCCPAA is a very important account for us and we need to do whatever we can to insure they come back next year."

"Yeah, we'd hate to lose the pencil pushing geeks."

"Those pencil pushing geeks contribute to paying your salary and I expect you and the rest of the staff to be on your very best."

I bit my lip in lieu of a response.

The rest of my talk with Buntemeyer went the way my talks with Buntemeyer usually go, him giving me the same old song and dance. He encouraged me to take a more active role in the hotel goings on and to become more of a team player. When he'd hired me he was under the impression I was some sort of super sleuth after I'd had a hand in solving a murder in the hotel. That was three months before and I suspected he was beginning to have second thoughts about my hire.

It was late in the day when I was summoned to the front desk. Mrs. Highsmith was retiring for the evening and wanted her jewelry placed into the safe. She was adamant about the fact I be the one to take care of it for her.

I dialed in the combination and opened the safe door, pulling out the tray corresponding with Mrs. Highsmith's room number. She took off her necklace and handed it to me, treating it like it was the most valuable possession in the world.

"You are sure my belongings will be safe here?"

I took it from her and laid it gently into the tray. "Yes, Mrs. Highsmith, you have nothing to worry about. It will be quite safe here."

The gaudy necklace was much lighter than it appeared, with hardly any weight to it at all. I guessed it was some kind of paint-ed tin for the most part, cheap costume jewelry, and I imagined my initial assessment of its value on the generous side.

You wouldn't know by the way Eleanor was going on about it. It may as well have been the Hope Diamond by the way she was acting.

She took off a thin bracelet and the earrings she was wearing and I placed them in along with the necklace. They didn't appear to be of any better quality.

"Have you had a chance to look into that other matter?" she asked.

"Yes ma'am, I have begun making some calls around town but I haven't turned up anything yet."

My answer disappointed her. I could see it in her face but she continued to smile and to talk to me with all the social graces I was used to getting from her. "Well, please do continue to look into it. I have the utmost faith that you will find my dear Patricia for me."

"If you could think of anything else that might be of some help, a name for example ..."

"Nothing comes to mind but I will certainly give it some thought. You know how young people are these days, free spirits and all, always doing what they want. I'm afraid it's just so hard to keep up with everything they do."

I wondered if there might be a little sadness in her eyes when she said it to me, if maybe her and her daughter's relationship might not be as kosher as she was letting on. There were a lot of things I was wondering about where Eleanor Highsmith was concerned.

Chapter Three

I WAS still relatively new in town and I hadn't made a lot in the way of friends. When I felt like company I usually ended up at Atlantic Beach and a little juke joint called Mack's Dive. Atlantic Beach and Mack's weren't the kind of places that saw a lot of people with my skin color but the people were friendly, the music was good and the drinks were cheap. Besides, I could always count on seeing the one person who was the closest thing I'd found to a friend so far.

She was a cute little dish named Tabitha but she went by Tabby. Her brother worked as the bartender and she waited tables part time. When she wasn't on the clock she could usually be found hanging out at the bar.

Tabby was around twenty, much younger than me. Probably much too young for some of the thoughts she conjured in my mind but I liked being around her just the same.

She had long dark hair that poured around her shoulders and expressive brown eyes, her face slender and taut, the kind that, in another time and place, might have launched a thousand ships. Her hourglass figure was about as perfect as possible and she was fond of extremely tight fitting dresses that buttoned up the front, though she rarely had use for all the buttons. Come to think of it, I was pretty fond of those dresses too, whenever

Tabby was wearing one.

Why Tabby took a liking to me, I have no idea. It's not like I'm the most personable guy but she seemed to get a kick out of having me around. We had almost nothing in common, aside from a penchant for the hooch. I was a good bit older, from another world and of a different pigmentation. It was perfectly natural that we became friends.

Mack's was lively. For the off season it was a decent crowd and Blind Eye Regis was in rare form, wailing away about the Blues that consumed his life and fueled his musical career. The horde of drunken Blues lovers were eating it up, dancing and singing along, hooting and hollering.

I was at the bar with Tabby staring down at a plate of something she called chitlins.

"Don't be such a sissy," she said laughing. "They're good. You're going to love them."

"These are really pig intestines?"

She shook her head in disgust. "What do you care? A pig's a pig. It all eats the same."

"I don't know about that. Some parts are meant to be cooked up and some just aren't."

Tabby turned to her brother behind the bar. "Randall, McKeller is afraid to try chitlins." For whatever reason, Tabby refused to call me by my first name, try as I might to get her to. It was OK by me. I was just glad she called me anything.

Randall gave me the kind of look reserved for lunatics and morons. "They're mighty tasty," he said. "If you don't want them I'll take 'em."

Tabby's brother was a big guy, wide and heavy, about four times the size of his sister. It didn't look like there was much he wouldn't be willing to eat.

"If I'm going to do this I'm going to need another drink."

I sat looking at the strange cuisine in front of me while Randall put up two more shot glasses of booze, one for me and one for Tabby.

By nature I was a whiskey drinker but Mack's didn't serve the real thing. Their version was local moonshine colored with iodine. It took a little getting used to but after the first couple you could hardly tell the difference and it packed more punch then the store bought stuff.

I shot back my drink and scooped up a fork full of chitlins, stuffing them into my mouth before the burn of the liquor faded away. Tabby and Randall sat staring with interest as I chewed.

It was a weird mix I wasn't used to tasting together, succulent and spicy, juicy and chewy. After the initial shock of chewing on the bowels of a pig, I had to admit they were quite good and I shoveled in another helping.

"See, I told you so," Tabby said with a chuckle.

Even Randall seemed to take pleasure in my approval of the local delicacy. It was one of the few times I'd ever seen him smile.

"How's things at the Big Digs?" Tabby asked. It was her nick name for the Ocean Forest Hotel.

"Things are fine," I answered through a mouthful of chitlins.

"They keeping you busy?"

I shrugged. "Not too busy. I'm more or less a babysitter for the rich and privileged these days."

"Just be thankful you got a job. Things are tough around here this time of year."

"It looks like you guys are doing all right," I replied, glancing around the half full room.

Tabby frowned a little. "Most of these people are drinking on tabs that won't be paid till springtime when the money starts rolling in."

"If you need some money—" I started to reach into my breast pocket but she put her hand on my arm, stopping me.

"No, I'm fine. It ain't so bad. I got everything I need."

Just then, we were interrupted by another young girl pulling at Tabby's shoulder and turning her around. "Can I talk to you, Tabby?"

The girl looked to be a few years older than Tabby with the same kind of slender figure and she had it stuffed into a white dress with black polka dots. There wasn't room for much else.

Her face was long and thin with sharp angular features and a darker complexion than Tabby's. She was a pretty girl but there was something anxious and nervous about her and her eyes looked wide and worried.

Tabby wrapped her arms around her and gave her the kind of hug you give someone you love and haven't seen for a long time. "Mona, how you been?"

"I'm good," the girl answered but her body language said different.

"Where you been hiding?"

"Working."

"Where?"

Mona glanced over to me. She gave me a suspicious leer, like she just realized how out of place I was.

"Mona, this is McKeller. He's a friend of mine. He's all right."

The look didn't let up.

The girl gave me half a nod, barely acknowledging me, and turned back to Tabby. "I need a place to stay tonight."

"Is everything OK?"

Mona nodded. "Yeah, everything's fine. I'm leaving town tomorrow."

"Are you in some kind of trouble?"

"No, it's nothing like that." Everything about her said it was exactly like that. "I just need a place to sleep tonight."

"Of course," Tabby said with a smile. "Anything you need."

"Thanks, that's a big help."

"Are you sure everything is OK?"

Mona nodded again.

"What about your job? I thought you were living in town."

"I can't go back there."

"What's going on, Mona?"

"I'm getting the hell out of here, finally. I'm shaking the sand off my shoes and getting out of this place, once and for all."

"Where are you going?"

Mona paused a second. The look on her face was somewhere between worry and defiance. "North," she said.

"North? That's it, you're just heading north?"

"Stuff happened, I can't talk about it just now. I got a one-way ticket out of this town and I'm going to start a new life."

"What's going on, Mona?"

"I'll tell you all about it later. I've got to go see somebody, but I'll be back at your place later."

"Are you in some kind of trouble?"

Mona tried to smile but it was a sad attempt. "Nothing I can't handle."

"Mona, what's going on?"

The thin girl in the polka dot dress shook her head side to side. "Everything's going to be all right. I just need to take care of something. I've got to go. I'll see you later tonight and I'll explain everything."

The two girls gave each other another quick hug and Mona was on her way. Tabby's gaze followed her friend as she worked her way across the room and out the door. She was trying to hide it but I could see the worry etched into her striking features.

"Is everything all right?"

"Yeah, I'm sure everything is fine. It's just Mona being Mona."

"Old friend?"

"One of my oldest, I've known Mona since I was a little girl. Her father used to work on my Dad's farm. We practically grew up as sisters."

"She doesn't seem like the farm girl type." Neither did Tabby.

"Getting off that farm was all she ever talked about. She was barely sixteen-years-old when she went off on her own."

"That's pretty young to be venturing out into the world."

"Mona was always older than her years."

"She seemed a little off kilter, like something was seriously wrong."

Tabby closed her eyes for a moment than opened them back up. "She's a sweetheart but she has a knack for getting herself into bad situations."

"Is there anything I can do to help?"

She looked up at me, those big brown eyes boiling over. "Yeah," she said. "As a matter of fact there is. You can buy me another drink."

I suppose you can guess what I did next.

Chapter Four

My usual routine is to get up around eleven or so. This infuriates my boss. He keeps telling me that half the day is over by the time I get going and he likes to point out that he's not paying me to sleep. When I heard the pounding at my door I assumed it was Buntemeyer with his usual berating. I was wrong.

It was Eleanor Highsmith at my door when I answered in a bathrobe, hung-over and barely coherent from the night before. That moonshine does a pretty good number on me. She seemed pretty adamant about getting me out of bed.

"Mr. McKeller, it's almost ten in the morning. Aren't there things you should be doing?"

I resisted the urge to slap her. "Like what?"

"Like finding out where my daughter is."

"Mrs. Highsmith, I can assure you that I am doing everything in my power to locate your daughter."

She gave me a look that told me she wasn't buying it. "You reek of alcohol."

"It's a new cologne I'm trying out."

"I would very much like to meet up with you on the terrace in fifteen minutes." It wasn't a request.

"Yes ma'am."

I went back into my room and took a quick bath, trying to

pull myself together and get myself into some semblance of sobriety. My head was pounding, my bum leg was throbbing and my mind was spinning. It seemed like the perfect way to start my day.

Mrs. Highsmith was sitting at a table, sipping tea when I arrived. I plopped my frame into the seat beside her and ordered a cup of coffee from a passing waiter. There was no doubt that she wasn't happy with me, but she ignored the state I was in and talked to me like I was a regular person.

"How do you plan on going about finding Patricia?"

"I've got to be honest with you. I'm not sure where to begin. You haven't given me much to work with. Patricia could be anywhere."

"She's not anywhere; she's in Myrtle Beach."

"Look, Patricia is a young girl. She's here in Myrtle Beach hanging out with her friends. She could be doing anything, sailing, fishing, golf…Why don't you just wait until she comes home?"

"That is not an option. I have only two more days in Myrtle Beach and I intend to see my daughter."

"Mrs. Highsmith, I am not a directory. I cannot just turn a page and tell you where your daughter is staying. I don't even know your daughter. I don't know her friends. I have no idea where she might be."

"Mr. McKeller, I am Eleanor Highsmith of the Greenville Highsmiths. My husband was the late Frederick Highsmith. I am also a paying guest of this establishment and I have asked you to do me one small favor. I do not understand why you can't put your considerable talents toward this one simple task."

It made me feel kind of bad when she put it that way.

Eleanor reached into her purse and produced a small photograph which she handed to me. It was a picture of a pretty young brunette. The girl looked fresh and healthy, the image of the All American Girl. She had a roundish face with plump cheeks, a slender chin and a sparkling smile. In the photo she looked happy and innocent and, even though the photograph was in black and white, I could tell her eyes were the bluest of blue.

"She's beautiful," I said, but not in a lecherous way.

Eleanor swallowed hard. "Yes, she is. She always has been. The picture was taken five months ago. Maybe it will help you locate her."

"I don't understand why you can't find out who she's staying with," I tried.

"I don't understand why you're being so difficult. My daughter is here in Myrtle Beach and you are the house detective of the Ocean Forest Hotel. All I'm asking you to do is find out where my daughter is staying."

I guess she didn't realize what a total fake I was when it came to detective work. She probably would have been better off calling the telephone operator. At least she would know where to begin.

I stuffed the picture into my jacket pocket. "I will do what I can."

"That is all I ask."

I gulped down a couple cups of coffee after Mrs. Highsmith left and headed back to my room. I had no idea how I was going to go about the task at hand and I needed some time to think. My room seemed as good a place as any.

There was something tugging at me. I wasn't even sure what it was. It was like things between Eleanor and her daughter weren't what they seemed to be, like there was something else going on.

I suspected some sort of quarrel between the two, a feud or wedge in their relationship. Maybe it was the reason Patricia had run off to Myrtle Beach in the first place. Maybe Eleanor Highsmith hadn't forgotten who it was her daughter was staying with at all and Patricia was making sure her mother didn't find out.

There had been something in the woman's eyes when she handed me the photograph of her daughter; it was a lost look bordering on desperation. I hadn't noticed it before but I was certain it was a look of regret and of the determination to right something that had gone terribly wrong. Whatever had happened between the two of them, she was counting on me to give her the chance to fix it. Of course, the other scenario was that I was totally off base and had no idea what I was talking about. This one seemed just as plausible.

Crazy or not, I felt a weird obligation to Eleanor. I didn't owe her anything, and I had no real clue what was going on between the two of them, but I felt like I needed to help. I can be a sap like that sometimes.

In the elevator, going up, freckled-faced Clifford was manning the controls. We'd had our differences in the past but the kid was beginning to grow on me. He was maybe seventeen and a little bit cocky, bright red hair and a smart ass grin always present on his face. Looking at him, it got me thinking.

"Hey, Clifford, what do kids do in this town?"

"Excuse me?"

"For fun, where do the kids go?"

Clifford smiled big. "There's lot's of fun things to do in town."

"Yeah, but what about the cool kids, the ones your age or maybe a little bit older, where do they go?"

Freckled Face thought on it for about a half a second. "There's not a lot going on this time of year but there's always the Pavilion."

"What's that?"

Chapter Five

THE Pavilion was located in the heart of Myrtle Beach. It had gone through many incarnations over the years, but now the large wooden structure housed a bandstand, food venders, game booths and a few primitive amusement rides. The front of the building, which faced the road, was enclosed and locked up for the off season, but the ocean side was open, a long planked veranda where the stage and some wooden benches sat. As far as the youth of the town were concerned, there wasn't a more happening place on the beach.

That said, the Pavilion in December wasn't exactly the same as it was during the height of the season. There were no venders selling their wares or bands playing the empty stage. The few rides had been packed up for the winter or buckled down for the off season.

Families from all over the area flocked to the Pavilion when it was in full swing but during the slow time there was no mistake it belonged to the local kids. It served as a gathering place and hang out for the next generation of Myrtle Beach-ers.

They were scattered about, grouped off in age brackets ranging from mid-teens to early twenties, none of them doing anything in particular, laughing, talking, cutting up. Boys were off on one side, whispering amongst themselves. Girls were on the other, talking, giggling and pretending to ignore the boys.

I spotted three girls on a bench. They appeared to be in Patricia Highsmith's age range and I made my approach, trying to be as nonchalant as possible.

"Hi," I said.

"Hiyh," they replied back in unison, their sweet Southern drawls like music in the crisp December air. They were cute little things, all wholesome and clean, full of innocence and optimism; they reminded me of Mom's apple pie.

"I was wondering if you could help me."

"Sure, mister," one answered.

"I'm looking for a girl—"

"Beat it, creep," another shot back and the three of them got up and walked away.

That went well.

My expertise in the detective field is fairly limited, I'm afraid. Walking up and gathering information from strangers wasn't exactly my forté. To this point most of my detecting involved following cheating husbands and wives. I was fine when it came to questioning bartenders and motel clerks but beyond that I was pretty much lost.

I decided another angle might be in order and I lit up a cigarette before taking another stab. For a while I leaned back on a wall and watched the goings on around me.

Most of it was regular kid stuff, laughing, playing, a lot of grab ass going on. It was winter vacation from school and they were enjoying their down time.

Older boys sat in a group on a small platform. I watched some of the others approach them from time to time, asking questions, passing on information. From the looks of it, they were a tougher crowd than most of the others. I got the sense they were the ones who ruled the area, the top of some kind of half assed hierarchy in the youth world.

I was just about to make my move when I was approached from the left.

"You got a light, mister?"

He was a scrawny kid, maybe eighteen years old and kind of scruffy looking. He wore beat up denim pants and an aviator's jacket that was too large and hung off him like a tent draped over an outhouse. His face was skinny and splotched with patches of peach fuzz, a lame attempt to grow out a manly beard. An unlit cigarette hung from his lips. He didn't fit in with the others.

I took out my lighter and lit his smoke.

"Thanks."

"Don't mention it."

The kid glanced around for a moment, getting a feel for the happenings around us. "You in the right place?" he finally asked.

"As far as I know."

"You some kind of cop or something?"

"No, I work at a hotel."

This seemed to appease him some. He nodded for a minute and took a long drag from his cigarette. "What brings you down here?"

"I'm looking for somebody."

"Well, I'm the guy to talk to about that. I know everybody around these parts." The kid had the usual Myrtle Beach accent. His voice was on the high side but with a gravely tone to it like he was purposely trying to beef it up. Everything about him, the clothes, the look, the body language, told me he was trying to put out a tough guy stance. I wasn't impressed. "Of course, I usually get paid for my services."

"What's your name?"

"They call me Cagney," he answered. "You sure you're not a cop?"

"I'm definitely not a cop."

"Who are you looking for?"

I paused a second, deciding which way to go with it. I figured the local angle might suit me better with this one. "I'm looking for a guy named Timothy Vincent."

Cagney spit on the ground beside him. "Hell, you don't need to go to Vincent. I can get you anything you need. I got connections in this town. What are you looking for?"

"What have you got?" It wasn't at all the way I thought the conversation would go. I figured I needed to play it out to see what was what.

"You're positive you ain't a cop?" he asked again.

"Contrary to popular belief, I'm positive."

"You looking to score some shine?"

"I can get moonshine in half the bars in Myrtle Beach. You're going to have to do better than that."

Cagney gave a twisted laugh. "What's your thing, buddy? You looking for a game, high stakes poker, roulette? You want to play the numbers? You looking for some smoke, some female companionship, what are you into?"

"What's Timothy Vincent into?"

His entire demeanor changed and he looked at me with suspicion. "Look, we're just talking. You ain't got nothing on me."

"I told you, I'm not a cop." I pulled a twenty from my pocket and showed it to him. "I'm just looking for a little information."

"I ain't no stool pigeon."

I shrugged my understanding and started to put my money away.

"Wait ..."

I paused and left the twenty spot dangling out in full view of both of us. The kid might have thought he was big time but he was pretty low budget and, judging from his appearance, I guessed it had been a while since he'd handled a twenty dollar bill.

"Anything I say won't go no farther than us, right?"

"As far as I'm concerned we never met."

Cagney snatched the bill out of my hand and stuffed it into his pants pocket. After surveying the area and making sure no one was paying us any attention, he began spilling what he knew.

"Vincent's a local, his family has been around for years. His old man was a trucker for the farm, Myrtle Beach Farms. Before that he was a logger back when this place was all about timber."

"That's all very interesting but I can do without the family tree. Tell me about Timothy."

"I can tell you he'd sock you one good if he heard you call him Timothy, I can tell you that." Cagney got a pretty good laugh out of his little joke. Once he'd stopped giggling like a little girl he continued on. "Vincent's been around this area since it was nothing. He knows this place like the back of his hand."

"I'll keep that in mind if I'm looking for a tour guide. Tell me about what Timothy is into these days."

"I s'pect Vincent has a hand in a little bit of everything. He started out running shine but that was small time for a guy like Vincent. He works as more of a middle man these days, a supplier if you will.

"He also has some side gigs he works. If you're looking for a big stakes game or a cock fight he's a guy to talk to. If you're lonely he's a guy who can provide some company, if you know what I mean."

"He runs a gambling and prostitution ring?"

Cagney laughed again. "Ring? This is Myrtle Beach, mister, not Las Vegas. He knows some people and he has some girls he works with. He's not like some kind of mob boss."

"He have a spot he works out of?"

"He used to keep some girls over top a restaurant up north of here, the Villa Roma, but the cops busted it awhile back. The gambling thing moves around, never in the same place twice."

"Do you know where he lives?"

The greasy kid shook his head no. "I hear he has a place in the country, a cabin or something but I don't know where. He's not the kind of guy to advertise stuff like that."

"What about his girls? Where are they working out of now?"

"Beats me, I haven't heard anything about it in a while. Not much going on in town this time of year."

"People don't get lonely in the winter time?"

"Sure they do but nobody has any money to do anything about it."

"Do you know any of his girls?"

"I see them around from time to time."

"You know one that goes by Patricia?"

"It doesn't ring a bell but then I don't know most of them by name. I just see them around is all."

I took the photograph of Patricia Highsmith from my breast pocket and held it up for him to see. "Does she look familiar?"

He studied the picture for a long time. It was almost creepy the way he studied it.

"She's a hot little number. I would remember if I seen her."

From there he didn't have much else to offer, nothing that could do me any good anyway. I made sure to tell him he could reach me at the Ocean Forest and if he could tell me where to find Vincent there was another twenty in it for him. We ended our little pow-wow and I went back to the car.

I had gotten my twenty-dollars-worth. I'm not in the habit of throwing money around like that, but I had some in the bank from a few months back. It was payment received for services not quite rendered with a bonus thrown in for almost getting framed for a murder. It was free money as far as I was concerned and I didn't mind putting it to good use.

Chapter Six

Usually, when I knock on the door of a guest I do it gentle and polite, a few quick raps to get their attention. I went with another approach when I knocked on the door of Eleanor Highsmith. I banged on the door with both fists, pounding for all I was worth. It took her a few moments to answer.

"Mr. McKeller, is something wrong?" she asked as she opened the door.

"You could say that." Without waiting to be invited in I walked past her, into the room,.

"Have you found Patricia?"

"I think maybe it's time you leveled with me."

"Whatever do you mean?"

"Do you want to tell me what's going on?"

Eleanor looked out of sorts, confused, maybe a little embarrassed. "I have no idea what you are talking about."

"What's going on, Eleanor?"

"Mr. McKeller, I don't like your tone."

"And I don't like being played. What's your deal? What are you doing here?"

"I'm here to visit with my daughter."

"Yeah, and you're from old family money in Greenville but your clothes are second hand and your priceless jewels are fake.

34

I've got a sneaking suspicion you're a fake too. Are you running some kind of con?"

She gasped in shock, still holding on to the facade.

"You knew your daughter wasn't staying with friends. You suspected she was in some sort of trouble and you wanted the Ocean Forest to find out for you. By the Ocean Forest, I mean me. That sounds like a clear case of fraud." I might have been bluffing the fraud angle but I figured it would put a scare into the old gal. I was right.

Eleanor collapsed to sit on the corner of the bed. Her shoulders slumped; her face was void of any expression.

"That first day, when you checked in, you knew my name, how?"

She looked up with confusion.

"I told you I was the house dick and you said, 'It's nice to meet you, Mr. McKeller'."

"I had heard of you." She sighed.

"From who?"

"Daniel and Tina Weatherspoon, I work for them as a maid. You may not remember them but they were guests at the Chilton wedding last September."

"You're a maid? How on earth can you afford to stay at the Ocean Forest?"

"My husband, Freddy, died a year ago. He left me a little insurance money."

"All right, but why me?"

"I heard them talking about how you solved the murder at the hotel. They said you were a brilliant detective. You solved two murders in one day."

It wasn't quite the way it went down that day but there was no reason to argue over semantics.

"There are other detectives."

"I've tried. They're all too eager to take your money but when it comes to getting results they don't mind dragging their feet."

"If you wanted to hire me, why not come clean; why the charade?" I could have also mentioned that my rates were much lower than a stay at the Ocean Forest.

"I'm a maid, Mr. McKeller. My husband worked as a pipe

fitter. We never had any money and our family name doesn't carry any clout. Nobody cares about the missing daughter of Ellen and Freddy Highsmith."

I didn't answer. I wasn't sure how.

"Do you have children, Mr. McKeller?"

A shake of my head was about all I could muster.

"I met Freddy later in life. I was almost thirty years old and didn't expect I'd ever have a family of my own. Freddy changed all that for me. Patty came along soon after and I went from being a lonely spinster to a wife and mother.

"Now that Freddy has passed, my daughter is all I have. She's all that's left of that life, Mr. McKeller. Without Patty I'm that lonely spinster again."

This time I couldn't even manage the head shake.

"My daughter is a good girl. She has a bit of a wild streak, but she's a kind and loving person. Patty has a history of joining up with the wrong crowd. She's never been in any kind of serious trouble but she has made some bad decisions.

"Patty met a boy, a man really. He was traveling through Greenville on business, monkey business if you ask me. He was the kind of hot shot who likes to throw money around to impress the young girls. I never liked Timothy from the moment I met him.

"The two became very friendly. When it was time for him to head back home she up and left with him. They snuck her things out in the middle of the night."

Ellen wrapped her arms around herself like she was cold. "She used to write at first, she really is a sweet girl. She didn't want me to worry. After a while the letters were slower coming. Eventually they stopped all together.

"I tried the police but they couldn't do anything. I hired a private investigator but he was more interested in taking my money than finding Patty.

"When I remembered hearing the Weatherspoons talk of the incredible job you did here and I knew you were the one to find Patty. I was afraid if you knew I didn't have any money you wouldn't take the case. I thought if I was a rich and important guest at the hotel I could convince you to look into it for me."

"You shouldn't have lied to me." It was all I could think to say.

"I know. I was desperate. I didn't know where else to turn. I suppose it was a silly idea."

"Sometimes children make choices in their lives. Sometimes they're the kind of choices parents don't like."

"It isn't like her not to write. She wouldn't let me worry like that. I'm afraid she's in some kind of trouble."

"What if she's not? What if she's happy where she is?"

"Then I deserve to hear that from her. If that's the case I will go home quietly and leave her alone."

I took a long look at Ellen Highsmith and I saw her clearly for the first time. She was a sad and broken woman, clinging to the most important thing left in her life. She was also a brave and gutsy dame who had gone to a lot of expense and trouble to secure my services. I didn't have the heart to tell her she was barking up the wrong tree, that there were plenty of better detectives out there with a lot more experience and expertise.

If I know one thing about myself it's that I'm a total sap with hardly the sense God gave a monkey. I guess that's why I decided to continue to look into Patty's disappearance. It's not like I had anything better to do.

"How much longer are you going to be in town?"

"Tomorrow is my last night in the Ocean Forest but I could move to a cheaper hotel. I can stay as long as I need to."

"If I decide to look into this we're going to have to lay down a few ground rules. Number one, no more lies."

"Of course," she said, her eyes lighting up with hope.

"No more holding back either. I need to know everything."

"And I will be more than willing to pay you whatever you require," Eleanor added.

I glanced over at the old velvet dress she was wearing, the gaudy costume jewelry across her neck and hanging from her ears. "We'll worry about that later."

From Ellen Highsmith's room, I went directly to the front desk. Buntemeyer was there with the desk clerk, checking in a couple of stiff looking characters with thinning hair and wire framed glasses, the first of the egg heads I guessed. He was just the one I wanted to see.

"Mr. Buntemeyer?"

"Yes, McKeller?"

"I just left Mrs. Highsmith's room. You had better get some-one up there."

"What's wrong?" He looked beyond worried.

"She saw a rat in her room. I saw it too."

Buntemeyer's expression turned to terror and he pulled me aside, out of ear shot from the incoming guests. "A rat in the Ocean Forest?"

"As big as a small dog."

Buntemeyer began barking orders to the clerk about getting the engineers up there, calling the exterminator.

"You know," I said, "a thing like this is not going to sit too well with a woman like Eleanor Highsmith. She's from a very important family and she has a lot of wealthy friends."

Buntemeyer gasped, almost choking on it.

"If I were you I would consider picking up her tab, putting her up for free for a few days. She is a Greenville Highsmith, after all. You know how they can be. The money's probably not that big a deal, but the gesture might go a long way."

"You are absolutely right, McKeller. That's a brilliant idea."

"It's the least we can do."

Chapter Seven

I HAD no idea where to look for Patty Highsmith. I barely knew how to get around town myself, much less find someone else. The Villa Roma restaurant seemed as good a place to start as any.

Kings Highway acts as a main thoroughfare for Myrtle Beach and the small communities to the north and south of it. It began its life as a trail blazed by local Indian tribes and was adopted by early settlers in the area to run goods up and down the coast. They say it was the route George Washington used during the Revolution to inspect the southern campaign.

These days it's a semi-improved road, paved in places, dirt in others. Around the downtown area it's littered with pockets of small businesses and houses, the occasional Mom and Pop hotel. The farther north you drive. the thinner things are where civilization is concerned. By the time you get past where you turn off for the Ocean Forest there's practically nothing. That is, until you get to the Villa Roma.

The restaurant sat in the middle of nowhere, on the left side of the road, a two story building that looked more like a regal Southern home than a place of business. A large porch on each floor sported stone columns holding up the overhang and a stone staircase coming in from the side. Out front was a four-foot-tall hand painted sign that said, "Villa Roma - Fine Italian Cuisine" with a thin plank tacked over it stating the place was closed for the season. It seemed like a strange spot to stick a nice restaurant, but I guess when your house specialty is young female flesh the farther off the beaten path the better.

I pulled up in front of the establishment and parked the car, got out to have a look. Up on the porch, I peered into the window. There was nothing high-brow about it but it looked clean and kept up, a half dozen tables scattered about with red and white checkered table cloths. The lights were off, but it was still bright enough to get a good feel for the inside. There was no sign of life stirring anywhere around.

Another set of steps led to the top porch and I climbed up, checking things out. My leg was aching as I'd been on my feet for a large portion of the day and I was beginning to feel it, the old war injury giving me fits. By the time I got to the top I was ready to sit down and give my bum leg a break.

Instead, I went over to the first window and peeked in. It was the smallest of bedrooms, with a single mattress, no sheets and a nightstand beside it. There wasn't room for much else. At the next window a hallway ran the length of the second floor with a closed door every few feet. There must have been ten of them, all told. In the third window was another bedroom set exactly like the first.

I was still staring in when a voice from ground level disturbed my train of thought.

"Hey you, what's the big idea?"

Down below me, staring up with an agitated look on his face was a stocky guy with a beer gut. He was tall with thick dark Italian features and he was wearing dirty work pants and a stained white cotton undershirt. He must have come from around back.

"Sorry," I responded. "I was just checking things out." I began to limp my way down the stairs.

"We're closed and this is private property."

I was moving as quick as I could but my leg wasn't cooperating, and I could tell the guy was impatient for me to get down. "Yeah, sorry about that. I just heard about your place and I wanted to come eat here. I didn't realize you were done for the season."

"Things are all closed up till springtime."

I was just reaching the bottom step and the Italian was there waiting for me. "I hear you guys have great food."

"It's a good meal at a reasonable price," he answered.

"I hear you guys offer some extras from time to time as well."

"Meatballs and pasta are my business. I wouldn't know about anything else."

"People say it's a place to come if you're looking for a good time."

"Are you some kind of cop?"

"No, I work over at the Ocean Forest. I'm just a guy looking to have a little fun."

He paused a second. "If you're looking for a real Italian dinner come back in the spring. Anything else and you're on your own."

"Look, I'm just talking but I hear you guys have some girls every once in a while, maybe a card game every now and again."

"I wouldn't know anything about that. I do the cooking here." His face and body were tense and it was fairly obvious he didn't care for my line of questioning.

"I understand Vincent is the guy to talk to about that stuff, Timothy Vincent. Do you know where I could find him?"

The guy shot me a growl of a look. "I cook the meatballs. I don't know from nothing."

I shrugged. "I'm new in town and I'm just looking for a place to spend my money."

"You can spend it here after we reopen if you're looking for some good grub. Other than that, I can't help you."

"You don't know of any other places I could try, do you?"

The Italian shook his head slow and angry-like. "I cook the meatballs." He grunted.

It was pretty obvious I wasn't getting anywhere with the Italian. I cut my ties and got back into the car. I didn't have a clue where to try next. My leg was killing me and I figured some self-medication was in order, so I decided to swing over to Atlantic Beach for a drink.

Chapter Eight

IT WAS just getting dark by the time I got there. Tabby was working the tables so I sat alone at the bar trying to converse with her brother Russell. Not the easiest of tasks. Whenever she got a break, Tabby would come over to keep me company.

Tonight she was wearing one of my favorites, a light blue dress that all but held her in, sleeveless and open in the front. Her hair was pulled back in a ponytail and she had a homemade choker around her throat of frayed twine and sea shells. She wore flat sandals.

She was running around pretty good and her face was covered in a mist of perspiration that glistened in the light, making her soft brown face look moist and alive.

"Two nights in a row?" Tabby asked, leaning on the bar beside me and waiting for Russell to make drinks for one of her tables.

"It must have been the chitlins."

Tabby laughed. "Must have been."

"Have you ever heard of a guy named Timothy Vincent?"

A scowl crossed her face. "Where did you hear that name?"

"One of the guests at the hotel."

"Vincent is bad news, stay away from him."

"You know him?"

"I reckon most folks around this way know Vincent, anybody that's been around for a spell."

"I hear he's got his fingers in a lot of pies."

"He gets around. There was a time when he tried to get me to work for him but I wasn't interested. He didn't want to take no for an answer."

I got a sudden vision of Tabby with some strange man in one of the small bedrooms over the Villa Roma. The image made me sick to my stomach.

Tabby wasn't the type of girl to end up like that. She was too smart. She might have been rural and country but she had more class and wits about her than most of the people who passed through the Ocean Forest.

"I'm glad you said no."

She smiled and gave a shrug. "I know enough to stay away from the likes of Vincent."

"Any idea where I could find him, these days?"

She wiped sweat from her forehead with the back of her hand and shook her head. "I haven't seen him around in ages. I heard he runs some business out of the Villa Roma every once in a while."

"If not there, where else could I look?"

"I wouldn't know. Vincent is the kind of guy who pops in and out when he wants to. I suspect this time of year he lays pretty low."

Russell had finished making her round of drinks and she loaded them onto a tray. Flashing me a smile, she hoisted it to shoulder height and turned away, heading to her table and back to work.

I turned back to my shot glass and prepared myself for another swig of moonshine. A towering presence hovered about me and I realized that big Russell had leaned over and was slouching in toward me. It made me a bit uneasy as Russell and I had never been particularly close.

"This guest at the hotel, he looking for a little something?" It seemed Russell had been listening to our conversation.

"Maybe."

Russell looked around and leaned back in. "Look, I don't get involved in that kind of stuff but there's a guy in town…"

"Yeah?"

"He runs some stuff. He's got some girls here in Atlantic Beach. He's got a place called the Sea Shack down by the water. I don't know exactly what this guest of yours is looking for but this guy has a bit of a selective inventory."

"Are you trying to say he doesn't offer much in the way of the lighter variety?"

Russell shrugged one shoulder. "A pretty gal is a pretty gal."

"I quite agree. Does this guy have a name?"

"Raddison Hayes. He's a big wig in these parts, so don't go to him unless you mean business. He's not the kind of guy who likes his time wasted."

"I'll keep that in mind. This guy at the hotel though, he's kind of an uppity type. I'm not sure how he'd feel about coming to Atlantic Beach. It's not really his style."

"That's not a problem. There's neutral sites around here people can meet where nobody asks any questions."

"That's good to know."

The big guy went back to work and I got working on another shot of booze. I was going over things in my mind, trying to figure out my next move. The Hayes guy was an interesting angle but I doubted it would do me any good. If he specialized in black women he wasn't likely to have anything to do with Patty Highsmith. I got the sense there were pretty strict racial lines a person didn't cross in this part of the country, even in that business.

There was a loud ruckus at the front door and I turned my attention to the commotion. People were moving fast, heading for the back of the room, a panic breaking out and the music coming to an abrupt stop.

I spotted white men in uniforms mixing it up with the locals, people getting shoved around and tossed aside. From the center of all the fuss, Sheriff Rufus Talbert came strolling in.

He was in full uniform with his hat cocked back on his head. There was a sour look on his puss and he was standing erect and military like, the kind of stance a man has when he means business.

"All right, everybody pipe down!"

A young man went to stand up but Talbert pushed him back in his chair, all forceful and mean. "Sit your black ass down," he snarled.

I'd seen Sheriff Talbert at work before, dealing with some of the area's more wealthy and influential people. He was a different person now and his demeanor and attitude were nothing like I had witnessed in the past. Now he was spiteful and ferocious, showing little if any regard for the people whose night he was disturbing.

"Most of you know who I am," he spat out. "You know how I run this county. I got no problem with ya'll as long as you keep to your selves and mind your business. I have a serious problem when folks, such as yourselves, go and commit crimes in my jurisdiction."

The room was dead still; each person hanging on the sheriff's every word. None of us had any idea what he was talking about.

"A girl was found earlier this evening just south of here. She was found on the beach with her throat cut. I suspect it happened sometime last night. Anybody know anything about a missing girl?"

Nobody let out so much as a peep.

"This girl was a young Negro, early twenties. She was a skinny little thing, looked like she might have been quite a looker. She was wearing a white dress with black polka dots. Does that ring any bells for anybody?"

Muffled whispering circled the room. My eyes shot directly to Tabby. Her eyes went wide with shock and she held the empty tray in both arms pressed up tight against her chest. She looked like somebody had kicked her in the back of the head.

"I got a suspicion that somebody knows something about what happened. Ain't nobody leaving this place till every one of you's talked to me and my men."

It was about that time the sheriff spotted me sitting at the bar and made a beeline in my direction. I wanted to go to Tabby but I figured I needed to deal with Talbert first. The rest of his deputies dispersed around the room and were taking statements from the clientele.

"You're a little out of your element, aren't you, McKeller?"

"What can I say? I'm a big fan of Blues music and chitlins."

"I heard you stayed in town. I hear you took up at the Ocean Forest, some kind of house dick or something."

"A guy's got to make a living."

"What brings you up this way?"

"I like the company."

"Do your employers know you patronize places like this?"

"I didn't know I had to clear it with the boss before I go to get a drink."

"This isn't the kind of place most respectable white men frequent."

"Oh, I don't know about that. It can't be all that bad. You're here, aren't you?"

The sheriff and I never got along particularly well but there was something different in his eyes this time. I could see the contempt he had for me in his face. I'm not sure if it was our past history or the people he found I was cavorting with.

"McKeller, why is it that every time somebody goes and gets themselves killed around here I turn around and find you?"

"I guess I'm just lucky like that."

"Always the smart ass ..." The sheriff's eyes wandered past me like his attention had been caught by something across the room. I turned my head to see what he was looking at and spotted a tall black man in a blue suit easing his way along the back wall and heading for the rear exit. He was trying to be inconspicuous and sneak by one of the deputies.

"Dale, stop that boy!" the sheriff yelled, pointing out the man.

The one in the suit made a break for the door but the closest deputy turned and cut him off, slamming him into the wall and pinning him face first against it. Sheriff Talbert was there in an instant. I followed along.

"Where in tarnation do you think you're going?" the sheriff asked.

"I was feeling a tad queasy. I thought I would get a breath of air," the guy grunted back, still pinned against the wall.

"You picked the wrong time for some fresh air, boy. What's your name?"

"Tyler Wilkins."

"What's your hurry to get out of here, Tyler?"

"I ain't in no hurry. I was coming right back."

"You know something about a missing girl?"

"No sir. I don't know nothing."

"Let me explain something to you, Tyler. When I see somebody try to sneak out of a room where we're questioning people about a murder it makes me wonder about stuff. It makes me wonder if this person might have something to hide. When I start thinking like that it makes me want to lock somebody up for a long spell, till they start wanting to talk."

"I don't know nothing, sheriff."

"Is that so? Well maybe an extended stay in County will jar your memory," Talbert said before turning to Dale, the deputy. "Take this boy into custody. We'll question him later."

"Wait…" Tyler said as he was being hauled away. "I know a girl. She was in here last night. I ain't seen her since and I didn't know nothing about her being missing, but she was wearing a white dress with black spots the last I seen her."

"This girl got a name?"

"Mona Cooper. She a local girl."

"How well you know this Mona?"

"I know her most of my life. Me and her was going together for a while."

"So, Mona was your girl, huh?"

"Not in a long time. We had a falling out some time back. I ain't seen her in ages, not till last night."

"Did you talk to her last night?"

"No sir. She came and went before I had a chance. I never even got to say hi."

"Did she talk to anyone else?"

"I seen her at the bar talking with Tabby. Her and Tabby was good friends, they growed up together," Tyler explained before pointing to me. "That there white fellow was there too."

Talbert turned to me. "I should have known." Then back to Tyler. "Which one is Tabby?"

Tyler pointed her out. She was up by the front of the room talking with one of the deputies. From the looks of it she was already explaining about seeing her friend the night before.

"You see anything else last night, Tyler?" the sheriff asked. "Anything I might be interested in?"

Tyler hesitated before answering. "I came in a bit before Mona. I was here when she showed up. When I was coming in I noticed Jarvis Brown hanging around out front, like he was waitin' on somebody."

"Jarvis Brown, is that right? Ain't that convenient?"

"Who is Jarvis Brown?" I asked.

The sheriff gave me a look. "Jarvis Brown is the Atlantic Beach equivalent to the Boogie Man."

"I ain't lying, Sheriff. He was out there big as life."

"Dale," Talbert said to his deputy, "go and fetch that pretty little thing for me. McKeller and her are going to have a long talk with me. After that, you can take this boy down town and show him our honeymoon suite."

The three of us sat down at a table while the deputies continued interrogating the crowd. Talbert wasn't too happy to be in our company by the way he acted.

"You want to explain to me why you didn't tell me you were talking with the dead Negro girl last night."

"Her name is Mona and you never asked." I looked over at Tabby. Her face was tense and flushed, a single tear rolling down her cheek.

Sheriff Talbert began grilling us on what we knew. Tabby gave him all the details about our encounter with Mona. I collaborated everything she said.

"So, this girl seemed like she was having some sort of problem?" he asked.

"She was nervous and anxious. Something was bothering her," I answered.

Tabby said, "I knew something was wrong but I didn't think too much about it. Mona was always high strung and a little dramatic about things. I just figured she had a fight with a man or something, like always."

"She had a lot of trouble with men, did she?"

"No more than most, I expect. Mona had boyfriends from time to time but they always seemed to let her down. Maybe she expected too much out of men."

"Just how many boyfriends are we talking about?"

"Mona was a beautiful girl. Every man in Atlantic Beach had his eye on her."

"That doesn't really answer my question."

"She had her share. Mona was always looking for something better. She wanted to get out of this town since she was a little girl. I think she latched onto men she thought were going to take her away from this life. When she realized they weren't what she was looking for she went on about her way."

"She was promiscuous," the sheriff said, all blunt and direct.

Tabby bit down on her lower lip, pausing before answering. "She was a free spirit. She loved to laugh and to have fun. She was a very popular girl and people loved being around her. Sometimes her zest for life got her in bad situations where men were concerned. Mona wasn't a tramp, if that's what you're asking."

"Was she seeing anyone in particular these days?"

"I wouldn't know. I hadn't seen her in such a long time."

"And last night she just showed up out of the blue and asked to stay at your place?"

"She said she was getting out of town. She wanted to sleep over at my place and she was supposed to come back after the bar closed."

"But she never showed up?"

Tabby shook her head slowly, side to side. "I waited around for a while and then I went to bed."

"How about Tyler Wilkins, you know him?"

"Tyler is a regular here. I've known him since we were kids. He and Mona used to go together but that was a long time ago."

"You don't know if they had been seeing each other recently?"

"I doubt it. I see Tyler all the time but I hadn't seen Mona in months."

The sheriff's questions kept coming but Tabby was running out of answers. She was able to tell the sheriff that Mona's father lived somewhere in the town of Conway but that was about it. She had no idea where Mona was staying, working or who she might have been seeing. She didn't have a clue what her friend might have been doing on a secluded stretch of beach in the middle of the night. There wasn't much more she could help with.

"I don't suppose you saw Jarvis Brown hanging about too, did you?"

Tabby shook her head. "No sir, I haven't seen Jarvis around these parts in ages."

"I had a feeling you might say that." Talbert wrapped up his questioning and stood up. He told us we were free to go.

"What's going to happen next?" Tabby asked.

Talbert took a deep breath, mulling it over in his mind. "We'll be holding on to Tyler a spell, see why he was in such a big hurry to sneak out of here. Something just don't sit right with that boy.

"We're going to need someone to come down to the station and ID the body. From everything you've told me I'm all but positive it's Mona Cooper, but if you could stop by and take a look it would be a big help. After that we'll see about contacting the father so he can make burial arrangements."

Tabby winced and nodded at the same time, like she understood what he was saying but the words physically hurt her to hear them. I was impressed by the way she was holding together. You could tell she was a hair away from breaking down completely.

After the sheriff left us, I placed my hand on the table over hers. "Are you all right?"

Tabby looked up at me and started to answer but the words got caught in her throat and her big brown eyes began to fill with water. She looked lost and confused as the tears began spilling down her cheeks and she tried to hold back the sobs erupting within her but it was no use. She had held them back as long as she could.

"Come on, I'll take you home."

I stood up and took hold of her arm, helping her stand and pulling her toward me. With my arm wrapped around her, I held her close to me and began guiding her toward the front door. Her body was limp and I could tell that if I were to let go of her she would collapse to the floor.

We got some looks on the way out the door, me with my arms around the pretty young black girl. Not all of them came from the sheriff and his men. It didn't bother me any.

Chapter Nine

Oᴜᴛsɪᴅᴇ, the night air was brisk by Baltimore standards but down right cold for South Carolina. I felt Tabby shudder in my grasp and I took off my jacket and hung it over her shoulders. She pulled it together in the front, holding it tight around her, and I held her close to me, supporting her as we walked. She was a mess, barely able to maneuver on her own, all of her weight on my side, wrapped in my arms.

Tabby gave me directions to her place, a third floor apartment around the corner, within easy walking distance. We strolled through the streets of Atlantic Beach, taking small cautious steps, in no hurry to get there.

Neither of us said much of anything. Tabby was a wreck and I imagine she was too overcome with grief to think of anything else. I, on the other hand, was disturbed at seeing her this way, as she had always been so strong and happy, but there was a selfish part of me that enjoyed having her in my arms. I'm a jerk like that.

We worked our way around the main drag and came to a couple of apartment buildings tucked in behind a hotel. A set of wooden steps lead up the back, old worn looking stairs that had seen better days and had clothes and bed sheets hanging from the railings, laundry drying in the night air.

I helped her climb the stairs one slow step at a time and before long we were at her door. She reached out from under my coat and turned the knob, opening it up and stepping inside and out of my grasp. I wasn't sure what to do and stood out on the landing for a few moments wondering if I should follow. It was, after all, the apartment of a single woman and I didn't want to do anything inappropriate.

After weighing my options, I decided to go in.

Tabby's apartment was small by any measure. There was almost nothing to it. Along one wall a bed extended out into the middle of the room with a medium sized bureau on the right and a flimsy table with two chairs off to the left. There was no stove and no icebox. The room was hardly large enough for the few furnishings it had.

The light was off but there was enough coming through the single window that I could see pretty clearly, dresses and such strewn about the room, hanging haphazardly over every piece of furniture. It was obvious Tabby wasn't the neatest of people.

She was sitting on the corner of the bed, still wrapped in my coat, with her head hanging low. The blinds were open and the light coming through sprayed across her in sections, dark sharp shadows separated every few inches down the contour of her.

Tabby lifted her head and looked at me, big browns wide and wet. A streak of light crossed at her eyes, shadow at her nose, light again at her mouth and chin, shadow at her neck. The sight of her took my breath away for a second.

I walked over and sat beside her without a word. She slid my coat off her shoulders and let it fall behind her, leaning on me and resting her head on my arm. We sat like that for what seemed an eternity, neither of us moving or saying anything. Eventually Tabby broke the silence.

"Who would do something like that?"

"I don't know. There are a lot of bad people in the world."

"I wish you could have known her, McKeller. Mona was such a sweetheart."

"It's a crying shame."

She scooted her head up my arm, until it was at my shoulder, lifting her chin and gazing up at me. I turned mine down and we ended up eye to eye, inches from each other's face.

"She didn't deserve what she got."

I wanted to answer her but couldn't. Her eyes held me paralyzed.

"Will you do me a favor, McKeller?"

At that moment I would have done anything short of murder for Tabby. I gave the slightest of nods. It was all I could manage.

"Will you find out who killed my friend?"

I wrinkled my brow, stunned at her request. It was about the last thing in the world I thought she was going to ask.

"You're a detective. You could you look into it and see what's going on? The police don't care nothing for some dead black girl. They won't hardly try to find out who killed Mona."

I still hadn't answered her. I still couldn't.

"I understand if you can't but if you could just ask around some …" The tears were back again. They formed at the corners of those bold beautiful eyes and rolled down her exquisite face. I watched them stream across her features, leaving moist trails alongside her delicate nose, her high cheeks, her full pouting lips.

"Of course," I said in a whisper. "I'll do what I can."

I couldn't take it any longer. I lowered my face the final few inches until our lips were touching and I kissed her soft and gentle like.

At first she didn't return my kiss but she didn't resist either. After a few seconds she began to kiss back, her soft lips caressing mine, her mouth moving with my lips, her tongue darting out ever so slightly.

Her hands were on each side of my face, pulling at me, and her kisses exploded into mine, a fury of pecks and nibbles in rapid succession, her head moving side to side, our mouths fused together. My hands were around her, one at the back of her head, holding her close, the other caressing her waist, back and hips, touching her in the way I had always wanted.

She let out soft whimpers and moans as we kissed and, each time she did, something boiled over inside me. I had lost all reason and self-control, my mind a maze of sensations; my body aching to be closer to her, reacting completely on its own to the lovely creature it was entwined with.

I laid her back on the bed, gently lowering her head to the

mattress and hovered over her. We continued to kiss and I reached down and placed my hand on the outside of her left calf. I slid it across the smooth surface of her skin and I could feel the muscles beneath contract and release with every movement she made. I wanted to touch every inch of her, my hand gliding up and around her knee, exploring the nook behind it, coming up farther across the outside of her thigh and under her dress.

We were swept up in a fit of passion, completely lost in each other, or so I thought. There had only been one other woman in my life that made me feel anything close. It was as near to perfection as I had ever experienced.

I felt two small hands on my chest and began to realize she was pushing me away. I stopped and let her gently shove me off her, rolling over and settling in on my back beside her.

"We can't …" Her voice was soft and raspy, breathless and weak.

"What?" I asked, trying to catch my breath.

"We can't do this. It won't work."

"It seemed to be working pretty well from where I am."

Tabby was breathing hard, lying beside me with her eyes closed. She shook her head slightly from side to side. "That's not the part I'm worried about. We can't do this, McKeller."

I rolled over on my side facing her. I reached out and touched her cheek with the back of my hand. "Why not?"

"You know why not. We come from different worlds."

"I don't care about any of that. I want you, Tabby."

Tabby opened her eyes and smiled. She took my hand and kissed it softly. "It wouldn't work. The world isn't like that."

"Don't worry about any of that right now."

"I'm not that kind of girl, McKeller. With me it's got to be all or nothing. It's the only way."

"Maybe we could make it work."

"You know better than that."

"All I know is how much I want to be with you." I leaned forward for a kiss but she stopped me, lifting her head and planting one on my forehead.

"You're a swell guy, Frankie. I wish it could be different but we both know how things are." It was the first time she'd ever called me by my first name.

"The hell with it, what do we care what anybody thinks?"

Her smile grew bigger but it wasn't a happy smile. "Let's say we tried. How is that going to work? Are you going to make me your girlfriend? Are you going to marry me one day and have babies with me?"

I didn't answer.

"McKeller, I couldn't even walk through the front door of the Big Digs with you. We wouldn't be allowed to eat in restaurants together. What kind of life would that be?"

"We could stay here in Atlantic Beach."

"Do you think that would be any better? Do you think there isn't bigotry here too?"

"I'm here all the time—"

"You're not dating a black girl. Trust me, things would be different. If anybody even knew you were here now it would change things."

"I'm not afraid of what people would think."

"Lucky for you I'm afraid enough for the both of us," she said. "You should go now."

I hesitated, trying to think of an argument, a way to convince her she was wrong. Glancing down across her, I took one last look at the landscape of her. She was lying on the bed, her left knee in the air, her right lying flat. Her dress was hiked up past mid-thigh and hanging off her right shoulder and her hair was tussled about, frayed out in every direction. Her gaze was fixed on me and her eyes were wide and sad.

I had nothing to offer. Without a word, I climbed out of bed, picked up my jacket and let myself out the door.

Chapter Ten

THE drive back to the Ocean Forest was frustrating to say the least. I wanted to roll the window down and yell obscenities, but I didn't figure that would solve much. It would take a lot more than some screaming and cussing to get Tabby out of my head.

I was cruising down a dirt portion of Kings Highway, getting closer to my turn off at Calhoun Road for the hotel when I noticed a light off to the right. It was in the middle of nowhere and barely visible. If I hadn't been there earlier in the day, I might not have paid it any attention. Maybe it was the fact I knew the Villa Roma was closed for the season.

I turned off my headlights and pulled the Studebaker into the far side of the sand parking lot. As quietly as I could, I opened the door and got out, taking special care not to slam it shut.

I crept up to the restaurant and climbed the stone stairs at the porch before inching my way to the window and peeking in. A few tables were pulled together in the center of the dining room and five guys were sitting around it playing cards. The Italian wasn't one of them. In the center of the table was a pile of money. It looked like a pretty decent pot.

Detective work was about the last thing in the world I was in the mood for. Most of me wanted to turn tail and head back home. Unfortunately, a small part wouldn't let me.

Patty Highsmith was still out there somewhere. Mona Cooper had been out there too but nobody cared enough to go out and find out what was going on with her. If someone had, maybe she wouldn't have ended up in the sand with her throat slit. I needed to make sure Patty didn't wind up the same way.

Standing by the front door, I took a quick inventory of everything I had on me, a half a pack of Lucky Strikes, a lighter, and almost two hundred dollars in cash. I had no weapons of any kind.

I rapped on the door three times. I could see the men moving about and jumping up. One guy threw a table cloth over the pile of money. Three headed toward the back and disappeared around the corner, one stayed by the table and the other one came to answer the door.

"What do you want?"

I took a deep breath and let it out. "I'm looking for a game," I said in my best tipsy voice.

"Go away. There's nothing like that here."

Reaching into my wallet, I pulled out my wad of cash and began thumbing through it, fanning it out for the guys to see. "I heard this is the place. I went out and got half a load on and I'm looking to lose some money."

One by one, I saw three heads peek back around the corner. I had their interest.

"Who are you?"

"My name is Frank and I work at the hotel. I'm new in town. I'm looking for a little action."

"Gambling is illegal in Myrtle Beach."

It was, but then so was liquor and that didn't seem to stop anybody. The local horse track had gotten by with it on a technicality, but now the city council, with the encouragement of the local church groups, was doing its best to shut that down. Most locals thought the track would be gone in less than a year.

"I won't tell if you don't."

The guy opened the door a few inches. "You a cop?" Why did it seem people were always asking me that?

"No. I work at the Ocean Forest."

"You know, if you were a cop and I asked you that you have

to tell me. It's the law," he said.

"I wouldn't know about that. I'm not a cop."

He looked back at the others and shrugged. All four shrugged back with looks on their faces like they'd all swallowed canaries. I was in.

Introductions were made. The guy's names were Ben, Joe, Larry, Ed and Steven—no Timothy and no Vincent. They were friendly enough, maybe a little guarded and tight lipped.

Their game was Five Card Stud with a twenty-five cent ante. I got the sense they played together a lot. They were decent players but none of them were going to quit their day jobs and head for Vegas. None of them were hardcore gamblers. They were the kind of fellows who played for fun, hoping to make a few extra bucks, praying they wouldn't lose too much.

I'm a fairly good card player, but I made sure I didn't show it that night. I folded good hands and played out the crap ones, losing as much money as I could and trying to raise them whenever possible. I ended up winning a few hands on accident by bluffing them too far. I wanted word to get around that some dumb yankee was in town throwing money around and losing it in a big way.

There's a word for guys like that and the professional scam artists can see them coming from a mile away. I was hoping to throw up a flare high enough for Timothy Vincent to see.

"You guys ever play for any real money?" I asked.

"This money looks pretty real to me," one of them replied.

"You know what I mean; don't you ever play for big stakes?"

They looked at me kind of funny. I was getting under their skin. I knew I was on the right track.

The game broke up in the early hours of the morning. I made a point to tell them again that I worked at the Ocean Forest Hotel. I gave them the number there and told them I was looking for a high stakes game. I was hoping they would pass it along.

All told, I had lost forty-five dollars for the night. Not a bad investment.

Chapter Eleven

Iᴛ was late by the time I got back to the hotel. I went in through the ground level entrance, under the green awning, hoping to swing by the Brookgreen Room. During the slow season they tended to wrap it up early and the bar was shut down for the night.

I needed a drink after the night I'd had and I walked back through the meat of the hotel, to my office. I turned on the light, pulled out a dirty glass and my bottle of whiskey from the filing cabinet and plopped myself down in the chair. The first three shots went down smooth, too smooth. I should have known that could mean trouble.

By the time I'd had my fill I had put more of a dent in that bottle than one man is meant to make in a fifth of whiskey. My head was swamped with things I didn't want to think about and even the hooch couldn't wipe them away. I felt like getting some fresh air so I grabbed what was left of the bottle and made for the back entrance of the hotel, the one that faced her.

You've got to wonder why a guy who hates the ocean would choose to live in a beach town. If I figure it out I'll let you know.

The Atlantic and I had a volatile relationship at best. We had ever since a day, two-and-a-half years ago, when I took some shrapnel to the leg at a place called Omaha Beach. You could say I'd had it out for her ever since.

I stumbled my way across the back lawn, crossing the road and walking down the planked path that led out to the sand. I stopped twenty yards from her and took a swig from the bottle.

She was feeling her oats that night. The moon was bright and the waves were larger than usual, crashing about and making a lot of noise in the night air. She wanted to make sure I knew she was there.

My mind flashed thoughts of a young brunette in a strange town up to her neck in who knows what. I thought of another young girl who hadn't got off so lucky, and I wondered what Mona Cooper had gotten herself neck deep into. What was it that would make a guy snuff the life of a kid like that?

There was another girl in my thoughts that night. This one was a sad, pretty thing who was looking for answers to why her friend ended up dead in the sand. This was the one who crept back into my head every time I tried to push her out. She was the one I yearned to be with, a yearning I'd had inside me for months but was afraid to do anything about it.

Tonight I had done something about it and it blew up in my face. I wondered how much different things would be between Tabby and me. I wondered how bad I had screwed things up between us.

The Atlantic kept tormenting me, the endless cycle of waves beating down on the sand, the deafening noise, the moonlight twinkling off her surface. The bitch was really putting it to me.

"What?" I screamed out at her. "What in the hell do you want from me?"

She answered me back a hundred times in a hundred different ways, but I was too dumb to understand any of them. A glimpse of an image on her surface reminded me of Tabby's smile.

I reared back and threw the whiskey bottle at her, heaving it out as far as I could. It barely got past the surf and she swallowed it up in a wave, mocking my inadequacy. She didn't even thank me for the drink.

"Why?" I yelled. "What do you want from me?"

I started yelling things at her, obscenities and threats, the kind of things a guy yells when he's on a whiskey drunk and half out of his mind with heartbreak. I yelled the things I had wanted to yell at her since I had moved to Myrtle Beach, since that day on Omaha. I yelled the things I had wanted to yell since earlier that night when I left Tabby's place.

After I got it out of my system I collapsed in the sand, drunk and tired. There was nothing left to yell. I looked back out over her, waves still pounding the shore, never letting up.

"Thanks," I whispered to her. "I owe you one."

I turned and began crawling back across the sand, eventually working my way back up to my feet and heading home to the Ocean Forest. I had to get some shut eye. I had things to do in the morning.

There was a little brunette out there somewhere I had never met, and she was counting on me to find her. There was a broken old woman in the hotel who was counting on me too.

There was another young girl lying on a slab in the morgue who I had met for about two minutes the night before. She was beyond counting on anybody for anything but I felt like I might owe her something too.

There was also Tabby. If by finding out who killed her friend I could relieve any amount of the suffering she was going through, it would be more than worth my time. If by finding the killer I could show her the kind of guy I was and win her affections, prove to her that we could one day be together, it would be worth everything I had.

I was juggling a lot of balls in the air. I wondered which ones would hit the ground before it was all over.

Mostly, I wished I had a clue to what I was doing. I wished I was in some way qualified to do what I was about to attempt.

Chapter Twelve

THEY say there are people who love to get up early in the day. They call them morning people, and these folks jump right out of bed at the crack of dawn and hop right into their day. If I ever meet one of these people first thing in the morning, there's a good chance somebody is getting shot.

Needless to say, I am not a morning person. I got out of bed early, anyway. I even managed breakfast with Ellen Highsmith.

There wasn't much I could tell her, but I assured her I was working on the case and had found a few leads I was checking out. This seemed to brighten her spirits. She insisted I keep her apprised to everything that was going on. I told her I would but decided to hold back on the things I had found out about Timothy Vincent. If she knew the details about the man her daughter had linked up with it would only cause her more worry.

After breakfast I left the hotel, climbing into the '46 Studebaker the Ocean Forest allowed me to use, one of my favorite job perks.

I was basically working on the cases of two young girls. They couldn't have had any less in common. One was black, one was white. One came from the cozy middle class suburbs of Greenville, South Carolina and the other came from the rural farmlands of Myrtle Beach. One was alive, I hoped, and the other was very much dead.

My first order of business was to head back up to Atlantic Beach and see Tabby. There was still the little business of identifying the body and I figured she might need a friend along.

I'm not going to lie. It was more than a little awkward when she answered the door. Neither of us knew quite what to say.

She was wearing a plain brown dress, bland and cut big, nothing like the dresses I was used to seeing her in, and she had a thick tan sweater over it. Her hair was pulled up in a bun and there were dark circles around her bloodshot eyes. She looked small and tired and I had to resist the urge to wrap my arms around her.

"McKeller..." she started to say.

"Look, about last night—" I began but she cut me off.

"It happened, no big deal." She forced a smile on her face, for my benefit I suspect.

"What do you say I give you a ride to the sheriff's office and we get this out of the way? Afterward, I'll buy you lunch."

Tabby nodded her acknowledgment, slow and somber. Neither of us was looking forward to the task at hand. We made the drive into Myrtle Beach in silence.

The sheriff's office sat on a little road off of Main Street. It wasn't much to look at from the outside. The inside wasn't much better.

His office was a little box of a room. It was cluttered with a couple of desks, a row of filing cabinets and a door leading to a back area, out of sight from public view. I figured it was where the jail cells were housed.

"We appreciate you coming by," the sheriff said to Tabby as we entered, ignoring me as best he could. He reached onto his desk and picked up an official looking form on a clipboard. "I just need to get some information before we take a look."

Tabby gave one nod.

"Can I have your full name?"

"Tabitha Rose Greenwood." I didn't know her middle name was Rose. It fit.

"Address?"

She gave it to him. He went on to ask her a half-dozen more

basic questions before tucking the clipboard under his arm. "OK, let's do this. She's over, across the street, at Doc's place."

He led the way and we followed. Doc Burns had a little office catty-corner to the sheriff. There was a clean, neat waiting room out front but we didn't wait. The sheriff walked directly through, leading us back to a series of examination rooms, sterile and hospital-like. We continued past to a small door in the back. The sheriff paused for a second, looking over at Tabby, before opening it up and stepping in.

They had her on a folding table in a storage room. A white sheet covered her and her legs were hanging off the end, dirty feet sticking out from under the cover. Around her was piled boxes and books, medical supplies the doctor no longer had use for.

The sheriff walked up to the table and flipped off the sheet like it was no big deal, like there wasn't a mutilated young girl sprawled across the table, Tabby let out a sigh and I saw her body go limp. I put my arm around her and held what little weight there was to her against me, giving her some kind of support.

Mona Cooper was sprawled out on a table just large enough for her torso. Her head was cocked to the side and a gash crossed her throat, clotted with dried blood. Her dress was muddy and dirty, ripped and stained with the reddish brown crust of what was once bright crimson and warm. Her left breast was exposed and there were purple bruises across her face and shoulders.

The eyes said it all. They were wide open and blank, a dull haze across them. I had looked into those eyes thirty six hours before, but it was difficult for me to remember how they appeared when they were backed by life, vibrant and seeing.

"Is this Mona Cooper?" the sheriff asked, no compassion in his voice.

Tabby nodded and covered her face with her hands, gentle sobs muffled in her palms.

The sheriff dropped the sheet and made a move for the door. "Thank you Miss Greenwood, you've been a big help."

"Can I have a minute?"

The sheriff looked confused.

"Can I have a minute with Mona?"

Talbert looked around the storage room, surveying it for

things Tabby might steal if given the opportunity, I imagine. He thought about it a second before answering. "I suppose that would be all right."

He left the room.

"Are you OK?" I asked her.

"I'll be fine."

I followed the sheriff out, glancing back as I closed the door behind me. Tabby had taken a handkerchief from her pocket and was beginning to clean the dried blood and dirt from Mona's face.

Chapter Thirteen

I stood outside the storage room, waiting for Tabby to finish. I was leaning against the wall with the sheriff across from me. He had barely talked to me since I got there but I didn't let that stand in the way.

"Where was Mona found?" I asked.

"She was found just north of the Ocean Forest and just south of Atlantic Beach, the old artillery range."

"Artillery range?"

"Yeah, during the war gunners trained here in Myrtle Beach, there was a stretch where they used to shoot at targets up along the coast. Nobody ever goes there anymore."

"Who found her?" I asked.

"A fisherman found her lying on the beach."

"From what I saw, it looked like she was roughed up pretty good. Do you figure she was raped?"

"She wasn't wearing panties. It's a possibility."

"Any suspects?"

"Tyler Wilkins is our main guy."

"Do you really think he had anything to do with it?"

"It's too soon to say. Right now he's all we have."

"What about that guy Tyler said he saw out front of Mack's?"

"Jarvis Brown?" The sheriff laughed. "Every time something

bad goes down in Atlantic Beach somebody or the other saw Jarvis Brown lurking about."

"Are you saying he's some kind of myth?"

"Oh, he's real all right. He's about the meanest, biggest son of a bitch in these parts. I've locked Jarvis up more times than I can remember."

"So, he's a repeat offender?"

"Jarvis has got a temper on him. It don't take much to set him off and when he does there's usually hell to pay. That temper of his has gotten him into trouble more times than any five men combined."

"What if Tyler actually saw him there that night?"

"First off, cutting a girl's throat isn't exactly Jarvis' style. He's more likely to beat you to death with his fists, presuming you make him angry enough.

"Secondly, we arrested Jarvis not three weeks ago after he done a number on his foreman at Myrtle Beach Farms, took three of my deputies to subdue him enough to get the cuffs on him. Last I heard, he's awaiting trial for attempted murder up in Conway. I don't expect we'll be hearing anymore of Jarvis Brown for a spell."

The sheriff paused and gave me that look of his. "What gives? Are you investigating this thing?"

"A friend of mine lost someone close to them. I'm just trying to help out."

"By friend, are you referring to that little darkie in there?"

"Her name is Tabby."

Talbert gave me a weird look. "What's up with you, McKeller? Why are you so cozy with the likes of her? You gettin' some of that?" He had a smutty smile on his face when he said it.

"She's a friend."

"You might want to take a little more care when choosing your friends."

"What's that supposed to mean?"

"It means there are lines drawn in the sand around these parts. Once you cross them it's hard to go back."

"I would think your main priority would be finding out who killed a young girl on the beach."

"Maybe things are different where you come from. Down here, we see things the way they are. There are people who conduct themselves in a certain manner. There are other kinds of people who don't. We find it's best to let those other kinds keep to themselves. They're going to do what they do, that's just the way they are. When people live like that, sometimes they end up on the beach with their throats cut."

"Are you saying she got what she deserved?"

"I'm saying things are what they are. We reap what we sow. If you live a certain way, chances are you're going to die a certain way."

"Mona Cooper was just a kid."

The sheriff took a step toward me and was standing in my face. "You're not a kid. You need to take a long look at where your priorities lie."

"Sheriff Talbert, a young woman was brutally murdered in your county. Isn't your job to find out who did it?"

He grinned at me. "I was elected to take care of the law abiding citizens of this county. As far as I'm concerned, the rest of them can kill themselves left and right."

"Are the rest of them the ones with the darker skin?"

"You're new down here. You don't know how it works yet. You might want to watch your back."

It was my turn to step forward. The sheriff and I were now nose to nose.

"I'm not really interested in your bullshit redneck philosophy lesson. A young girl was murdered on your watch. It doesn't matter what color her skin was, she deserves the same kind of justice as anyone else."

The door opened at my right and Tabby came walking out. "Is everything all right?" she asked.

I was still staring into Sheriff Talbert's eyes. "Everything is fine."

There was something different about Tabby when she came out of the storage room. I had expected the same fragile grieving kid but something had come over her. There was a determination in her eyes and a strength about her I hadn't seen earlier. It was like the old Tabby was back.

"Sheriff, I want to talk to Tyler Wilkins." She wasn't asking.

She turned and walked through the examination area, leaving the sheriff and me looking at each other. From her tone it seemed she had her mind pretty well made up. We rushed behind her to catch up.

"This is very unorthodox," the sheriff said as he opened the door at the back of his office. "Tyler Wilkins is the prime suspect in a murder investigation." He was explaining to Tabby why he shouldn't let her speak with him but he was doing it just the same. Maybe he saw the same look in her eyes that I saw and figured there was no use arguing.

Through the door was a narrow walkway with bars lining the right side, three empty cages. We continued down to the far end where a fourth barred door was. The door was fixed to another cell but this one was small and cramped without even the modest bunks that adorned the others. Tyler Wilkins was on the other side of the bars, sitting on the floor with his back against the far wall.

His blue suit was wrinkled and grimy, covered in dirt and dust. There was a small tear at the seam of the right shoulder. Tyler's face was dirty too but the dirt didn't hide the bruise on his cheek or the swelling in his right eye. He looked despondent and depressed. Why wouldn't he?

Tabby took a long look at him and his surroundings and glanced back up to the three empty cells we had passed. She didn't say a word but I knew what she was thinking.

"How are you, Tyler?" she asked.

Tyler grinned. "I've been better."

"They feeding you OK?"

"It ain't bad food, when it comes."

Tabby turned to the sheriff. "Do you think we could get this man some water, maybe a wash rag so he can clean up?"

Talbert glared at her for a moment. "I'll see what I can do." He turned and walked off, leaving us alone with Tyler.

"What happened to your eye?" she asked, once the sheriff was gone.

"They weren't too keen on how I was answering their questions."

Tabby sighed.

"What did you tell them?" I asked.

Tyler didn't answer. He looked at Tabby instead.

"It's all right," she told him, "McKeller is a friend of mine. He's a private eye and he's looking into Mona's death. You can talk to him."

He turned back to me. "I told them the truth. I told them I hadn't seen or heard from Mona in a coon's age. I saw her that night she came in but I never even talked to her. I stayed in the bar till they closed down and then I went home and went to sleep."

"They got nothing on you. They're only holding you because they don't have anything else."

"They don't need to have anything on him," Tabby said. I ignored the remark and continued to talk to Tyler.

"When's the last time you saw Mona, before the other night?"

"I don't recall, six months or more."

"Do you know what she had been up to, where she was working?"

He shook his head. "She was working for Raddison awhile back but that was a long time ago. I heard she got a job working for a white family in town but I don't know for sure."

At the mention of Raddison Hayes, I looked over at Tabby. She didn't seem to react to the name at all. I thought maybe she might.

"What did she do for Raddison?"

"I suspect she done whatever he told her to do."

"Do you know where she lived?"

The head shake again. "She used to keep a place near Tabby but she moved. I guess she moved in with the family she was working for."

"Does she have any friends or family that might know what she was doing?"

"Mona always had a lot of friends. Most of them are in Atlantic Beach. I don't know that she kept in touch with near anybody after she moved. It was like she done fell off the face of the earth. She got a father lives in Conway, last I heard."

"You don't know if she was in any trouble or anything?"

"I wouldn't know."

The questions were coming to me slower by now. "Why were you sneaking out of the bar?" I thought to ask.

Tyler shrugged. "I don't know. I got scared. Cops always scare me."

"What about this Jarvis Brown character? Do you really think you saw him outside of Mack's?"

"I seen him clear as day. Walked right past him on the way in. Jarvis ain't the kind of fellow that's easy to miss. He's about as big as a man can be."

"The sheriff says Jarvis is being held up in Conway for attempted murder."

"I don't know nothing bout that but I seen him, that's for sure."

I tried to think of something else to ask him but I was coming up dry. My detective skills were failing me and I had no idea what to do next. It's not like I had gotten anything out of Tyler I could go on.

"I imagine they're going to keep you in here awhile. They don't have anybody else and they're hoping you'll break down and give them something."

"I ain't got nothing to give them."

"I know."

"Are you going to be OK?" Tabby asked him.

"I reckon so. It ain't like I got any other option, do I?"

"I'll talk to the sheriff but I don't know that it will do any good," I said.

"Thank you, Mr. McKeller. I appreciate that."

I motioned to Tabby that we should be going.

"You go ahead. I'll be along shortly."

The sheriff was out in the office. There was a bucket of water with an old rag hanging over it sitting on the desk but it didn't look like he was in any big hurry to get it back to Tyler.

"You've got the wrong guy," I told him.

"Says you."

"His connection to Mona Cooper dried up a long time ago."

"That's what he keeps telling me."

"Why are you holding him?"

"I'm holding him in custody because he tried to sneak out of the bar. That and because I can."

Sheriff Talbert had his own way of doing things, and I had serious doubts anything I could say was going to make any difference.

Tabby came out a few minutes later and we left together. On our way back to the car, I asked her if I could buy her a cup of coffee or some lunch. After what we'd experienced that morning, I was guessing it would be the Joe as neither of us would have much of an appetite.

She looked around the main drag of town, the shops and stores, the diners on the corners. "What world do you live in, McKeller? Where do you think the two of us could sit down and have lunch together?"

Chapter Fourteen

I TOOK Tabby back home after. The ride was about as pleasant and awkward as the one down, what with that four hundred pound gorilla sitting there and all. Neither of us said much of anything. When I pulled up in front of her place I started to get out, offering to walk her to her door.

"No, that's OK," she replied. She didn't say it in an unfriendly way but her message was clear just the same.

"I'll start asking around. If I hear anything I'll let you know." I used my best professional voice. The one that's supposed to convey that I have some clue as to what I'm doing.

"Thanks, McKeller. I really appreciate it." Her voice was soft and her eyes were wide and trusting, everything about her screaming of the confidence she had in me, the gratitude she was feeling. It made me pray I wouldn't screw up.

From Tabby's I headed back to the Ocean Forest. I was a salaried employee after all and I was expected to log in some time in the building, even if my daily duties were vague at best.

Buntemeyer was standing at the front desk with a clerk when I walked in. He had a look on his face like I might be just the person he wanted to see.

"McKeller, you're just the person I wanted to see," he said.

"What can I do you out of?"

"How are things going with the Highsmith dilemma?"

"I'm working on it."

"We need to see this thing through. Mrs. Highsmith is extremely distraught and I have assured her that we will resolve her situation in an expeditious manner."

He seemed pretty concerned with seeing that Eleanor, or Ellen as it was, was more than satisfied with the service she received at the Ocean Forest, as though her opinion could make or break the reputation of the hotel. If only he knew.

"I gather she's calmed down after her little incident?"

Buntemeyer cleared his throat. "Yes, she was more than understanding. I assured her that things like that never happen at the Ocean Forest and I invited her to stay on as our guest until her daughter can be located."

"That's mighty nice of you."

"I thought it was the very least we could do after the trauma she has suffered." He said it as though it had been his idea. "I have had the exterminators in combing through the hotel but they haven't found any sign of our ... little problem."

"Maybe it was a fluke thing, one rat wandering in."

Buntemeyer shushed me. "McKeller, we do not say that word aloud. The last thing we want is for word to get around that the Ocean Forest is infested with rodents."

I nodded my understanding. "I'm going down to my office to make a few phone calls."

"I trust this is in regards to Patricia Highsmith?"

"Of course," I answered. I turned and started off when the clerk called me back.

"Wait, Mr. McKeller, I have a message for you."

"What kind of message?"

The clerk was middle-aged and skinny, all arms and legs with a big head and flat brown hair. He was rummaging through a stack of papers in front of him. "You had a call while you were out. They asked for a Frank McKeller and I told you you weren't in. They left a number," he explained as he handed me a slip of paper.

The paper had my name at the top and a phone number below it. "They didn't leave a name?"

"No, they hung up before I could get one."

"Did they say what it was about?"

"No."

"Was it a man or a woman?"

"It was a man. He just said to give you that number."

"Thanks."

I proceeded down to my office and sat looking at the phone number for a minute or so. It seemed odd for a guy to leave a number out of the blue without a name or any explanation. There was only one way to solve that probing mystery.

A man's voice answered on the other end. "Yeah?"

"This is Frank McKeller. I got a message to call this number."

"Yeah, McKeller, right…"

"And you are?"

"Let me ask you, McKeller, you aren't some kind of cop are you?" Again with the cop thing.

"No, not at all."

"It's just that I heard from a friend that you might be looking for a game."

"I'm always looking for a game."

"I have some friends in town. We like to get together for a game every now and again. We're always looking for new players."

"What kind of stakes are we talking?"

"We don't play nickel ante, if you know what I mean."

"Are we talking high rollers or what?"

"Well, it's not like you're going to be sitting across from Howard Hughes or anything but we like to make it worth our while."

"Sounds interesting. I'm still pretty new in town and I'm trying to figure where a guy can go for a good time. I don't mind throwing some money around but I don't want to spend my Friday nights sitting around and drinking milk with a bunch of old men."

The guy laughed. "I know what you mean. You don't have to worry. We try to make sure all the usual vices are represented."

"Count me in. Where and when?"

"Tonight at ten, back at the Villa Roma." For a restaurant that was closed for the season it certainly seemed to be a popular hangout.

"I'll be there."

"Go around the back and knock on the door. Ask for Joey."

"Are you Joey?"

The guy paused. "Yeah, I'm Joey."

It wasn't Timothy Vincent but at least it was a start. I guessed that it was the crowd Vincent ran with anyway. Maybe Timothy might even make an appearance.

I hung up the phone and dialed the sheriff's office. Talbert was one of the last people I wanted to speak with but I didn't have a lot of options.

"What do you want, McKeller?" he asked in a tone that said he wasn't much interested in what I wanted either.

"I wanted to know if you got a hold of Mona's father."

"Yeah, I talked to him a little while ago. He's coming in from Conway to claim the body. He'll be here tomorrow afternoon."

I started to ask another question but the good sheriff had already hung up on me. If I were the sensitive type I might have started thinking Talbert wasn't very fond of me.

My next call was to the Myrtle Beach Train Depot. It rang about four dozen times before a woman with a husky voice answered. I asked about incoming trains from Conway.

"From Conway? Where else are they going to come from?" There was only one line into Myrtle Beach and it was a straight stretch that ran back and forth between the two towns.

The train had already come and gone for the day. The next one was scheduled for noon the next. I figured there was a good chance Mona Cooper's father might be on that one. I also figured I should probably be there to meet him when he came in.

The familiar ache was creeping into my bum leg and I knew it would be throbbing before long. The pain was always there to some degree but it came and went in intensity. I could tell a good one was coming on.

The bottle I usually kept in my filing cabinet was gone. I hadn't replaced it since my night on the beach or I probably would have pulled it out for a swig. There was always the Brook-green Room.

Tempting as it was, I decided maybe it would be better if I lay off the booze for now. It was a long time before ten o'clock and I didn't want to start too early. There was a good chance I might need to have my wits about me. I figured I could suck up the pain for a while. It wouldn't be the first time I had to.

Chapter Fifteen

THE Villa Roma looked deserted from the outside. The sand lot was empty and the lights were low; you had to look hard to see any on at all. I drove around the back and found five cars parked behind the building, tucked off so you couldn't see them from Kings Highway. These guys were more careful than the amateurs I played with the night before.

I walked up to the beat up wooden door and rapped hard. The door opened a few inches and I couldn't see who was behind it. "What do you want?"

"I'm here to see Joey. My name is McKeller."

The door opened the rest of the way and I found myself face to face with the Italian I had met the other day. He gave me half a snarl, looking over me with distrust in his eyes.

"Through there," he said, motioning with his head the direction he wanted me to go.

I continued on through the kitchen. It was a cluttered little room with an old stove and oven off to one side and a large wooden table in the center. The table was covered with cut vegetables with a long butcher's knife lying off to the side. On the stove was a huge pot cooking, and the smell of rich spicy sauce simmering inside it made me hungry.

Past the kitchen, a swinging door opened up to the dining

area I had played cards in before. The tables were moved around some, with two pushed together in the center and the others pulled out of the way, chairs scattered about and turned in to the main table. It gave the room more space and made it seem bigger and more comfortable.

Guys were sitting around on the outlying chairs, cigars and drinks in their hands. There were six of them all together, ages ranging from mid-twenties to early forties. They were laughing and cutting up. Nobody was playing cards yet.

There were girls in the room too. One was a scrawny redhead in a short dress, her hair long and wild looking. She appeared to be in her twenties and she had long, sharp features. She wasn't the cutest thing I had ever seen but she was getting a lot of attention from three of the guys in the room.

The other girl looked younger, maybe eighteen at most. She was blonde and pretty, short and scrawny like she was just growing into her womanly curves. Her hair was pulled back and she was wearing a light blue cotton dress that buttoned all the way down the front, the top four undone. She had it pulled out across the front of her, trying to show off some cleavage but there wasn't much to show off.

The blonde was wearing a lot of makeup and I could see a patch of acne under the rouge on her right cheek. Her lashes were long and fake-looking and they fluttered when she laughed. She was sitting on the lap of one of the men and, from where I was standing, it looked like she was flirting for all she was worth.

A stocky guy in a white shirt and tie stepped up to me. He had light hair with a reddish tint, combed perfectly, parted in the center. His small eyes and the straight set of his mouth gave his wide face a strict business-like look about it.

"You McKeller?"

"Yeah. You Joey?"

He nodded. "Glad you could make it." He poured a drink from a brown jug and handed it to me. "The best around," he informed me as I took a sip.

It tasted a lot like turpentine but without the smooth aftertaste. I could tell the moment it hit my tongue that it had more kick than the stuff they served at Mack's.

"Nice."

He grinned wide, happy that I approved of the moonshine. "I got a connection."

I took another swallow.

Joey offered me a cigar which I accepted. He lit it for me with a wooden match and watched intently as I drew in a puff. I'm not much of a cigar guy and wouldn't know the difference between a Cuban and a nickel cigar but I could tell he was awaiting my opinion.

"Very good." I nodded.

"We do it up right at these things. Its ten bucks to get in. That covers the booze, the cigars and the food. Everything else will cost you. We start out at five a hand and take it from there, no limits on the betting. The girls are on their own, you work it out with them."

I reached into my pocket and pulled out a wad of money, making sure to show it off as I fished through it for a ten spot. Joey's eyes lit up when he saw it. I sensed others around the room had noticed it too.

After handing him my cover fee, he called the room together and the boys began taking seats around the table. The girls drifted off into the background and let us get settled in.

Introductions were next, a bunch of names that I forgot almost immediately. None of them were Timothy Vincent. We began playing.

These guys were better players than the night before. They took it seriously and they were all concentration with every hand. The first pot got up to fifty-four dollars, the second sixty-eight.

I raised with a pair of deuces on the first. I folded with three kings on the second. They were feeling me out, and I wanted to make sure I came across as the pigeon I was advertised to be.

On the third hand, the pretty blonde planted herself in my lap.

"Hi."

"Hi," I answered back.

"You're cute."

"You're not so bad yourself. You got a name?"

"Claire," she said.

"It's nice to meet you, Claire."

"I always wanted to learn how to play cards. It looks like fun."

"Maybe I could teach you sometime."

She glanced at my hand. "It looks so confusing."

I was holding nothing, five cards with no connection to each other. It was a sucker hand. Joey raised ten dollars and I saw his bet.

I picked two cards at random and tossed them down. "Two," I said.

The girl watched as I took my two from the dealer and slid them between my other three cards. These two had even less to do with the three I was holding.

Joey raised another ten. I saw him again.

This is the way it went for a while. When I had nothing Joey was raising all over the place. When I was dealt something decent he saw fit to either bet low or fold.

Claire was shooting him signals, I was sure of it. I couldn't tell how she was doing it but I knew she was. Joey always knew how to bet with what I was holding.

By the time I was down two bills I announced I needed a break. "You guys are creaming me. I'm taking a breather."

"We could go upstairs for a spell," Claire suggested.

"Yeah, that would be nice."

The blonde stood and took my hand, guiding me up and across the room, out around the corner to a flight of stairs. I followed behind as she led me up and into the narrow hallway I had seen from the window before. We went into the first room on the right.

I sat on the corner of the small bed with Claire hovering over me, playfully toying with the fabric of her dress in her small fingers. She had a sly smile on her face and she was batting her lashes at me, making her eyes go all wide and innocent.

"You want to have some fun?" she asked.

"Sure."

"It will cost you ten dollars plus tip."

"What's an average tip?"

"A buck or two." she sighed. "I got five once."

"At twelve bucks a pop I'm guessing a girl can make a nice living."

Claire giggled. "I don't get to keep it all. I work for a guy. I do pretty well though. I can make thirty dollars on a good night."

That was almost as much as I pulled in a week at the Ocean Forest. I took a twenty out of my pocket and handed it to her.

"I ain't got any change."

"That's all right, I don't want any."

Her eyes got big and excited. "Wow, thanks."

She no longer looked anything close to eighteen. She seemed more frail and little girl like and it was a little sad to see the joy my twenty bucks put on her face.

I'm not going to lie to you. It's not like I didn't consider it. She was a pretty little thing, all wholesome and fresh looking. It's not like it was outside the realm of possibilities.

My problem was I was pretty fond of looking at myself in the mirror in the morning. I wasn't sure I could still do that if I took advantage of what that twenty dollars bought me.

Claire leaned in and tried to kiss me, but I gently pushed her back, guiding her down onto the bed beside me. She sat looking at me, confused, maybe a little offended. "What's wrong?"

"This is going to be the easiest twenty bucks you ever made."

"Look, I don't do any kinky stuff."

"That's all right, I just want to talk."

Now she looked really confused.

"Who is this guy you work for?"

"Are you a cop?"

"No."

"He's just a guy, is all."

"This guy named Timothy Vincent, by any chance?"

I hit a nerve and Claire stiffened. The color drained out of her face. "What's it to you?"

"I need to talk to him."

"I don't know any Vincent." She was lying.

"I'm looking for a girl."

"The last time I checked you have one sitting beside you."

"This girl's name is Patty. She's about your age."

Claire shoved the twenty back in my chest. "Keep your money, I don't want it."

"You keep it. I just want a couple of answers. Nobody has to know we ever had this talk."

"I don't know nothing."

"You work for Vincent."

She shrugged. She was eying the money in her fist and I could tell she wanted it.

"I don't care what Vincent is into. It's none of my business. I just need to find the girl. Her mother is in town and she's worried. She's gone to a lot of trouble to find her daughter and I'm just trying to help out."

"Patty is fine." The words made me exhale. It was the first time I'd had any confirmation she was still alive.

"She's with Vincent?"

Claire nodded, slow and stiff. "She's his girl."

"Does that mean she doesn't work for him?"

The young girl looked into my eyes. "I used to be his girl too."

"Where can I find Vincent?"

"Look, mister, you don't know what you're getting into here. You don't want to mess with Vincent."

"Tell me about him."

"Vincent runs half of what goes on in this town. He's got connections all over the place. He's smart too. He knows how to keep himself out of trouble."

"Where does he live?"

"Out in the country somewhere. I've been there before but I don't know how to get there. It's way down some old dirt road. It's like a fortress."

"If he's such an important guy, why does he hole up in some shack in the woods?"

"Vincent has a lot of friends but he has a lot of enemies too. He plans on taking over this whole county one day. Things like that don't sit well with some people."

"Are you going to see him tonight?"

She shook her head. "I never know when I'm going to see Vincent."

"How does he get his money?"

"Sometimes he comes and gets it. Sometimes I give it to Joey and he takes care of it."

"Joey works for Vincent?"

"Not really, they have an arrangement. Vincent lets him take care of some of the business in return for part of the action."

"So, if Joey doesn't work for him, what does Vincent get in return?"

"Protection. Joey's brother is the sheriff."

I didn't see that one coming. "Sheriff Talbert?" I asked, like Myrtle Beach had another sheriff.

"I don't think the sheriff is too happy about it but he turns his head from time to time. He still harasses us enough to keep us in line, let us know he's in charge. When it comes to the other stuff he looks the other way."

"Didn't this place get busted not too long ago?"

"Things were getting pretty crazy. I was making all kinds of money and this place was crowded most nights. It was the sheriff's way of telling Vincent and Joey to tone it down."

"That's a hell of a system they have down here."

"They call it the Good Ole Boy System and it's the way things are done down here."

"You think the sheriff has a hand in it?"

"No way, he ain't like that. He lets things go on the way they always have but he tries to keep them under wraps as best he can."

"Let's get back to Vincent. Where can I find him?"

"There's a place up north of here he likes to go to. It's an old roadhouse, not much to look at. They run a rough crowd. There's always trouble. It's a hangout for the old time locals. The sheriff wouldn't even think of going out there."

"Why doesn't he run his operation from there?"

"The kind of folks Vincent caters to wouldn't be caught dead in a place like that. It's too rough for most. I'm sure he does some business out of there but his money comes from down this end, the law abiding people looking for a little fun."

"What's this place called?"

"Betsy's Tavern. You head up past North Myrtle Beach, when you come to an old burned out tobacco barn there's a four way intersection, a dirt road really. You make a left and it's back there about a mile or so."

"You think he might be there?"

"He's there a lot."

"What about Patty?"

"Sometimes, but he keeps a pretty tight leash on her. That's the way he does to the new girls. That's the way he done with me."

"Do you think he's put her to work yet?"

"I don't know but if he hasn't it won't be long."

I took a long look at the pretty young girl. If not for the tight dress and thick makeup she could have been somebody's kid sister.

"We should get back downstairs," she said. "If we don't, I'm going to have to charge you more money." Claire said it matter-of-fact, like it was just the way her business was.

I stood up and we moved to the door. Before I could open it, she stopped and gave me a glare. "If anybody asks, I showed you a real good time."

"The best," I agreed.

Back downstairs the game was going strong and I could tell they were anxious to get me back in. I figured I'd had enough cards for the night and the two hundred dollars I lost was more than enough for the information I'd gathered. The boys were going to have to find themselves another pigeon for the night. I had another stop to make.

"What do you mean, you have to go?" Joey pleaded. "We're just getting started."

"Not me. I've got to run."

"Come on, Frank, your luck is bound to change."

I gave him a look. "I somehow doubt that."

Chapter Sixteen

FROM the Villa Roma, I got into the Ocean Forest's Studebaker and headed north. When I was passing the turn for Atlantic Beach I had the urge to veer off and go see Tabby but I decided not to. Instead, I continued to follow the directions Claire had given me to get to Betsy's Tavern.

The girl hadn't been kidding when she said it was in the middle of nowhere. I made the turn at the dirt intersection, after the burned-out tobacco barn, and crept through the pitch black for what seemed like forever. Finally, I caught a glimpse of a light up ahead. It turned out to be a single neon sign advertising something called Pearl, which I assumed was a beer. I figured I had found Betsy's.

If not for the neon I might have driven right by the place. Not only was it stuck out in the boondocks but there was hardly anything to it. It wasn't much more than an old barn converted into a bar and it was painted dark on the outside, easy to miss. There was a look to it like it had been condemned some time before but no one bothered to tell anybody.

The inside wasn't any better. A plywood bar ran down the length of the left side and there were a few tables, along with a pool table, scattered to the right. It was dimly lit and smoky with an old jukebox off in the corner blaring away a Hank Williams song.

The place had just over a half dozen people in it, mostly men. A middle-aged woman was working the bar. She had a hard look about her, plump cheeks and a scowl so deep it looked like it was always there. The only other woman was younger and thin, sickly thin in the way Olive Oil is in the Popeye cartoons. She was hanging around the pool table giggling with a couple of guys.

The men in the room were all dressed down, dungarees and pullover shirts, no ties or jackets. They ranged in ages from the very young to the extremely old, and all of them made a point to give me a glare as I entered the room. I ignored the looks I was getting and took a seat at the makeshift bar.

"What are you having, Mack?" the bartender asked me.

"Whiskey with a water back."

She hesitated for a moment, looking me over, before turning around and fixing my drink. When she came back she slammed down a couple of glasses, one with two fingers of brown liquid, the other tall and filled to the brim with a liquid just a shade less brown than the whiskey. I decided to forgo the water and threw back my shot.

"How's business?" I asked, sliding my glass forward for a refill.

"About the same as usual."

"I heard this is the place to come if you're looking for some action."

"I wouldn't know anything about that."

"Where can a guy go to find a little company around here?"

She motioned over to Olive Oil. "You could go over and try to get into the Shelly sweepstakes. She gets pretty friendly with a few drinks in her but you're up against some stiff competition."

I looked back over to the skinny girl. She was leaned over the table and eying a pool shot with two men close by and over her shoulder. She looked unsteady as she pulled back and thrust her stick forward, missing the cue ball completely and bursting into laughter.

"Is Vincent around tonight?"

"You know Vincent?"

"We have mutual friends. I hear he's a guy to talk to."

"I wouldn't know anything about that either," she said, pausing again before adding, "I ain't seen him all night."

"Do you expect him in tonight?"

"I don't expect nothing."

"Any idea of how I could get in touch with him?"

"I wouldn't know. I just sling the drinks."

"Are you Betsy?"

"My mother was Betsy. My name is Madge."

"Nice to meet you, Madge." I toasted her with my glass and shot back another.

Somebody took the stool beside me and I looked over to see a large beast of a man glaring back at me. He was a wide load with broad shoulders and a thick chest, the frame of a corn fed country boy stuffed in filthy clothes. His head was shaved, his face broad and serious, eyebrows turned down. Pudgy fingers circled a beer mug that seemed lost in his grasp and black dirt caked under his fingernails.

"Nice suit," he said in a heavy southern drawl.

"Thanks."

"I ain't never seen the likes of you in here."

"It's my first time."

"We don't get many outsiders up this way, especially not no yankees."

I cringed and told myself to play nice and stay cool. "Maybe you're not advertising enough. Did you ever consider running a radio spot?"

The big guy's face froze over like he hadn't understood a word I said. His lips dipped down into a stiff frown. "We don't take too kindly to strangers barging in on our place."

"I'm just having a drink."

"This is kind of a long round about way to go and get a drink."

"I heard this is a hopping joint."

"He was asking about Vincent," the bartender added.

"What you want with Vincent?"

"I'm just a guy looking to have a good time. I heard Vincent is the guy who can make that happen."

"I like to have a good time too. You know what I like to do for fun?"

I was guessing that it had something to do with farm animals but I decided to keep it to myself. "No, what?"

"I like to beat the tar out of damnyankees."

This did not sound good to me.

"That sounds like a lot of fun but how about I buy you a drink instead?"

"How about you buy me all the drinks I want and then I'll decide whether or not to kick your ass?"

"Madge, can I get a couple of drinks over here?"

Big boy didn't take his eyes off me while the bartender set up a couple of drinks for us. Things were about as strange as strange gets and I was running scenarios through my head, none of them working out in my favor.

"Are you a friend of Vincent's?" I asked the big guy.

"Everybody is a friend of Vincent's."

"I was just down at the Villa Roma playing cards with some of his buddies. They told me to check this place out."

"They told you wrong."

"Look, I'm not looking for any trouble. I just want to talk to Vincent."

The large man picked up his beer glass and chugged it dry in seconds. He slammed it down and ordered me to buy him another one. I motioned for Madge to set up another.

"Thirsty, huh?"

"Among other things ..."

He downed the second one even quicker and saluted me with his mug, indicating it was time for me to spring for a fresh beer. I wasn't relishing the idea of being the big guy's patsy but I figured, in the kind of place I was in, I couldn't be into him for more than sixty cents. If nothing else, I was buying myself some time.

I bought him another and then another. He was slamming them back pretty quick and I could see they were starting to catch up to him as he was beginning to slur his words. On the next round, I told Madge to make them Boiler Makers and she put up shots and beers for both of us.

I saluted the big redneck with my shot glass and drank it down, chasing it with a few swallows of beer. He did the same. He threw back the whiskey and began chugging his beer back.

This was when I stood and picked up the stool beside me, holding it by the legs and swinging it into the big boy with everything I had. The heavy wood seat hit the back of his skull as his head was tilted back and drinking. It sounded like a lead pipe hitting a side of beef and the legs shattered off as his head went forward, the glass flying across the room and shattering against the wall. I hit him again with the busted stool as his body went limp across the bar, face down and motionless.

The place was dead quiet except for Hank singing about sharing a doghouse with a big old dog. All eyes were on me but nobody made a move. I had half expected to be fighting off the locals and getting the stuffing beat out of me by this point but no one seemed overly concerned with the fact I had knocked out their buddy. I got the feeling this sort of thing wasn't all that uncommon at Betsy's. It might not have been one of my brighter moves, but I have a problem with guys taking advantage of my good nature.

I reached into my pocket and pulled out some bills, tossing them on the bar top. "That's for the drinks." I threw down another five. "That's for the stool."

The big guy was making slight moaning sounds under his breath. He was still pretty much unconscious but he was beginning to stir. I threw down another dollar.

"Buy him a beer when he wakes up."

I turned and walked out of the bar like it was the most natural thing in the world. As I went out the door, I could hear the voices and commotion start back up.

My trip to Betsy's had been much more than a waste of time. I figured I had probably hurt my chances of finding Patty Highsmith in the long run. Timothy Vincent still wouldn't know I was looking for her but he was bound to hear of my brawl in his hang out. Once he talked to Joey about the stranger they took two bills off of, he was likely to start putting two and two together.

It was just another example of how little I knew about this detective thing. I cussed myself the whole ride back.

Chapter Seventeen

My plan was to go straight back to the hotel but the closer I got to Atlantic Beach the more I started thinking about Tabby. As much as I knew it wasn't a good idea, I made the left and headed into the heart of the town.

I parked my car outside of Mack's Dive and sat thinking for a few minutes. Seeing her earlier in the day had been awkward and I imagined seeing her now wouldn't be much better. The thing to do was to keep my distance for a while, at least until I had something to report on Mona.

Looking down the street, toward the water, I saw another light in a window. I wondered if it might be the Sea Shack, Raddison Hayes' bar.

The place was right off the beach, dark and long. The side facing the road was enclosed but the back was open and tables were spread out where people could sit and look out over the ocean. It was nice in a rundown, second hand kind of way. None of the tables or chairs matched and they had a worn look to them, but they seemed clean and kept up. A young man stood behind a bar toward the back and there were only three or four customers hanging around.

The bartender gave me a dirty look as I took a seat in front of him.

"I'll take whatever passes for whiskey in here."

He seemed a tad leery about serving me but he did anyway. I nursed my drink for a little bit and cased the joint. The few patrons in the Sea Shack were checking me out too. It was as if I was somehow out of place.

"Quiet night?" I asked the kid behind the bar.

He kept staring at me and didn't bother to answer, like he wasn't sure what to make of me. He wasn't exactly making me feel welcome. I ordered another shot and he gave it to me without a word.

"Are you always so talkative?"

"You want something else?" he answered back in a snarl.

"Is Raddison around tonight?"

The dirty look got dirtier. "Who wants to know?"

"My name is McKeller."

Without another word, he set down the glass he was drying and walked out from behind the bar, across the room and out a doorway to the side. I turned my attentions back to my drink. It wasn't bad, overall, but then I was getting used to rot gut moonshine.

"He's in the office. You can go back." The kid had crept up behind me and was standing over my shoulder. He made no effort to point the way as I turned around and stood up. I figured the office was back the way he had gone. It was.

Raddison Hayes' office made mine look like a ballroom. It was still a cramped, cluttered, box of a room with an oversized mahogany desk taking up most of the space. He sat behind it, leaning back in a chair with his arms crossed in front of him. Hayes was a big man, broad shouldered and tall. His features were thick and rugged, and his skin was dark except for a light bleached scar on his right cheek. He looked like the kind of guy who had mixed it up more than his share of times. He didn't seem too impressed with me either way as I entered.

"You wanted to talk to me?" he asked in a low baritone voice.

"My name's McKeller."

"So I heard."

"I work out at the Ocean Forest."

Hayes didn't respond at all. It was like I hadn't said anything that interested him yet.

"I understand Mona Cooper used to work for you."

"What's it to you?"

"Maybe you heard but they found her on a stretch of deserted beach with her throat cut."

"Yeah, I heard. What's that got to do with me?"

"Nothing as far as I know, I'm just trying to find a little background information on Mona."

"I don't think I'll be able to help you."

"She did work for you, didn't she?"

"I don't make it a policy to discuss my business affairs with strangers."

"That's probably a good idea, considering your line of work."

He didn't answer.

"How long ago did she work for you?"

"What's a white boy like you give a shit about a dead black girl?"

"She was a friend of a friend."

Raddison Hayes got up from behind his desk and came around to where he was standing in front of me. He stood a good five inches taller than me and he wanted to make sure I knew it. "I don't know nothing about nothing."

"Was she one of your girls?"

"You some kind of copper?"

"I get that a lot but no."

I barely had the words out of my mouth when he slammed me back against the wall with his frame leaned hard into me. His left hand was under my chin pushing it up and back, his right was at my throat and I could feel the sharp tip of a knife jabbing at the skin on my neck. He was holding it pinched between his fingers with just the point protruding out; the way a guy does when he wants to leave scars but not do any lethal damage. It was the way a guy holds a knife when he knows what he's doing.

"You better start talking, white boy. What are you doing here?" His breath was sour in my face and his eyes were wide with anger.

"I'm trying to find out what happened to Mona," I managed to get out, straining to keep the point of the knife from going any deeper.

"Who's this friend of yours, that family she was working for?"

"No, I'm a friend of Tabby's."

I thought I sensed the knife let up on my throat some but I wasn't in a position to test the space he was giving me. "How do you know Tabby?"

"She's a friend. I met her when I moved down here."

Raddison shook his head slightly, never taking his eyes off mine. "That don't make no sense at all."

"I'm the house dick at the Ocean Forest Hotel. Tabby's a sweet kid, I met her at Mack's a few months back and we became friends. She asked me to look into Mona's death."

I could see him trying to read me, to get a fix on who I was and whether or not anything I was saying was more than bullshit. "Why did you come to me?"

"I heard Mona used to work for you."

"Did Tabby tell you that?"

"No, I heard it from somebody at Mack's."

"What else did you hear?"

"I heard you were the kind of guy who can supply somebody with things that are hard to come by."

"So you figured Mona was one of my whores and I might have something to do with it?"

"I didn't figure anything. I just wanted to ask some questions is all."

"My advice to you, McKeller, is to forget everything you heard." He pushed the edge of the knife back into my throat for effect. "You don't know nothing about nothing. If you're smart, you'll stay that way."

"I'm just trying to help out a friend."

"We take care of our own in these parts. If there's any helping to be done, Tabby's got friends of her own that can help her."

"What about Mona? Didn't she have any friends that could help her out?"

"Maybe you're not getting what I'm trying to tell you. This ain't none of your concern."

"A young girl was murdered."

He eased up on the hold he had on me and put the knife away. The look he was giving me was pure hatred. "If I were you I'd be real careful about whose business you stick your nose into. There's some that ain't as friendly as me.

"Does that mean you're not going to answer my questions?" I asked, rubbing the spot on my neck and feeling for blood.

"This conversation is over. Consider yourself lucky it ended the way it did."

"Do you know who the family was she was working for?"

"You can let yourself out."

I started to leave but stopped in the doorway. Raddison Hayes was staring back at me, motionless and full of anger. "Look, I don't care how you make your money. I'm no altar boy myself but Mona Cooper is dead and I intend to find out who did it and why. From where I'm standing the color of hers or my skin shouldn't make any difference."

From there I went back out to the bar and paid my tab before leaving. It had been another disaster as far as I could see. I hadn't learned a single thing.

That's not actually true. I did learn one thing. I learned Raddison Hayes was pretty handy with a knife.

Chapter Eighteen

THE following morning I arose early again and had breakfast with Ellen Highsmith for the second day in a row. She wasn't her usual chipper self and I could see the strain of worrying about her daughter weighing on her. When I told her I had talked to a girl who had seen her recently, she seemed to perk up some. At the news that Patty was safe and sound, she perked up even more.

"I can't thank you enough," she said to me, taking my hand and squeezing it in hers.

"Don't mention it."

"Do you have any idea where she is?"

I bobbed my head back and forth, somewhere between a nod and a head shake. "I've got an idea but I don't know for sure yet. She's here in town or somewhere just outside. She's with Timothy Vincent."

"That awful man." She didn't know the half of it.

"I know she's safe and she's being taken care of." It might have been a stretch but there was no need to worry Ellen any more than I had to. "I've talked to some people. They're around but I haven't been able to pinpoint where just yet. I'm getting close."

"Please, do continue, Mr. McKeller. I have the utmost confidence in your abilities."

That made one of us.

"I'll keep you posted and let you know if I turn up anything."

"I don't know how I'll ever be able to repay you."

Being repaid by Mrs. Highsmith was the last of my worries. I was still wondering if I had the wherewithal to get the job done.

After breakfast I went about my daily routine at the hotel, checking out the common areas, inspecting the hallways and depositing some valuables into the safe. More of the pencil necked bean counters had checked in and quite few of them wanted money and whatnot placed in the hotel safe. By the time I felt I done enough to keep Buntemeyer at bay, it was close to noon and I headed off to the Myrtle Beach Train Depot.

I didn't need a description to figure out who Clarence Cooper was. After the train pulled in and most of the passengers got off, a tall thin black man came strolling down the steps of the last car. He was taller than I had expected, well over six feet, and he was wearing a black suit that looked like it had seen better days, carrying a small brown suitcase.

Although he was thin and old, he was in no way frail looking, standing erect and proud. His face wore the telltale signs of age but there was a strength about it, the kind you see in a man who has worked hard his entire life. His eyes were sunken in and hazed over, as you might expect, and he walked slow and surely, his shoulders back and chest out. Curly white hair receded up his forehead with matching white brows.

I approached him. "Mr. Cooper?"

He looked a bit startled, like he wasn't expecting to be met at the station.

"My name is Frank McKeller. I'm a private investigator and I'm looking into Mona's case."

He held out his hand and we shook. He had a strong firm handshake. There was nothing soft or dainty about it, nothing that revealed the fact he was there to retrieve the body of his dead daughter.

"Clarence Cooper," he replied in a sturdy voice.

"I was wondering if I might have a few minutes of your time? I have a car out front. I could drive you to the sheriff's office."

"That would be fine."

I took his bag and we walked around to the front of the depot to where I was parked. I put his luggage in the trunk and we climbed into the car. The sheriff's office was only about two minutes away so I waited to start the car and began asking questions.

"When is the last time you saw Mona?"

"She came up to visit a couple of months ago."

"How was she doing?"

"She was well."

"So, there was nothing troubling her?"

"Not that she ever mentioned."

"Where was she working?"

"She worked for a family in town, housekeeping."

"Do you know the name, where they lived?"

Mr. Cooper hesitated, looking me over with curiosity, sizing me up. "Exactly just how did you come to be investigating my Mona's death?"

I let out a small sigh. What he wanted to ask was why a white man was looking into the death of his black daughter. "I only met your daughter once, Mr. Cooper, and it wasn't but a couple of minutes. She was a beautiful young woman and she seemed like a sweet kid. I'm very sorry for your loss. It just so happens that I'm friends with her friend, Tabby. Tabby asked me to look into the matter."

"I see." His response was short with a tinge of formality to it.

"That family she was working for?"

"The Baker family," he said as he reached into his breast pocket and pulled out an envelope. "The address is on here. He's a lawyer, the wife is from one of the more prominent families in the area. From what I could tell, Mona was getting along pretty well there."

"Can I hold on to this?"

"That's the last letter I got from my daughter."

"I'll see that you get it back." I slipped the envelope into my jacket. "Did she ever mention anything about a big move she was planning?"

Her father let out a chuckle but it wasn't a happy kind of laugh. It sounded more like I had reminded him of something it hurt to think about. "My Mona has been talking about making a big move for about as long as I can remember."

"Did she say anything to you about making that move now?"

He shook his head. "I reckon she would have told me about it when the time was right."

"I wouldn't think there would be a lot of money in house-keeping. How do you think she was able to save up for this big move?"

"Knowing Mona, I reckon she put aside everything she made. She didn't have no bills to pay, the Bakers took care of her room and board."

"Was she seeing someone, a boyfriend maybe."

"She didn't say. She didn't talk a lot about that kind of thing, not with me anyway."

"Did she have a lot of boyfriends?"

The old man gave me a hard look. "Mona was a good girl. She was full of fire and as independent as they come. She was a big dreamer and she had a young heart, liked to live her life as she saw fit but, in the end, she was always a good girl."

"Yes sir, I understand."

Mr. Cooper gave a couple of knowing nods. "How is Tabby?"

"She's taking it pretty hard, as you can imagine."

"Those two was always thick. They was like sisters."

"That's what she said."

"I'm sorry you didn't have the chance to know my daughter, Mr. McKeller."

"So am I. Tabby speaks very highly of her."

He nodded some more. "Those two were like sisters," he said again and I noticed a tremble and weakness to his voice for the first time.

"Did Mona ever mention a man by the name of Raddison Hayes?" I felt like a heel for even bringing it up, like just mentioning the name in the same sentence as Mona's might tarnish her memory in some way.

"Not that I recall." The sturdiness had returned to his voice, the moment of weakness passing.

"Did she mention any friends she might have been seeing recently?"

"From what I understand, she spent most of her time looking

over the Baker children and household."

"You don't know of any enemies she might have had?"

"Mona wasn't the type of girl to make enemies. Everybody loved Mona."

I was about out of questions to ask, my detective skills coming up short, as usual. I suggested that we head over to the sheriff's office and Mr. Cooper agreed.

Sheriff Talbert was sitting at the desk in his office, talking to one of his deputies when we arrived. He seemed relaxed and jovial and he even made an effort to be polite and somewhat understanding with Mona's father. After he had taken down the necessary information from him, he turned to his deputy.

"Dale, escort Mr. Cooper over to Doc's to see his daughter."

The deputy and Clarence Cooper went on their way, toward the grizzly task at hand and I was left alone with Sheriff Talbert.

"You're getting quite friendly with these people, aren't you?"

"Is that against the law?"

"I can't figure you out, McKeller."

"Why is that?"

"When I first met you, you were hob-knobbing with the finest families around these parts. You were rubbing elbows with the social elite."

"We all know how that turned out."

"Look at you now. What do you think you're doing?"

"I'm trying to help out some people who lost someone dear to them."

"You never struck me as the good Samaritan type."

"What can I say? I'm working on my Good Samaritan Merit badge."

"Ain't nothing I can say that's going to change nothing, one way or the other I suppose."

"Do you know anything about the family she was working for?"

The sheriff had a look on his face like I'd just asked him to solve an atomic theory problem. He had no idea what I was talking about.

"She did housekeeping for a family in town, their name is Baker," I explained as I pulled the envelope out of my pocket and rattled off the address.

"Mathew Baker," he said, "he's a lawyer here in town. He's a fine upstanding citizen with a beautiful wife and three kids."

"You didn't know Mona was working for him?"

"How would I? Girls like that tend to jump around from job to job."

"I thought you might want to look into it as part of your investigation."

"How we run our investigation is none of your business."

I knew right then the only investigating Sheriff Talbert was doing on the Mona Cooper murder was holding Tyler Wilkins in custody until he confessed.

"Do you have any other leads, a murder weapon or anything?"

"Not a thing."

"Did you at least search the area where her body was found?"

"We took a look but didn't find anything but her shoes. One of them was missing a heel. I figure she lost it in the struggle, probably buried in sand by now."

"It was out on a deserted beach, did you find any footprints leading out?"

"None of my deputies reported seeing any."

"Are you telling me you never went out to the crime scene yourself?"

"McKeller, I'm a very busy man. I have people who take care of those things."

"A young girl was murdered in your jurisdiction and you can't even take time out of your busy schedule to look at the crime scene?"

"Before you get all high and mighty, maybe I should explain a few things to you. Mona Cooper wasn't exactly some church going daisy who spent her time tip toeing through the tulips.

"She ran away from home when she was sixteen-years-old. According to Tyler Wilkins she had at least five jobs over the last three years. She worked in bars, drank heavily and consorted with men. At one time she was in the employ of one Raddison Hayes. Do you know who that is? Do you have any idea what he deals in?"

I thought about pointing out it was the same thing his brother dealt in but I held my tongue. "So she deserved to get her throat cut, is that it?"

The sheriff took a deep breath, gathering himself together. "I don't like to see anyone die by the hands of another but some people put themselves in positions where the likelihood of things like that happening are greatly increased. Mona Cooper did that to herself and there ain't nothing can change that now. I'm not going to waste the tax payer's money or my time trying to find out how some tart went and got herself killed."

There it was, all plain and simple. Mona Cooper was a whore and whores pretty much deserve what they get.

"With the people she ran with, it's a wonder it didn't happen earlier," he continued.

I started to say something but the sheriff cut me off. "I have a lot of work to do, McKeller. I don't have time for this. If you want to wait here for Mona's father that's fine but this conversation is over."

He walked away, over to the filing cabinets, shuffling papers and trying to look busy.

When Mr. Cooper and the deputy got back I was sitting off to the side reading a three month old issue of Life Magazine. Cooper looked bad. He looked like a guy who had just taken two shotgun blasts to the chest. He looked like a guy who had just seen the dead body of his little girl.

Talbert and Mr. Cooper talked briefly. They spoke of arrangements to be made and of places to be called, the details of having Mona's body transported and prepared for burial. There was almost something sympathetic in Talbert's voice as they discussed the grave matter. For a second I thought he might actually have a soul.

After they were finished, I took Mr. Cooper out to the car and offered him a ride. He wanted to go to Atlantic Beach and see Tabby. That was fine by me. I wanted to see her too.

The old man sat straight and stiff in his seat as we drove, never uttering a word. There wasn't much to say.

Tabby wasn't at her place so we headed over to Mack's where we found her inside preparing the joint for opening. She ran up to him when she saw him and they came together in an emotional hug, standing in place holding each other for all they were worth. Mutual sobs ran together, her head in his chest, his face buried in her hair.

I stepped outside for a cigarette and to give the two some space. It was a sad and private moment that I didn't need to be a part of.

The streets of Atlantic Beach were bare, hardly a soul lurking about. The place looked a lot more rundown in the daylight. At night it was alive and festering with energy, a center hub of activity and entertainment. The sunlight washed all that away and revealed the steamy underbelly of a decrepit part of town where buildings were held together with plywood and two by fours. Makeshift shacks had been added onto and painted haphazardly with whatever colors they could find. Windows were missing and blankets and rags hung in place of curtains, doors even.

There were grills made of metal drums, cut in half, sitting out in alleys and behind businesses, some supported on rigged wooden platforms, others dug into the dirt. They served as kitchens for the local eateries and they were as primitive as things got in the middle of twentieth century America. You weren't likely to see anything like them in the white part of town.

From down the street, toward the water, I saw a large man in a brown suit coming out of a building and heading my way. It was Raddison Hayes and I guessed he'd seen me from the Sea Shack. I took a deep breath and waited for him to make his way toward me, hoping he left the knife back in his office. I doubted he had.

Chapter Nineteen

"We need to talk," Hayes said to me as he approached.

"OK, shoot." I probably could have chosen a better phrase.

"I asked around about you. They say you're on the up and up. Tabby says you're OK."

"That's good to hear."

"I checked you out. You served in the Army, overseas, won the Purple Heart at Omaha Beach. You're a regular war hero."

I was a lot of things. A war hero wasn't one of them.

"After the war you went back to Baltimore and opened up a detective agency. From what I can tell you were barely getting by, strictly low budget." He was making a point to let me know he had connections and sources to find out information. Money will do that, no matter what the color of your skin.

"You came down here for the Chilton wedding in September and somehow managed to solve a big time murder case, even though the sheriff got most of the credit. That's when they offered you the job to stay on as the house dick of the Ocean Forest."

"Can you tell me what color socks I've got on?"

"I'm guessing white." He was right.

"OK, you had me checked out, so what?"

"We don't take too kindly to strangers poking around in our affairs down this way."

"So I hear."

"When I see a white man sticking his nose in stuff he ain't got no business sticking it into it makes me start a wondering."

"I told you I'm just trying to help a friend."

"Maybe that's so and maybe it ain't. Mona was a friend of mine. I'd like to see whoever done this to her get what's coming to him."

"That's what I want too"

"I was thinking maybe it wouldn't be so bad if you were to keep looking into it."

"Does that mean you're willing to answer some questions?"

Hayes gave a crooked smile. "I ain't one to speak out of turn, especially where business is concerned. You don't need to know nothing about me and what I do."

"I've already got a pretty good idea of what you do."

"What you think you know ain't here nor there."

"When exactly was it that Mona worked for you?"

Raddison took a deep breath. "I ain't going to answer nothing like that. That's my business."

"I guess that means you're not going to tell me what she did for you either?"

He shook his head. "What's done is done."

"Let me get this straight. You're telling me that it's OK if I keep investigating Mona's murder but you're not willing to cough up any information. Is that right?"

"That's not what I said. I ain't willing to tell you nothing that don't need to be told."

"What are you willing to tell me?"

"There's somebody you might need and go see."

"Who would that be?"

"There's a fellow not far from here that goes by Doc Pearson."

"What kind of doctor is he?"

"He ain't no real doctor but doctors is expensive. People in these parts don't always have the money to go see the real thing. Doc Pearson ain't never been to school or nothing but he's always been real good at fixing people. He's the one people go to see when they're feeling ill. Hell, he done birthed half the babies in Atlantic Beach, I suspect."

"I'm feeling pretty good. I don't think I need to see a doctor."

"Well, that's up to you, I'm just saying…"

"You think this Doc Pearson might be able to tell me something I don't know?"

"I reckon there's a lot Doc Pearson could tell, you don't know."

Raddison Hayes turned and started to walk off, back toward the Sea Shack. I called after him with another question. "What can you tell me about Timothy Vincent?"

Hayes stopped in his tracks and turned back around with a funny look on his face. "What do you want with Vincent?"

"It's an unrelated matter."

"You best stay away from that one. Vincent is trouble, always has been."

"You know where I could find him?"

Hayes shook his head, not in a "no" kind of way, more in a "crazy white boy" kind of way. "He hangs in a place up north of here…"

"Betsy's Tavern?"

"That would be the place."

"Anywhere else I could look?"

"I s'pect you keep asking around about Vincent and you won't have to look real hard. He hears you're looking for him, he'll turn up whether you like it or not."

"How about you? Do you ever have any dealings with Vincent?"

"You know better than that. Me and you don't talk none about business."

With that he turned and started to walk away. "What about Jarvis Brown?" I called after him. "Do you know him?"

Raddison stopped and turned back to me. "Timothy Vincent, Jarvis Brown, you looking to get yourself beat down, McKeller? If I was you, I'd go barking up some other trees."

"Tyler Wilkens says he saw Jarvis Brown hanging around Mack's that night."

"Anybody else see him?"

"No."

"I figure when a mans being held for something he says he

didn't do he's liable to see a lot of things. I ain't seen Jarvis around in ages.

"Cutting a girl's throat ain't exactly the way he goes about things, anyway. He'd about beat a man to death over a chicken bone if he decided he wanted it bad enough, or if he was pissed off enough. I don't figure him for a flat out killer, though. Wouldn't be no reason for him to kill Mona."

"Did she know Jarvis Brown?"

"Say, what kind of detective are you? Isn't Jarvis in jail for attempted murder or something? I heard he beat four men half to death with his bare hands."

"I didn't ask you that."

Raddison hesitated. "I don't believe they were acquainted. I'm sure she knew of him, like most folks do, but Jarvis was never really the sociable kind and she never mentioned knowing him to me."

With that, he turned around and walked away, back toward the Sea Shack.

I lit another smoke, leaning back on the front wall of Mack's Dive, taking in the sights. I wasn't ready to go back inside. What was going on in there was family business and I wasn't going to intrude.

After a while, Tabby came walking out. Her eyes were red and her face was drawn, she looked exhausted. I took my hat off as she approached and held it down in front of me.

"Mr. Cooper's going to stay here a spell."

I gave a half nod, acknowledging I was no longer needed. "Are you all right?"

She tried to smile but it didn't look like she had the energy. "I'm fine. Thanks for taking care of him today and bringing him out here."

"No problem."

"You've been a really big help, McKeller, I can't thank you enough."

"Don't mention it. If you need anything just call the hotel." I put my fedora back on and started to walk away.

"He likes you," she said. I stopped and looked back at her. "He says you were very nice to him today and he appreciates you looking into Mona's death. He said you have a good soul."

"I like him too. He seems like a good guy."

The smile she had tried before eased itself onto her pretty face. For a second she looked the way she always had, the way she looked in my head when I thought of her. It gave me a warm feeling to see that part of her again, to know it was still inside there somewhere, lurking under the sadness and despair she was wallowing in.

I smiled back and went on my way.

Chapter Twenty

THE ride back to the hotel was slow and easy. I was taking my time, in no hurry to get anywhere. My mind was wandering, half thoughts and possibilities popping in and out, disappearing from my consciousness before I even grasped what they were. It had been awhile since I had let my brain relax in such a way.

I had gone about three miles south of Atlantic Beach when I spotted a dirt road off to the left. I had noticed it before but never paid it much attention. Part of me wondered if it might lead back to the old artillery range where Mona Cooper's body had been found. Maybe it was something I needed to check out.

The road was a straight shot back toward the ocean, a make-shift access overgrown with vines and shrubs, like it hadn't seen much use in a year or more. A sign warning of dangerous explosives peeked out from some brush and leaves so I figured I was on the right track.

Up at the nearside of the sand dunes, guarded by a patch of tall sea grass and weeds, a cleared piece of land looked like it might have been some sort of staging area. Matted down dirt and sand, a place which had seen heavy traffic, could be where trucks were loaded and unloaded, artillery pieces drug in and out.

I pulled in and got out of the car, noticing an array of tire prints on the ground around me. Most were probably from the deputy's vehicles and ambulance used to investigate the crime scene and remove the body. I wondered if any might belong to the car driven by Mona Cooper's murderer. Too bad nobody thought to check that out when she was found.

The place was deserted and secluded. The only sounds were of the ocean waves crashing about in the distance. The wind was whipping pretty good and there was a decent chill in the air. Maybe not the kind of chill you get in Baltimore in the middle of December, but it made me shiver just the same and I pulled my old trench coat out from the back seat and wrapped it around me. All this time living in South Carolina's mild climate was thinning out my blood and I wasn't any good at dealing with the cold anymore.

I walked up through the sea grass and over the dunes, out to where the sand opened up against the Atlantic. She greeted me with her usual dance, an assortment of foaming waves slapping at the shoreline and a salty breeze in my face mixed with sprinklings of grit and wet.

"Yeah, it's good to see you again too."

There wasn't a soul in sight as I glanced up and down the beach, a vast flat stretch of emptiness that ran across her front, as far as the eye could see. It would have been easy to imagine I was the only living person left on the face of the earth.

It didn't look much like an artillery range. I tried to imagine what it might have looked like during the war, with the large guns lined up along the beach, manned by teams of gunners. Old barges and boats would have floated out on the horizon, decrepit targets placed out there for the men to shoot at, honing their skills for live combat. Once they had taken their fill of shells, the useless boats would sink quietly into the waves, swallowed up by the ocean, becoming man made reefs, homes and feeding grounds for her fish and sea life. Now, all that was left was the sand and water, emptiness and skyline.

What would it have been like for Mona Cooper to be standing on the same stretch of loneliness with only her killer by her side? I wondered about her screams in the night, mixing with the sound of the pounding Atlantic, lost in the openness of the world laid out before her. How small would she have sounded under the crashing waves and howling winds as she screamed and cried and pleaded for her life?

The Atlantic would have heard her cries. She would have been the lone witness to the dreaded deed but Mona Cooper would have been better off screaming and pleading with a brick wall. The Atlantic wasn't prone to sympathy or compassion. I knew that much first hand. She wasn't the kind of woman to intercede with the folly of mankind. She was just as likely to swallow you up and spit you out as she was in lending anything in the way of help or comfort. That's the way she operated and nobody was any the wiser to her methods than me. She wouldn't have shown any more interest than she showed to the boats and barges and incoming shells that exploded and burned in her bosom.

I walked up and down the beach, looking for something I didn't expect to find, a clue as to why Mona Cooper's life had been snuffed out. The Atlantic continued to torment me as I went about my futile chore, laughing at me with every step I took.

My coat was pulled in tight around me and my hands were in my pockets, my body clenched, fighting off the cold. I wandered back up into the dunes and trudged through the thick sand, cluttered with grass and debris, sprinkled with sea shells and driftwood. Off in the distance I caught sight of something that looked out of place.

Half hidden under the browning vegetation and partially buried in the sand was a white swatch of fabric. I reached down and grabbed a corner of it in two fingers and gently pulled it out of the dirt.

It was a pair of woman's panties, thin plain and white. They were of a dainty size, the kind worn by a young girl with a slim figure. The left was ripped at the waist and down the side with both leg openings hanging in shreds, like they might if they had been torn from her body while she kicked and fought for her life. They were ripped in the way they might have been had they been torn off with one hand by a rapist as he holds a girl down in the sand and has his way with her.

I balled them up and placed them in the pocket of my coat, trying not to imagine how horrible the last minutes of Mona Cooper's life must have been.

A particularly loud wave hit the shore and I glanced back up at the Atlantic. I couldn't tell if she was trying to tell me something or if she was just flexing her muscles, showing me how tiny and inconsequential I was. She knew something I didn't. What I wasn't sure of was whether she wanted to relay this information to me or merely make sure I was aware where we both stood on the food chain. I guessed it was the later.

I went straight back to the hotel, thinking I should maybe put in some time and remind Buntemeyer why I was still on the payroll. I went up the front steps, across the porch and into the lobby.

"McKeller," someone said as I was passing through, on the way to my office.

Curtis, the desk clerk was waving me down. He told me I had a visitor and he pointed across the lobby to where the over-stuffed chairs and sofas sat on oriental rugs. Just rising above the back of one of the chairs, I spotted the top of a small blonde head. I walked around to see who it was.

"I'm guessing you weren't expecting to see me, huh?" the girl said in a quiet, bashful voice. I almost didn't recognize her from the Villa Roma.

In the daylight she looked thinner and paler than I remembered or maybe it was the contrast created by the swollen purple eye and the fat lip on her small frail features.

"What happened to you?"

She tried to force a smile but I could tell it hurt too much. "I didn't know where else to go."

"Did Vincent do this to you?"

Claire paused, tears welling in her eyes. "Some guy got the hell whacked out of him at Betsy's. It was the same night I saw you. This guy was asking about Vincent too."

I took a deep breath, hoping I didn't know where the story was heading; hoping the bruises and black eye weren't my fault.

"Vincent came around asking me about you," she continued. "He figures it was the same guy. He wanted to know what I told you."

"I'm sorry. I didn't mean to get you in any trouble."

Claire gave one quick nod. "It's a tough break but I've had tougher."

"What did you tell him?"

"What do you think I told him? I told him a guy was in asking where he could find him and I told him where he hung out."

"What did he say?"

"That's when he did the number on my eye. Then he wanted to know what else you were asking about."

"Did you tell him I was looking for Patty?"

"It never came up and I didn't volunteer any more than I had to, even after he punched me in the mouth."

"I didn't mean to put you in the middle of all this."

"Yeah, well, you did and I figure that's worth a little more than twenty bucks."

"Can I buy you lunch?"

"I figure you owe me more than lunch."

I took a seat in the chair beside her. "Maybe I do. Let me ask you something. After I give you this money, what then? Are you going back to Vincent?"

"No way, that son of a bitch has put his hands on me for the last time. I'm never going back there."

"So, where to then?"

"I don't know. I'm getting out of here, Charleston maybe."

"You got any family?"

"None to speak of."

"Your plan is to just get some money and head out of town?"

She shrugged her boney shoulders at me. "Maybe."

"The last train out of town has already left for today. You're not going anywhere before tomorrow unless you want to hoof it."

"I got places I can go."

"Why don't you stay here tonight and rest up? You look like you could use it."

Claire gave me a sour look. "That would cost you a lot more than last time."

"It's not like that. I'll get you your own room."

The young girl's eyes got wide and she looked around the lobby of the Ocean Forest. I gathered it wasn't the kind of hotel she was used to staying in. "Here?"

"I get a discount for working here," I told her.

"What about my money?"

"We'll talk about it later. One more thing, how did you find me?"

"I heard Joey tell Vincent you worked here."

I took Claire over to the front desk and got her registered under a fake name. If anybody came looking for a young blonde, I told the clerk to keep his mouth shut. Curtis didn't seem too happy about it as he took her through the process and got her signed in. He kept looking at her as if she were out of place and me like I was out of my mind for suggesting it. I tried to put him at ease by telling him she was a friend of Mrs. Highsmith's daughter and she was helping me find her. I assured him that Buntemeyer wouldn't have a problem with it and that he'd be more than happy to pick up the tab. I was hoping I was right.

After I got her settled in and had some food sent up to her room, I figured I'd get back out on the road for some more snooping. Again, I had proven to myself that I didn't have a clue as to what I was doing. My latest blunder had ended with a young girl getting her face beat in. How's that for professional detective work?

As far as Timothy Vincent went, I was pretty certain that now that he knew I was looking for him I was likely to get a visit from somebody sooner or later. He wasn't the type to let loose ends hang around. I only hoped I hadn't botched it enough that he'd stash Patty somewhere I couldn't find her. The thing I still had going for me was he didn't know I was looking for Patty.

What I did have was a few leads on the Mona Cooper case I could check out. Leads might be a stretch but at least I had some places and people I needed to go see. It was all I had.

Chapter Twenty-One

MATHEW and Rita Baker lived in a spacious two-story house just south of Myrtle Beach proper, on a road called Waccamaw Street. It was a comfortable looking and well-kept building in a quiet neighborhood with the proverbial white picket fence around it. As I approached the front door, I could hear dogs barking and kids yelling in the background. I knocked.

In a few minutes the door swung open and a woman's face appeared at the opening. She looked to be in her mid-to-late thirties with soft brown hair and brilliant green eyes. Her face was pleasant and a tad plump with the early signs of aging beginning to show. She wasn't at all unattractive but I could see she had been quite a looker not too long before.

"Can I help you?" She squinted into the sun outside, and her voice sounded sharp and impatient. She was holding a young child in her arms, maybe two years old, supporting it on her hip with a tight grip. Her hair was long but pulled back and falling out in strands, hanging in her eyes and somewhat out of place.

"Mrs. Baker?" I asked.

"Yes?"

"My name is McKeller. I'm investigating the death of Mona Cooper."

Everything about her softened when she heard me speak the

name. The frustration disappeared from her face and was replaced with a melancholy, like I'd triggered her grief.

She sighed. "Please come in."

I followed her through the door and past the front parlor, back to the rear of the house and the kitchen. She sat the child on the floor next to where two others, slightly older, were playing with blocks. The kids were laughing with each other and the barks of a dog could be heard coming from the back yard. There was a large pot cooking on the stove, and the room was cluttered with plates and cups, children's clothes and toys.

Rita Baker moved over to the pot and began stirring its contents. "You'll have to excuse the mess. Ever since Mona…" She paused and took a deep breath. "Things have been in a shambles since Mona has been gone. I'm positively lost without her."

"How long did she work for you?"

"I don't know, somewhere around eight or nine months, I suppose. It feels like it was longer."

I began going through my usual list of questions, the ones I always seemed to ask and the ones which never seemed to turn up any new information. What I found out was Mona Cooper had seemed happy and content, showed no signs of being involved in any trouble, didn't appear to have a boyfriend and hadn't been involved in a romantic dispute that Mrs. Baker knew anything about. It was the same stuff I always found out.

"Mona did a good job for you?" I asked.

Rita smiled. "Mona was a godsend. She was so wonderful. The children adored her."

"And you and Mr. Baker got along well with her?"

"Mona and I got along splendidly. She was a pleasure to be around. I can't begin to tell you how many hours we sat around talking, laughing. She was an absolute joy."

"Your husband felt the same way?"

"Well, my husband is a lawyer. He works in Conway and he's away from home quite a bit. He never spent the time with her that I did. They weren't all that close but he thought the world of her as well. We both agreed she did a terrific job."

"Did she ever speak about moving away from Myrtle Beach?"

Rita laughed out loud. "That's all she ever talked about. She had big plans. She was going to move up north, a big city, New York maybe. She was saving up for it."

"You think she had saved enough to make the move?"

"I wouldn't know about that. She didn't mention anything about going anytime soon."

"Did she ever talk about her friends or family?"

"She has a father who lives in Conway. I know she has friends in Atlantic Beach but she didn't talk about them much, not with me anyway."

"Did she ever mention a guy she used to work for, Raddison Hayes?"

"No."

"Did she ever talk about what she did before she came to work for you?"

"Not really, nothing specific anyway. I know she had a bunch of jobs."

"Did she go out much?"

Rita shook her head. "No, not at all, she was saving her money for her move. She went to see her father awhile back but other than that it was just out for groceries and what not."

"How about visitors?"

"Never."

"When she first came here, did she seem afraid, like she was running away from anything?"

"Heavens no, she seemed fine and very happy to be here."

I was getting nowhere. Nothing she was telling me was shedding any light on the life or death of Mona Cooper. The more questions I asked the less I felt I knew about the dead girl, and my list of questions was drying up.

"How about your husband, is there any chance I could talk to him?"

"Sure. He works long hours though. The truth is I'm usually in bed by the time he gets home. I don't see him much myself. You can catch him on the weekend or you could go to his office in Conway. but he's got a big case coming up so he's very busy these days. My husband works for the District Attorney's office."

"So, his interaction with Mona was minimal?"

"He usually gets home late. Mona would make sure to have a plate of food waiting on him but I doubt they saw each other much."

"The night ... it happened. Can you tell me anything about that night?"

She shrugged. "It was a night just like any other. I went to bed early. I remember my husband came in pretty late. I didn't even know Mona had gone out."

"Do you think it would be possible for me to see her room?" I asked.

"Of course." Rita put a lid on her pot and wiped her hands before leading me through the house and up the stairs.

Mona's room was the last one on the left, on the back side of the house with the master bedroom up front and the kid's rooms in between. It was small but cozy and immaculate, decorated with a down home feel. The single bed was perfectly made and a hand sewn quilt was folded neatly at the foot of it. To the right sat a medium-sized oak dresser and on top of it was a glass vase filled with dried dead carnations sagging over the lip.

"Nice flowers," I commented, looking back at Rita Baker. She was standing in the doorway, leaning against the doorjamb. Her eyes were wet and wide and she had a lost, distant look on her face. It appeared as though she were afraid to enter the room.

"I don't know where she got them. I don't grow carnations." Her voice was thin and strained.

I opened up the top drawer and began poking through the white cotton underthings it was full of. Stuffed in under the fabrics were a few cards and envelopes, snapshots sandwiched between.

Pulling them out and sorting through them, I began to examine them closer. The envelopes were all addressed from Conway, her father's name neatly printed in the top left corner. There was a birthday card and a postcard from New York City which hadn't ever been mailed.

The photographs were mostly of people I had never seen. One of them was of the Baker family. Mona was in a few of them at various stages of her life. There was even one with her and Tabby, arm in arm, standing out in front of an old barn. They were smiling big and their hair was blowing back away from their faces, they couldn't have been more than thirteen or fourteen years old.

Under that I found a smaller card, the kind you get with flowers. It was from a florist shop called Bartlett's. There was no note or signature written on it, only a small heart drawn in the center.

"Would it be all right if I held onto this stuff for a while?"

Rita hesitated, uneasy with my request. "I was planning on sending all her things to her father."

"I'll see that he gets them."

"I guess that would be fine."

We made small talk for a while longer, mostly Rita saying nice things about Mona, how she missed her. I realized I had gotten about as much out of Rita Baker as I was going to get, which wasn't a lot.

Chapter Twenty-Two

I THOUGHT about visiting Mathew Baker in Conway but I didn't feel like making the almost two hour drive. Instead I decided to head back up through Myrtle Beach and pay my buddy, Sheriff Talbert a quick visit.

He was sitting at his desk doing paperwork when I walked in and he barely looked up enough to acknowledge me as I approached. Deputy Dale was off to a corner, reading the newspaper.

"You're like a bad rash that won't go away, McKeller," Talbert said without lifting his eyes from the papers in front of him.

"It's nice to see you too, Sheriff."

"To what do I owe this pleasure?"

I pulled the ripped pair of panties from my pocket and tossed them onto the stack of papers on the desk. The sheriff paused before sticking his pencil under them and lifting them into the air, examining them.

"I would have figured you for a boxer's guy."

"Do you see how they're ripped, like they were torn off?"

"Where did you get these?"

"I found them on the beach. I guess your crack homicide team missed them during their thorough investigation of the crime scene."

Talbert looked down at the torn panties for a few seconds.

"You don't even know if they belonged to Mona Cooper."

"Yeah, maybe they came off one of the other girls who were raped and murdered on that stretch of beach."

"What's your point?"

"I believe they call it a clue. Police use them to solve crimes."

"Well, in that case, I'll get somebody right on this." He said it sarcastically like he had no intention or interest in bothering with them.

"What did the doctor say?"

"About what?"

"About Mona Cooper?"

"What do you think he said? She died from a stab wound to the throat."

"Was she raped?"

"He didn't say."

"Did he examine the body?"

"He examined it as much as he had to. Cause of death was established."

"He didn't check to see if she'd been raped?"

"Doc Burns is an old country doctor. He's not a medical examiner."

"You're really going to do this, aren't you?"

"Do what?"

"Sweep this whole thing under the rug until it goes away."

"In case you've forgotten, we're holding a suspect in custody."

"Yeah, while the real killer is out there running loose."

"McKeller, I have work to do. Is there something else you wanted?"

I was boiling mad. This pretentious jerk was dragging his feet and he wasn't even making an attempt to hide it. Tempting as it was to bring up our old arguments, I decided to go in another direction.

Word was probably out on the streets that I was looking for Timothy Vincent. What did I have to lose? This was one of my tried and true detective methods, throwing things up in the air to see where they landed.

"What can you tell me about Timothy Vincent?"

The sheriff's eyes got wide with surprise. It looked like it was the last thing in the world he'd expected out of me. I guess word hadn't made it back to him about what I'd been up to.

"Timothy Vincent ain't got nothing to do with Mona Cooper."

"I didn't say he did. What can you tell me about him?"

"Vincent's a local boy. I knew his daddy. He's got a bit of a wild streak in him."

"A wild streak? That's putting it kind of mild, don't you think? From what I hear, he's into a little bit of everything, gambling, moonshine, girls…"

"You don't know what you're talking about." The sheriff's voice took on a hard edge.

"No? I hear he and your brother have got a pretty good thing going."

"You hear wrong," Talbert said, standing up and assuming a tough guy stance. "I suggest you get back to the hotel and stop listening to local gossip."

"Maybe it's all talk but it would be mighty convenient, wouldn't it? Running a little racket on the side and having your brother to watch your back, make sure you don't get into any trouble."

"You're walking a very thin and dangerous line, McKeller. We don't take too kindly to wild accusations in these parts."

"Apparently, there are a lot of things you do different in these parts, like choosing when and when not to uphold the law you were sworn to protect."

"You have no idea what you're talking about." He was so angry spit was flickering out of his mouth when he spoke and his face had turned a beet red.

"Where can I find Vincent?"

"I wouldn't know. It's not my turn to watch him."

"Your brother would know, wouldn't he?"

"What is this all about?"

"I've got business with Vincent. I need to talk to him and I think you can make that happen."

Talbert didn't answer, just stood there glaring at me.

"I couldn't give a rat's ass how your brother makes his living. I don't even care about this good ole boy thing you guys have going down here. As far as I'm concerned it doesn't make a zip to me until it gets in the way of doing what I've got to do.

"I need to talk with Timothy Vincent. If I have to overturn every rock in this two bit town and expose every dirty secret for fifty miles to do it, so be it."

"Are you threatening me?"

I gave him the friendliest smile I could muster. "Of course not, Sheriff. I'm just asking for a little help from the local law enforcement officials."

"You might want to be careful about what you ask for," he snarled back.

"Thanks for the advice. I'll keep that in mind."

"Dale?" the sheriff asked, still looking at me.

"Yeah?" Dale answered.

"Has the Cooper girl's body been taken away yet?"

"No, it's still over Doc's. They're coming to get her later today."

"Run over there and ask Doc to re-examine the body. Tell him to check and see if he can tell whether she'd been raped before she got killed."

"Yes, Sheriff, right away." Dale rushed out the front door. Talbert was still glaring at me.

"As far as that other matter goes, I'll make some calls and see if I can arrange a meeting between you and Timothy Vincent. I believe you're barking up the wrong tree but I'll see what I can do."

"Thanks, that's awfully peachy of you."

He sat back down and went back to his paperwork, or at least he tried to look like he was. I could see the rage boiling inside of him. Talbert wasn't the kind of guy who was used to being pushed around and I wondered if I had taken it too far. Pushing buttons was one thing but making enemies out of the guy who ran the town was another.

There was nothing I could do about that now. The deed was done and the dye was cast. Now it was just a question of waiting to see how it all spilled out and what ended up getting stained.

"Thanks again for your help," I said as I turned and made my way out the door. The sheriff didn't bother to answer me.

As I walked out and headed back to the car I made one decision. I decided from here on out I would always make sure I had my trusty .45 Automatic on my person. It's better to be safe than sorry and I wondered how safe anything was going to be after my latest blunder.

Chapter Twenty-Three

Back at the Ocean Forest, I went straight to my room and retrieved my pistol. I made sure it was loaded and oiled and I stuck it in a holster at the back of my belt. From there I went to Claire's room.

She was in good spirits, enjoying her deluxe surroundings. The swelling in her face hadn't gone down any but she'd cleaned up some and it didn't look quite as bad as before. Claire was wearing a flimsy little slip and had her hair pulled back. She looked thinner and younger than earlier.

"This place is great," she said with a smile. "Did you know they have running salt water?"

"Yeah."

"What's that for?"

"Beats the hell out of me but the guests seem to like it."

"Do you think I could get some more food?" she asked, all innocent and shy. She didn't look like the gal I met turning tricks in the Italian restaurant anymore. Now she just looked like what she was, a naive kid.

"Sure, just call down and tell them what you want. Tell them I said it was alright."

Her smile got even bigger. The sight of it tugged at my heart and made me want to join in, to get lost in her youthful wonder and enthusiasm.

What kind of monster could take something this sweet and pure and use it like Vincent had? What kind of freak of nature could look at a girl like her and see dollar signs? What kind of ruthless bastard could raise a hand to something as wholesome as this skinny little kid? It made me hate him all the more.

I took her over to the bed and sat her down, me standing over her. "I need you to stay in this room. You can't go anywhere."

"Not even to the pool?"

"Things could get kind of hairy here. Vincent knows I'm on his tail. He's going to come looking for me soon. I need to know that you're not going to get caught in the middle of this mess."

Her eyes were big and confused.

"If he finds out you're here he's going to come after you. I don't think he's the kind of guy who likes to lose girls."

Claire nodded.

"Is there anything you can tell me about him that might be of some use? Does he pack a weapon?"

"A knife, I think. I've never seen him with a gun."

"That's good to know." It made the .45 on my back seem bigger somehow.

"Of course, Harley does."

"Who's Harley?"

"Harley is his sidekick or body guard or something. He's always around him. He's a big guy, lots of muscles. Harley always has a gun with him."

"Does he tend to travel with anybody else?"

"Not usually, Joey sometimes."

"That's a big help. At least I know what I'm up against."

"Are you going to be OK, Mr. McKeller?"

"Yeah, I'll be fine. Just in case though, if anything does happen to me, go to the front desk. There will be an envelope back there for you with some money in it. Take it and get out of town. Do you understand?"

"Why don't you just give it to me now?"

"I don't want that money burning a hole in your pocket and giving you any ideas about leaving this room. I want you to stay put."

"How much money are we talking about?"

"Enough to get you out of Myrtle Beach."

Claire nodded again. I tried to reinforce how important it was for her to lay low and stay out of sight for a while and I hoped she was getting it. She was on the telephone ordering a cheeseburger and French Fries when I left her.

Next I stopped by Eleanor's room to touch base. I told her I had some leads and I hoped to have something more concrete soon. This seemed to appease her.

From there I went to the front desk and placed two hundred dollars in an envelope with Claire's name on it. I placed it in the safe, in the drawer corresponding with Claire's room number.

I've got to be honest. I was having serious second thoughts on how I'd handled this thing until now. I felt like I was on the top of a lot of people's hit list and I wondered if maybe I'd caused a few too many waves.

Things felt like they were closing in on me and I still didn't have a clue as to how deep a hole I'd dug for myself. All I knew was it was time to watch my own back.

I had just closed the safe door when Buntemeyer came calling. He had that familiar agitated look on his face.

"McKeller, what's going on here? Who is the girl you put up on the fourth floor?"

"She's a friend of Patricia Highsmith. She's helping me find her."

"This is highly irregular."

"Things in the Highsmith case have taken a strange turn. I'm afraid Patricia might be in some kind of trouble."

This made Buntemeyer perk up and take notice. I doubt if it had anything to do with any real concern he had for the Highsmith girl but he wanted to keep her mother happy. He also wanted to keep the Ocean Forest Hotel as far away from any kind of scandal as possible.

"Of course, we want to help out wherever we can in this matter but I hope you're looking out for the reputation of the hotel as well."

"That is my primary concern. We can't let it leak out that the daughter of one of our prominent guests was involved in any sort of misdoing."

Buntemeyer gave me the kind of look a guy gets when he's speaking gibberish to a squirrel. He had no idea what I was talking about and that's the way I wanted to keep it.

"I got a look at that girl when she came in," he said in a confused voice. "She doesn't look like the type of girl to be associated with a Greenville Highsmith."

I gave him a knowing nod. "That girl's family makes the Highsmiths look like paupers."

Buntemeyer's eyes got as big as golf balls. I could almost see the dollar signs flashing up behind them. "Well then, whatever it is you're doing ... keep on doing it."

It was good advice. If I'd had any idea of what I was doing I might have followed it.

From there I wandered down stairs to the Brookgreen Room for a quick belt and a little quiet time to get my thoughts together. A few of the accountant types sat around in shirts and ties, sipping on gin and tonics. They were a humdrum bunch, starched shirts and straight laced. Not a one of them looked like they could so much as spell the word fun. I could only imagine how boring this convention of theirs was going to be.

I was working on my second shot of booze, sitting back on my bar stool and sorting through what I knew, which wasn't much. Mona Cooper had been murdered on a secluded stretch of beach just south of Atlantic Beach just hours after I had seen her at Mack's. She'd worked for the Bakers and led a relatively reclusive lifestyle. She'd had no boyfriends or suitors that anyone was aware of. So where did the carnations come from, and why hadn't she bothered to throw them away after they died? I could only guess she'd kept them for sentimental reasons, the way young girls do. That told me there was a man out there somewhere she was involved with. So, when did she find time to see a man without anybody knowing?

The Raddison Hayes angle continued to gnaw at my gut as well. I knew she had worked for him and I knew what he did. Putting the two together I wasn't coming up with the kind of answer I wanted. It wasn't the way I wanted her friends and family to remember her.

Something was bothering her the night I met her. She'd said

she had something to take care of and she was leaving town. What was it she needed to see to, and did it have anything to do with getting her killed? I also kept wondering why Tyler Wilkens had claimed to see Jarvis Brown at Mack's that night, a guy I knew was being held in jail. As usual, I had more questions than answers.

Where Patty Highsmith was concerned I had even less. Aside from knowing she was with Timothy Vincent I had nothing. The only thing I had accomplished on that front was ruffling a few feathers and getting another young girl beaten up, and I figured that wasn't a good thing.

Sitting my ass on a bar stool all afternoon wasn't going to get me any closer to where I needed to be so I decided to get back to work. I didn't have much to go on but I did have that little tidbit Raddison Hayes had thrown me. It wasn't much but it was a place to start.

I was on my way out of the bar when Deputy Dale came walking in. He caught me at the door.

"Howdy, McKeller."

"Deputy," I nodded.

"I just left Doc Burns'."

"And?"

"He said he couldn't be sure but, judging by the bruising and what not, there's a fairly good chance she was raped. That, along with the under things you found, would make it mighty likely."

"I figured as much," I said, turning to leave. Deputy Dale stopped me.

"Look, the sheriff, he ain't all bad. He's stuck in his ways is all. He's done a lot of good for this town."

I didn't answer.

"I ain't saying I agree with everything he does but he ain't all bad. People in these parts are used to what they're used to. Change happens real slow in a town like this. People know what they growed up with, that don't make it right."

"Why are you telling me this?"

"Not everybody is like Sheriff Talbert around here."

"Did he send you?"

"He don't know I'm here."

"Why did you come?"

"I take my job serious. I took an oath to uphold the law and I figure that's about as important as anything a man can do."

"Until it's some black girl who goes and gets herself killed?"

"Like I said, not everybody around here is like Sheriff Talbert. We don't all feel that way. I figure people is people and no matter what color they are they all deserve the same kind of justice. I figure when somebody gets killed they got the right to know the law is going to try and find out who done it. Everybody deserves that much."

"Are you offering to help?"

Deputy Dale shrugged his shoulders. "We don't deal with a lot of killings here in Myrtle Beach. It don't happen much and when it does it's usually pretty easy to figure out. A woman shoots her drunk husband, two boys get all tanked up and one gets his head bashed in, stuff like that. I don't know exactly what I can do but I intend to look into this matter as best I can. I figure Mona deserves that."

"Have you talked to Tyler Wilkens?"

"Yeah, I questioned him some."

"Is he still claiming he saw Jarvis Brown out in front of Mack's that night?"

Deputy Dale's cheeks turned red and he looked like he was suddenly uncomfortable, maybe embarrassed.

"What is it?" I asked, sensing something was up.

"It's Jarvis Brown. Up at the courthouse, they're usually pretty good at keeping us up to date with the goings on but we never got the word on Jarvis. Usually somebody will call."

"What about Jarvis?"

"They done lowered the charges to assault and battery. He's out on bail."

"When did this happen?"

"Four days ago."

"So, he was out of jail the night Mona Cooper was murdered?"

"It looks that way."

"That means Tyler could be telling the truth. If Jarvis Brown was there that night, he should be on the short list of suspects. Somebody needs to check that out."

"McKeller, I've known Jarvis Brown since he's been out of diapers. He's as mean and ornery as they come, he's got a temper that's always getting him in trouble, but he wouldn't have no reason to kill Mona Cooper. He just ain't like that."

"He was being held for attempted murder, wasn't he?"

"After his boss done got him all riled up. Jarvis ain't never been in trouble but for one thing, losing his temper and starting fights. He ain't the kind to take a girl out to the beach and cut her throat."

"That being said, you have an eyewitness placing him at the scene and he has a history of violence. Don't you think that's something you might want to look into?"

Deputy Dale looked even more embarrassed and uncomfortable. "I suppose it's something I could ask around about."

I couldn't help but smile. "There you go, Dale. You're starting to think like a real live law enforcement officer. There might be hope for you yet."

"Don't get your hopes up. I know Jarvis and he just ain't the type."

"That's all right. Every person we eliminate gets us closer to the real killer."

"Look, McKeller, we don't need to let Sheriff Talbert know about what's going on. He don't need to know we had this little talk."

"We could pinky swear if it makes you feel better."

"I don't reckon that's necessary."

"Why are you doing this, Deputy?"

"Because it's the right thing and because it's my job."

I gave him a nod. There wasn't anything else that needed to be said.

From the Brookgreen Room, I walked out the lower entrance of the hotel and around to the big sand parking lot outside of the amphitheater, where most everyone parked and where the Ocean Forest Studebaker was waiting for me.

My talk with the deputy had sparked something in me. I had been dealing with the wrong sort of people for some time now. The likes of Talbert and Vincent and Raddison Hayes had consumed my thoughts for days and it was good to see that there were other kinds of people in this town as well.

The more I thought about it the more I realized they were all around me. For every Talbert I'd met there had been a Deputy Dale, an Ellen Highsmith or a Tabby. For every Vincent there was a Rita Baker or Clarence Cooper and for every Raddison Hayes there was a sweet lost kid like Claire. I guess the thing my talk with Deputy Dale really sparked in me was a kind of hope for the community that I lived in and was attempting to make my home.

Chapter Twenty-Four

Doc Pearson's place was on the outskirts of Atlantic Beach. It was a well-kept little house with a thriving garden in the front yard. There seemed to be every kind of plant imaginable out there, but not much in the way of flowers. I wondered if they weren't herbs and remedies for his quaint and rural medical practice.

I'd gone into town first and spent some time asking around about Doc Pearson, where I could find him. At first people seemed reluctant to talk to me but it was obvious they all knew who I was asking about. Finally I got the information I was looking for, after assuring people I meant no harm to Doc Pearson.

I went in through the gate and up the walkway, and knocked on the door. An old black man answered. He appeared to be in his late sixties and was a stout man with broad features and white receding hair. He greeted me with a smile.

"Can I help you?"

"My name is McKeller and I'm investigating the death of Mona Cooper."

The smile dissipated from his face. "Poor sweet little thing …"

"I was told I should speak with you."

Doc Pearson opened his door wider and motioned me in. The place was small, but clean and cozy. Nothing about it looked anything like a doctor's office but instead like a normal living room.

"I suppose you know about what I do?" the old man asked me.

"I understand you're some kind of doctor."

"I'm not a doctor in the traditional sense of the word. I've never been to medical school or anything. I'm what you could call a healer. People come to me when they're feeling ill and I do what I can for them."

"Did Mona Cooper come to see you?"

"Mona has been coming to see me since she was born." He flashed me a toothy grin. "I brought her into this world and I've been looking after her ever since."

"When was the last time you saw her?"

The smile faded again. "She came to see me a few days before she died."

"Was she sick?"

Doc Pearson hesitated. "I know I'm not a real doctor, Mr. McKeller, but I do believe what the patient tells me is private."

"Yes sir, I understand and I'm not trying to put you in a bad spot. Anything you tell me would be between us. I wouldn't want to do anything to tarnish her memory. I'm just trying to find out who killed her and why."

He thought on that for a while, mulling it over in his mind, trying to decide whether or not to talk to me.

"I suppose there's no reason to keep it secret now," he said with a sigh. "I wouldn't want this to get around but Mona wasn't exactly sick, she was with child."

I can only imagine how wide my eyes got. It was about the last thing in the world I'd expected to hear. "Mona was pregnant?"

"I reckon she was about two months along or more. She got worried when her menstruation wasn't coming regular like it was supposed to and she came to see me. I think she knew what I was going to tell her before I even examined her."

"How did she take the news?"

"About how you'd expect a single young girl with big plans for her future would."

"Did she say who the father was?"

"No, she was pretty upset. She kept going on about how it wasn't possible and how it was going to mess up everything. I asked her about the father but she didn't tell me much of anything."

"You didn't know of anyone she was seeing, did you?"

"I hadn't seen Mona in ages. I couldn't tell you what she'd been up to. I got the feeling, whoever the father was, it wasn't somebody she was planning on settling down with."

I paused before asking my next question. "Did she mention any desire to…terminate the pregnancy?"

"I'm afraid that's not something I'm qualified to take care of. She wouldn't have asked me about that. She was pretty upset about the whole thing and she kept asking me what she should do but I didn't know what to tell her.

"I suggested she talk with the young man who helped get her into this predicament. I told her she needed to sit down with him and tell him what was what."

"What did she say to that?"

"She said she couldn't, it was impossible. She said it was going to ruin everything."

"She was pretty shaken, huh?"

"I tried to calm her as best I could. I assured her that this sort of thing has been happening to women for as long as there have been men around."

"What did she say to that?"

"She said I didn't understand, that this was the worst thing that could happen."

"What do you think she meant by that?"

"Your guess is as good as mine. Young girls can be highly emotional. When something like that happens it can seem like the end of the world. Many girls think they can never get through it but they always do. Nature has a way of working itself out."

"Mona didn't get through it."

"No, I guess she didn't but it certainly wasn't the pregnancy that killed her."

"I'm wondering if it was a contributing factor."

"I'm afraid that's not my expertise, Mr. McKeller. I diagnose the conditions and try to help where I can, bring people what comfort I can offer."

"Was this the first time she'd ever found herself in this condition?"

"She didn't have any children."

"That's not what I asked."

He gave me a look. "As far as I'm aware, she had never been pregnant before."

"But it's not out of the realm of possibilities. She could have gotten herself pregnant and had it taken care of and she could still get pregnant again, right?"

"Well, she couldn't have gotten herself pregnant, she'd need some help in that department but it's possible."

"I'm just asking."

"Mr. McKeller, did you know Mona Cooper?"

"Not really, I met her once, just before—"

"Mona liked to live large but she was a good girl. She had a heart on her the size of Horry County."

"Did she say anything else that might be of any help?"

"She was awfully upset. She said a lot of things but I can't think of anything else that would be of help."

"Did she ask about traveling in her condition?"

His eyes lit up like I had caused him to remember something he'd forgotten. "As a matter of fact, she did. She asked if she could take a long train ride in her condition."

"What did you tell her?"

"I told her the truth. I told her women have been doing much tougher things in that condition over the centuries. I told her she'd be fine."

I walked out of Doc Pearson's in a daze. The news of Mona's pregnancy was a bombshell but it didn't go a long way in helping me find her killer. I wondered how it fit in with what happened to her, if it even had anything to do with it. My guess was I needed to find out who the father of her unborn baby was.

My car was still parked over on Main Street, in front of Mack's. Against my better judgment, I decided to slip in for a quick drink. Tabby was working the tables and I took a seat at the bar with Randall.

"The usual?" he asked.

"Yeah, sounds good." He put up a shot glass and I threw it back before glancing around the room. Tabby was busy, she shot me a look and a half smile and went about her business.

Far off in the back corner I caught a glimpse of a familiar

face. It wasn't one I particularly wanted to see, but it was familiar just the same and I felt like maybe the two of us should have a little chat. I ordered another drink and took it with me, over to where Raddison Hayes was sitting.

He was at a table with a woman on each arm, voluptuous and buxom. The three were laughing and drinking, empty shot glasses lined up in front of them. They didn't notice me approach.

"You lost or something?" I asked.

Hayes stopped laughing and turned to stare at me for a moment before saying, "As a local business owner, sometimes it's good to get out and support your fellow owners."

"How did you know?"

Raddison leaned into the girl on his right and whispered something into her ear. She got up and took the other girl by the arm, leading her away from the table and leaving Hayes and me relatively alone.

"How did you know she had been to see Doc Pearson?"

"You hear things."

"You knew she was pregnant."

"I heard a rumor floating around."

"What rumor? Where would you hear something like that? Doc Pearson doesn't strike me as the kind to talk out of school."

"People talk."

I shot back my moonshine for some quick liquid courage and took the seat across from him at the table.

"What people? Who else knew about Mona's condition?"

"It only takes one."

I took a deep breath, preparing myself for the confrontation. Moonshine and testosterone are a dangerous mix and I could feel the two simmering inside of me, a highly combustible and volatile combination. "Maybe you knew all along. Maybe you're the one who sent her over to see Doc Pearson in the first place."

"What are you blubbering about?"

"Maybe you knew all along because it was your baby."

Hayes let out a loud belly laugh. "Mine? Is that what you've come up with, that I got Mona pregnant?"

"It makes sense. You had a history with her. She used to work for you. How else would you have known about the baby?"

"If that was the case, why would I send you over there?"

It was my turn to hesitate. "I don't know. Maybe you're playing some kind of game. Maybe you're the type who likes to flaunt stuff."

"Maybe you haven't got a clue."

"How angry were you when she left to go work for the Bakers?"

Hayes laughed again.

"It's bad for business when your girls go off to find new professions, isn't it?"

He was still smiling but the laugh had drifted away and his eyes became dark and serious, fixed on me.

"How did this go down, Raddison? Did Mona sneak off and leave you in the middle of night? Is that why she never came back to visit her friends in Atlantic Beach, because she was afraid of bumping into you?"

"Mona wasn't afraid of near nothing." He grunted back.

"She was afraid of you though, wasn't she? She was afraid of being forced back into that lifestyle, the life she'd managed to escape from. She was afraid of what you'd do when you found her again."

"You ain't got a lick of sense about you."

"You found her again somehow, didn't you? Did you track her down or did you happen upon her? However it happened, you got her back in your sights. Maybe you contacted her and told her things would be different. Maybe you even sent her flowers and made promises you never intended to keep. You convinced her to meet you."

"Flowers, what in the hell are you talking about?"

"You're not the kind of man who lets things get away from you, are you? Once you were with her again you had to show her who was boss. Is that how it went down? Is that how you ended up having your way with her? Is that how she ended up getting pregnant?"

Hayes didn't answer. He just sat there glaring back at me, stewing in his own anger.

"Mona tried to go back to her new life and get away from you again. She was saving up for her trip to get as far away from you as she could but things took a funny turn. She found out she was pregnant and that threw a monkey wrench into her whole plan. Did she come looking to you for help or was it something else? Maybe she was looking for some hush money."

Raddison Hayes shook his head. "What are you smoking, McKeller?"

"Maybe you promised her some money for her trip. Maybe you told her to meet you but instead of giving her the dough you took her out to a deserted stretch of beach and you raped her. After that, you were in too deep. There weren't many other options. Maybe that's when you slit her throat with that knife you're so handy with and left her out there in the middle of nowhere to die."

Hayes leaned forward in his chair, still staring into my eyes with hatred. When he spoke his voice was low and calm. "Why don't you and me go somewhere more private to talk about this."

"I like it right here."

He smiled some and cocked his head to one side. "You're not very good at this, are you? Now let me ask you something … How on God's green earth did you ever solve them there murders at the Ocean Forest? Is this here how you done it, by spouting out every crazy thing you can think of?"

"What's so crazy about it? If I'm wrong tell me how it really went down, tell me about when Mona was working for you."

"I done told you, my business ain't none of your concern."

"Where Mona Cooper is concerned, everything is my business."

"So that's how you figure it, huh? You figure it was me that got her pregnant and it was me that took her out there and done those things to her?"

"It's on the short list of possibilities."

"I don't take kindly to accusations."

"I'd think you'd be used to it by now, what with your line of work."

"I got half a mind to beat that nonsense out of you."

I stood up, our glazes locked on each other's. He followed suit and we were standing across the table from each other. "Well, it's not going to be like last time."

Hayes' grin got wider. "I can promise you that."

From out of nowhere, Tabby appeared at my side. She placed

a hand on my shoulder. "Is everything OK?" she asked.

"Sure it is. Raddison and I were just having a little pow-wow."

"Yeah, a regular bull session," he added.

She looked over at him and back at me. "Don't you boys go and do anything stupid now. I'd hate to have to bar either one of you from here."

"Don't you worry about that, Miss Tabby," Radisson said, all mild and agreeable. "Ain't going to be no trouble here tonight. I was just fixing to leave."

She stood there for a few moments looking us over, trying to get a read on what was going on. "Ok, then," she said as she turned and walked away, back to work.

"You're lucky I feel the way I do about Tabby. Out of respect for her I'm going to let this slide…for now."

"Lucky me."

"Out of respect for Mona's memory, I'm going to give you the benefit of the doubt and figure you're just grabbing at straws and trying to stir things up because you got nothing else. So long as this talk of ours stays between us I'm going to let it be but if I find you been talking this nonsense around town you and me are going to have issues."

"Well, I'd hate to have issues with you, Raddison. You and I have been getting along so splendidly until now."

"You best watch your step, white boy."

"You might want to watch yours too."

Hayes reached down and picked up a shot glass from the table and threw it back, drinking it in a quick effortless gulp. He motioned for the two girls he came with to return and the three left Mack's without another word. Tabby was back at my side before he was out the door.

"What was that all about?"

"Research."

"What's that supposed to mean?"

"It means he knows more than he's letting on about Mona."

"You think he knows something?"

"I think he knows a lot. Things are starting to surface. Why didn't you tell me Mona worked for Hayes?"

"What does that have to do with anything?"

"Maybe it has everything to do with everything. The fact that she was one of his girls shines a whole different light on the situation. It puts her in the middle of a lot of fireworks."

"She worked at the Sea Shack. She did the same thing I do."

"Is that all she did?"

Tabby's eyes got wide and she let out a gasp. "What are you saying? You think Mona was some kind of whore?"

"I'm saying she worked for Hayes and we all know what he's into."

"You got it all wrong, McKeller."

"Do I? I know she was your friend but she bounced around a lot. She got herself involved with some bad people."

"So that means she must have been whoring around?"

"Look, Tabby, I'm trying to get to the bottom of this and I'm not trying to drag Mona's name through the mud but if I'm going to find out what happened I need to know the truth, the whole dirty truth, no matter how ugly it gets."

"You want to know the truth?"

"Of course I do."

"After my daddy lost his farm, we were in a bad way. We didn't have nowhere to go and my family needed money bad. I had to get a job and I went to see Raddison Hayes. I told him what was what and he hired me on the spot. I worked for Raddison nearly a year before I started at Mack's."

This one caught me off guard. I wasn't sure what to say. "What did you do for him?" I finally settled on.

"I done the same thing as Mona did," she replied blankly. "So, what does that make me?"

"Tabby," I started to say but she cut me off.

"I think you should leave now."

"Tabby, I didn't mean to—"

"I think you should leave now," she said again.

Chapter Twenty-Five

I WAS in a foul mood by the time I got back to the hotel. My entire world was in disarray. Of all the people in the world to be angry with me, Tabby was the last one I wanted. The fact that I had insulted both her and her departed friend made me feel queasy in the stomach and flat out pissed at myself.

Just the same, there was something about Raddison Hayes that didn't sit right with me. Maybe I didn't have all the details figured out but I was fairly positive there was something there, more than he was letting on to. Not that he was letting on to all that much.

The connection was there. Somewhere behind it I figured there might be a motive to go with it. The how's and why's were all I needed to fill in the gaps. That's kind of like saying if I only had wings I could fly.

The Jarvis Brown thing was gnawing at me too. If Raddison Hayes wasn't my man, I figured there was a good chance Brown might be. Of course, I had no motive or connection with Mona to back it up but the fact he'd been seen there that night was enough to keep the wheels turning in my head. If there was any kind of connection with Jarvis Brown and Mona Cooper, I needed to find it.

As I walked through the front door of the Ocean Forest, I

was greeted by a panic-stricken desk clerk. He looked about as distraught as anybody I'd seen in quite a while.

"Thank goodness you're back," Curtis said as I came in. "I didn't know who to call or what to do. They've gone crazy. They're out of control. The other guests are complaining—"

"Calm down. What are you talking about?"

"It's them. They're raving lunatics. I tried talking to them but they won't listen," He was blabbering on like a madman.

"Exactly who are we talking about?"

"Them... those guys... the accountants."

"The accountants have gone crazy?"

"I've never seen anything like it. They're animals."

"The CPA's?" I asked, still not sure we were talking about the same guys.

"Yes, they've taken over the seventh floor. They're wreaking havoc."

"The pencil neck guys with the ties and the glasses?"

"Those are the ones."

"I'll take care of it." This I had to see.

Clifford was manning the elevator and I told him to take me up to the seventh floor.

"You sure you want to go up there? It ain't a pretty sight."

"Just get this shoebox moving," I grunted back.

I could hear the hoots and hollering before the doors even opened. Once they did I was greeted with one of the strangest sights I had witnessed in a long while.

There were about fifteen of them total. They were the same fellows I had seen around the hotel for the past few days, the number crunching dweebs in stiff shirts and wing-tips. Now they were something different. They had transformed into a pack of drunken gluttonous dogs in the midst of a full-blown feeding frenzy. If there had been a chandelier in the hallway these guys would have been swinging from it.

Most of them were holding bottles, quarts of beer, pints of liquor; one guy even had a jug of moonshine cradled under his arm. Some of them were in sleeveless under-shirts with their suspenders hanging down at their sides. Three of them were still in their white collared shirts and ties but their trousers were gone and they wore only socks and boxer shorts.

A couple of them were wrestling in the middle of the hallway. Four others had a Hispanic chamber maid cornered at the far end of the corridor. She looked scared and disheveled and she was slapping at their hands as they reached for her, trying to grab at the hem of her uniform skirt. Her other hand was holding the collar of her blouse closed, her knees pressed together in a defensive stance and she was yelling at them in Spanish. I don't know what she was saying but I don't think she was asking for tax advice.

"What in the hell is going on here?"

Some of them stopped to look back at me. Some of them didn't. All of them went back to what they were doing in just moments.

I stalked down the hallway, shoving drunks out of my way as I went. When I got to the two guys wrestling, I put my foot into the side of the guy on top and gave him a shove, sending him toppling over.

"All right boys, the party's over," I kept saying.

At the end of the corridor, I stepped in between the maid and her would-be attackers. The men groaned with disappointment when I got in their way.

"What the hell do you guys think you're doing?"

"We're just having a little fun," one of them answered.

"Assaulting hotel employees does not qualify as fun." I turned to the frightened girl. "It's OK, you can go now."

"Gracias," she smiled back before crossing herself and taking off toward the elevator. She got her share of whistles and cat calls as she scampered away.

"All right, that's enough. The fun is over. I want everybody to gather themselves up and head back to your rooms."

"What's the big idea?" one guy moaned.

"Who died and made you boss?" another asked.

"I'm the guy who's going to throw each one of you out on your cans if you don't straighten up and fly right. Now let's get a move on it."

"We're just blowing off a little steam. We're not hurting anybody."

"What you are is drunk and rowdy and disturbing our other guests. Besides that, what you were doing to that poor girl carries three to five in some states. If you go along quietly, we'll sweep this whole thing under the rug, but if you're going to start a ruckus I'm going to have to start physically tossing you out of here one at a time."

"There's a lot of us and only one of you," a guy said, standing up straight and pulling his shoulders back. Some of the others agreed and the crowd began to murmur.

"How about I start with you?" I suggested back to him. His shoulders slouched a bit and he didn't seem to be standing quite as erect. He was tough enough when he was speaking for the group, but when I called him out he slunk down a few notches.

"Anybody else?" Nobody responded with anything more than a groan. "All right then, let's get this mess cleaned up and everybody head on back to their room. We'll forget this ever happened."

"Look, Bud, we didn't mean no harm. We've been working hard all year and we just wanted to have a little fun. We weren't going to hurt that pretty little girl or nothing. We were just looking for a little female companionship is all. We were planning on treating her real nice."

"You've got a hell of a way of showing it," I responded. "You guys had that poor thing scared half out of her mind."

A bunch of them had their heads hanging low, offering half-assed apologies under their breath.

"You guys ought to be ashamed of yourselves. How would you like it if somebody did that to you?"

"If it was her I'd like it a lot," one answered and they all busted into laughter.

"That's no way to treat a lady. You guys are lucky nobody called the cops."

"Hell, Mack, we were just trying to talk her into hanging out with us. We even offered her money just to stick around and be a part of the party."

"There's a word for that and it's illegal in this state."

"We're having us a party. What's a party without girls?"

"Yeah, we just wanted something soft and pretty to look at."

"Looked to me like you guys were doing more than just look-ing," I pointed out.

"Well, maybe we got a little out of hand, but we did mean nothing by it. We're just having some fun. We wouldn't have hurt her."

"Guys, look, I like women as much as the next guy. I'm a big fan but there are proper ways of doing things. You can't hold someone against their will. It's just not right."

"How about you? Do you know any girls you could call? We've got money. We'll be good."

"Forget it. This party is over for tonight." They let out a collec-tive groan. "Pack it up and get back to your rooms. If I get called back up here I'm going to start booting people out on their ear."

It was fairly obvious they weren't ready to call it a night, but they began dispersing and making their way back to their rooms. I waited until the area was clear and headed back downstairs.

Believe it or not, I decided a drink was in order. It had been a long day and my leg was killing me. I bellied up to the bar at the Brookgreen Room. The second shot of booze was still burning its way down my throat when I was interrupted from my left. A tall, younger guy in a tan suit was sitting next to me.

"Howdy," he said, toasting his glass in my direction. The guy was slim with wide shoulders and dark hair. He had pitch black eyes and a thin mustache across his upper lip.

"Hi," I answered, not really interested in small talk.

"You're McKeller, aren't you?"

"Yeah, that's me."

"You're the house dick here, right?"

"Yeah, that's right."

"I wonder if you could answer a question for me."

"Sure thing."

"Why would the house dick at the Ocean Forest Hotel be looking for me?"

"Excuse me?"

"I keep hearing about this guy who's been running around town and asking about me. I did some checking and I figured out that guy is you."

If there is anything to that expression about your blood running cold I guess it happened to me right there and then. I looked over my shoulder and caught a glimpse of a muscle bound blonde man sitting at a table alone and staring me down. I could only guess it was the Harley guy Claire had told me about.

"I hear you walloped a friend of mine over the head with a bar stool," Timothy Vincent said to me.

"Sorry about that but it needed to be done. He's not the most polite person I ever met."

"No, I guess Billy Bob isn't at that. So do you want to tell me why you've been hunting me down?"

My head was spinning and I had a tight twisting sensation in the pit of my stomach. This wasn't the way I expected to meet up with Vincent and he caught me off guard. It was time for some fast thinking and my brain was stuck in second gear.

"I hear you're the guy to talk to in this town."

"I got'a be honest with you, McKeller. When I hear about people asking around about me it tends to make me a little nervous. I'm not such a nice guy to be around when I get nervous."

"Nerves are a tough thing. You might want to get that checked out."

"Do you want to tell me why you're so intent on finding me? Do you and me have something I need to know about?"

Vincent was a smart guy. I could tell in the first minute of talking with him. Maybe he wasn't book smart but I could tell he was the kind of guy who could see through a cloud of bullshit pretty easily. If I was going to play this off without tipping my hand I needed to be cool about it. I figured I had a few directions I could go and I wasn't sure which one would play right. Until the very second I said it, I wasn't sure which cards I was going to lay on the table.

"I work here at the hotel," I said. "Part of my job is to take care of the guests. Sometimes we have people come in and they have very specific requests. Sometimes these requests are the kinds of things you can't go pick up at the five-and-dime."

He looked me over for a bit. "I'm listening."

"Take now for example. Right now I've got about a hundred accountants here at the hotel. They're here for their annual convention and some of them are a little bored with the daily meetings and business routine they're going through. Some of them are looking to have a good time and they're asking me where to go for that."

"I guess even accountants need to cut loose from time to time."

"The thing is I'm relatively new in town. I don't know where a guy goes to find those things that you can't get on Main Street. I don't really have the connections here in Myrtle Beach. I asked around and I heard you're the guy to talk to."

"What exactly are they looking for?"

"I'd say they're looking for the same things most married men away from home for a long weekend are looking for."

"I might be able to help you there."

"The way I see it, I'd be bringing you the business. I figure that should be worth a little something."

"So, you're looking to be cut into the action."

"Nothing major, I figure some kind of finder's fee would be in order, maybe a small percentage of the take."

Vincent gave me a look, like he was scanning me for flaws. I couldn't tell if he was buying my story or trying to figure out how to dispose of my body.

"You're the detective here at the hotel. What does that actually mean?"

"It means the Ocean Forest throws me some chump change every week, hardly enough to get by on. It also means that I'm not actually any sort of law enforcement official. My only affiliation is with the hotel so you've got no need to worry about me."

"What do these boys have in mind?"

"They're looking for a good time, a party, some booze, maybe a few girls."

"That could be arranged."

"How's your selection as far as the girls go?"

"I reckon it's about the best this side of the Sunset Lodge."

"What's that?"

"It's a place down just north of Georgetown, about as famous as it gets in these parts. It's kind of a hike and they ain't going to come to you."

"One of my guys had a special request. He's looking for

something on the young side, likes them brunette with blue eyes. Says he'll pay extra."

This caused Vincent to shoot me a funny look. I wondered if I had pushed it too far and given him too much, maybe alerted him to what I was after.

"This ain't no mail order service. He'll take what I got or he can go someplace else."

"I was just passing it along, trying to keep the customers happy."

"I understand you know how to get to the Villa Roma. You bring your boys up there tomorrow night around ten. Tell them to bring their money. I can promise you they won't be disappointed." He finished off his drink and stood up, straightening his jacket. "As far as me and you go, we'll see how we do and I'll throw you what I think is appropriate after."

"Sounds good. In the meantime, is there a number I can reach you if I need?"

"You'll see me tomorrow at the Villa Roma."

He left on that note. I sat there by myself, wondering what on earth I was going to do next. I had managed to smoke him out and make him show himself, but now that I had I didn't have a clue what to do next. I was flying blind, as usual.

If Patty Highsmith was one of the girls he brought along the next night it would solve one of my problems, but it might open up a whole other can of worms. I still didn't know if she wanted to be found. For all I knew she might be very happy setting up house with the likes of Vincent.

If she was looking to be rescued there was the question of how to go about it. Was I supposed to pull out my .45 and shoot my way out? Was I going to sneak her out the back door? Either way, if it turned out she wanted to go, I got the feeling Vincent wasn't going to give her up without a fight.

Chapter Twenty-Six

THAT familiar banging on my door woke me up once again. I lay there for a few minutes trying to figure out who it was. The raps were too hard and heavy to be Eleanor. I hadn't heard Claire's knock yet but I imagined it would be less intense, so I ruled her out as well. Judging by the force and repetition, I decided it must be Buntemeyer, my boss. I also decided he wasn't happy with me for some reason.

"What did I do now?" I asked as I opened the door.

"Do you know what time it is?"

"I'm going to go out on a limb and say later than you think I ought to be sleeping."

"I just left Henderson in 714."

"I hope you didn't leave him on my account."

"Would you care to tell me about what happened last night?"

"What part of last night would you like to hear about?"

"How about the part where you insulted a group of paying guests and ordered them back to their rooms?"

"Did you happen to hear about the shenanigans they were pulling when I walked in on them?"

"My understanding is they were having a little party."

"If by little party you mean, drunk and disorderly, felony kidnapping and assault and battery, then yeah. They were having a little party."

"McKeller, let me explain something to you. We, at the Ocean Forest Hotel, are here to cater to the guests every need. If a few guests wish to gather in the corridor for cocktails, so be it."

"Things were getting out of hand. Somebody had to do something."

"Mr. Henderson is under the impression that he and his people are under some sort of house arrest."

"Look, give me a few minutes to splash some cold water in my face and run a razor across my chin and I'll go talk to him. I'll straighten it all out."

"I think maybe you've done enough damage."

I gave him one of those looks. "Trust me," I told him, "I think I know how to make it all better."

Henderson turned out to be an agreeable bloke, especially after I filled him in on what I had in mind. From there on he was putty in my hands. I'd caught him coming out of one of his meetings on the first floor and recognized him at once. He'd been the guy with no pants and a jug of shine the night before.

"How many girls?" were the first words out of his mouth.

"I don't know exactly but I'm guessing there will be plenty."

I could almost hear his mouth watering.

"How many guys do you think would be interested?" I asked.

"All of them," he shot back before adding, "but let's not tell everyone. We want to keep this under our hats and make sure it doesn't get back to the big shots. We'll keep the party on the small side, say about twenty."

"OK then, small it is, an intimate little gathering for twenty of your closest buddies."

I told him to pass the word around and to meet me, with the others, in the lobby around nine thirty. It turned out about half of them had cars so getting us all up to the Villa Roma wasn't going to be a problem.

There was the little issue of that grating feeling in the back of my skull. It was the first time I'd ever played pimp for a bunch of horny bean counters and I wasn't exactly sure how I felt about it. I tried to tell myself that whatever happened between consenting adults was none of my business, whether I'd arranged the meeting or not. The other thing I kept telling myself was if it got me a step closer to finding Patty Highsmith it would be more than worth it.

From there I swung by Eleanor's room and gave her a vague rundown, basically telling her I had some leads and felt like I was getting closer. I didn't let on to anything else I was up to.

Next it was over to Claire's room where I found a bored teenage girl climbing the walls and itching to get out. The novelty of staying at the Ocean Forest had worn off and now she felt more like a captive than a pampered guest.

"I can't stand it anymore. The walls are closing in on me. I need to get out of here. I need to get some fresh air and sunshine."

"I don't think that's such a great idea."

"You're not the one stuck in this hotel room twenty-four hours a day."

"You act like you've been here for a month. It's only been a day."

"It feels like a month."

"Just stay put awhile longer."

"What's it going to hurt if I go down to use the pool?"

"It's going to hurt a lot if you get spotted by the wrong person."

"In case you haven't noticed, we're at the Ocean Forest Hotel. It's not the kind of place Vincent and his boys hang out."

I took a deep breath. "It might interest you to know that Vincent was in this very hotel last night. He came looking for me like I told you he would."

"Vincent was here?" This caught her attention and caused her to perk up and take notice. "What did he want? Did he ask about me?"

"He came to find out why I was looking for him. He doesn't know you're here and I'd like to keep it that way?"

"What did you tell him?"

"I made him a business proposition. I'm meeting up with him later tonight."

Claire gave me the once over. "I hope you know what you're doing."

"That makes two of us."

"I take it he still doesn't know you're looking for Patty?"

"Not as far as I can tell."

"You better be careful."

"That's my plan," I said as I slipped my gray felt fedora on my noggin and pulled the brim down low on my face. "In the meantime, you be a good girl and keep your fanny in this room. Order yourself some more food."

"That's all I do is eat, sleep and stare out the window. What kind of life is that?"

"It's called playing it safe and it's not going to be for much longer."

"If Vincent has already been here and he's meeting you later tonight, why can't I go down to the pool? It's not like he has any reason to come back."

"Claire, give me a break here. I'm doing this for your own good. Stop fighting me on this."

She let out and exasperated sigh. "I don't know what the big deal is?"

"One more day and we'll figure something out."

Claire shrugged her skinny shoulders in the air. It was one of those moves that aren't designed to say anything one way or the other, a polite way to tell a guy to go fly a kite, a childish pout. You could look at her and see that headstrong kid pushing to cut loose, that teenage girl who's sure she knows everything and nobody can convince her otherwise. I got the feeling she was heading for the downstairs pool as soon as I was gone. What could I do? It's not like I could tie her to the bed posts.

"Don't do anything stupid," I said as I made my way out the door.

Claire didn't answer.

Chapter Twenty-Seven

As I came out of the elevator and through the lobby I passed pockets of CPAs clustered together like pencils in pockets. A few of them gave me winks and grins, the occasional knowing nod. Word had gotten out about our upcoming foray and I had gone from villain to hero overnight.

I was passing by the front desk when the clerk beckoned me over. He was an older, dumpy sort of guy who always looked like he was bored with being there.

"McKeller, you've got a visitor," he informed me.

I glanced around the lobby, looking for someone who might be looking for me.

"Down at the service entrance," he said.

That was weird. Why would anyone want to meet me back where the deliveries came in and the employees reported for work when they could come up to the elegant and comfortable lobby.

The service entrance was located on the south end of the hotel, off to the side. It was a convenient place to bring in the daily essentials to keep the hotel running with easy access to the kitchen and worker areas. I came out of the double doors and saw one of the last people I expected to see.

Tabby looked good. Her hair was down and she was wearing a conservative Navy blue dress with a thick brown sweater wrapped over it. She was off to the side with her arms crossed, dazing out at a spot far away.

Now I knew why it had to be the service entrance. Tabby wouldn't be allowed to use the front door because of the color of her skin.

"Hi," I said as I approached her.

She gave me a soft smile and tilted her head slightly to one side, a cute, girlish move she probably wasn't aware she was doing but one that sent shivers up my spine. "Hi," she said back.

"Is everything OK?"

Tabby nodded. "Yeah, everything is fine. I wanted to let you know Mona's getting buried on Saturday morning. I needed to talk to you too."

Her chin was down slightly and she looked up at me with her big browns about as wide as they could go. Peering down into them, I could feel my insides begin to melt away.

"I'm sorry about last night," she said in a shy quiet voice.

"Forget it, I was out of line."

"No, you were just doing your job. I guess you have to explore every angle when you're investigating something like this."

"I didn't mean to hurt your feelings or insult Mona's memory in any way."

"I know that."

"I should have handled it better."

"You were doing what you felt you had to. You're doing me a favor by looking into this, I know that."

"I'd do anything for you, Tabby."

Her smile got bigger. "I know that too. I just figured maybe I could help clear some things up for you. There's some things folks don't talk much about around here."

"Things like Raddison Hayes?"

"For one."

"I think I have a pretty good read on Raddison Hayes."

"Everybody knows about some of the stuff Raddison does but that's not all there is to him. He's not all bad."

"You're going to defend Hayes?"

"No...well, yes, kind of. We all know how he makes his money and that is what it is but he can be more than that too. When I needed help he was there for me, the same thing with Mona."

"How many of the girls who work for him did he start out helping?"

"Most of them, I suspect."

"I understand what you're trying to do, Tabby, but let's face facts. Raddison Hayes is a sadistic bastard who preys on the weaknesses of others. He makes his money at the expense of other people. He uses them for his own benefit.

"By the grace of God, you didn't end up working for him in that way, maybe you were too smart for that, but for every one of you there are probably four more girls who didn't get off as lucky."

"Girls like Mona?" she asked me. "Is that what you think?"

I didn't have the heart to answer her.

"You don't get it, McKeller. Mona wouldn't have done it that way. It ain't who she was. She was stronger and smarter than I'll ever be."

"Sometimes desperation can make a person do things."

"It wasn't like that. Raddison's not like that. He's not going to push a girl into that. There are too many who are willing."

"Tabby, I know you loved Mona and you're trying to protect her but—"

She cut me off. "No, I'm telling you how it was. Mona never did that for him. I know it for fact. She needed work and he hired her for the Sea Shack. She waited tables and worked the bar from time to time.

"I told you how she was, so outgoing and full of life. Everybody that knew her loved her. After a while, Raddison took a shining to her. They didn't have much in common. They were two totally different kinds of people. I think Raddison saw something in her, something all his money and power couldn't buy. He saw a life with Mona he never had before."

"You're telling me Raddison Hayes was in love with Mona?"

Tabby hesitated. "She saw something in him too. I don't know exactly what the attraction was. He was older and he had that lifestyle, maybe it was the money and power, maybe she knew that under all that was a good heart, I don't know. For him, it was something clean and pure, nothing like the other things in his life. He saw possibilities in Mona he never had with anyone else."

"How long were they a couple?"

"Near about a year, I suppose. She broke it off just before she went to live with that white family in town. He asked her to marry him. She could have had it all, the money, the big house. She could have been one of the most important women in all of Atlantic Beach."

"It sounds like everything she always wanted," I said.

"You didn't know Mona. She dreamed big but she was a good girl at heart. She didn't want everything that came with it. She didn't want to be married to a gangster. She knew he was a good man underneath it all but she couldn't live with knowing where his money came from."

"How did he take it?"

"It near about killed him at first. She broke his heart. I do believe that Mona was the true love of his life. Being the kind of man he was, he pulled himself together and got back to business."

"Did he try to contact her, to bring her back?"

"I don't think so. Raddison respected her wishes. He understood why she couldn't be with him."

"Raddison doesn't seem like the type to take rejection well."

"He loved Mona and he wanted her to be happy. I suppose a man like Raddison could have gone out and found her. He could have tried to force her to come back but Raddison ain't like that, especially where Mona was concerned."

"You have a knack for seeing the best in people, don't you?" I said. She didn't answer me. "Maybe sometimes you see it when it's not there."

"It's usually there, McKeller. Sometimes you just have dig harder to find it is all."

"OK, so Raddison and Mona were a couple. He fell hard for her. Maybe that explains why he's so reticent about talking about her, maybe it doesn't. Could be it opens up a whole other list of questions and possibilities."

"I wouldn't know about that. You're the detective. I just thought you ought to know how things were."

"What about Jarvis Brown?"

"What about him?"

"Do you know him?"

"I see him around from time to time. I've waited on him before but I've never really had much to do with him. He always seemed like a time bomb ready to go off and I've always tried to keep my distance."

"What about Mona?"

"The same. We all knew who he was and what he was like. We just handled him with kid gloves and tried to give him a wide berth. I'm sure she waited on him a time or two at the Sea Shack but she wouldn't have had anything to do with him either."

"You're sure they were never friends, maybe more?"

Tabby gasped. "Never in a million years. Mona was too smart to have anything to do with Jarvis Brown."

"She ended up with Raddison Hayes. That wasn't very smart."

"That was different. Raddison is what he is, but he's no Jarvis Brown."

"You're positive?"

"I knew Mona better than anyone else in this world. There is no way in heaven or earth she would have ever had anything to do with Jarvis."

"OK, it was just a thought."

She gave me a nod and started to turn to walk away but I stopped her. "Wait," I said, fishing into my breast pocket. "I have some things of Mona's. I got them from the Baker house. I was going to give them to Mr. Cooper when I was finished with them but there's one I think you should have."

I pulled out the stack of photo's I'd found in Mona's dresser and began sorting through them. When I got to the one of her and Tabby, the one of the two of them in front of the barn as young girls, I pulled it out and handed it to her.

Her eyes went misty and her smile softened. She stood staring at it silently for a minute or so. "I remember when this was taken. We were just kids."

I still had the bunch of cards and photos in my hand and I noticed the corner of one sticking out. It was the card from the florist I assumed came with the dead flowers, the one with the heart drawn on it. I flashed it to Tabby.

"Do you think this came from Raddison?" I asked.

"I wouldn't know."

"Does he read and write?"

"A little, not much. Enough to keep up with his books and

such but that's about it. There's a lot of folks in these parts who don't read and write so good."

"A guy like that might be the kind to draw a heart instead of signing his name."

"It could be the kind of guy who doesn't want to put his name on anything too."

"That still sounds like Raddison Hayes to me."

"I don't know about any of that."

"What about this florist shop, Bartlett's?"

"I never heard of it."

"There were some dead flowers in her room. It looked like they'd been there for a while. Do you think they might have been from Raddison?"

She shrugged again. "As far as I know they hadn't seen each other since she broke it off. I have no idea."

I put the stack back in my pocket. "Maybe it's nothing."

"Thanks for the picture," she said with a sigh. "I've got to get going."

"Can I give you a ride?"

"No thanks. Russell is waiting in the parking lot."

"OK, maybe I'll see you up at Mack's?"

"Yeah, that would be nice. I like it when you stop by."

Tabby gave me one of her signature smiles and turned and walked away. I stood there watching her go until she was out of sight.

I still had the florist's card in my hand as I walked back through the hotel and back up to the front desk. I tossed it onto the counter top in front of the desk clerk.

"You ever hear of this place?"

He examined the card for a few moments. "Bartlett's? Never heard of it."

"You don't know if it's local?"

"I've lived in Myrtle Beach all of my life. I know this town like the back of my hand. There ain't never been no Bartlett's Florist Shop here."

How weird was that? How did a girl who longed to go somewhere else but never made it out of town end up getting flowers from someplace else? It didn't seem to make any sense.

Chapter Twenty-Eight

AFTER driving around aimlessly for a bit I ended up at the Kozy Korner for a cup of Joe. The place had its usual assortment of old timers and locals sitting around talking everything from sports to local goings on to current events. The owner, a friendly Greek man, was perched in a booth dunking biscuits in a saucer of coffee.

I was at the counter, half paying attention, consumed by my own thoughts.

Tabby's revelation was sticking to the inside of my brain like salt water taffy. If everything she told me was true it altered the scenario I had laid out in my head but I wasn't sure it changed things so much.

There was still a deep connection between Mona and Raddison Hayes. Even if she hadn't been one of his working girls there was a deep tie between the two, maybe enough for him to go to great extents to bring her back in the fold. If things went bad it might have even been enough for him to blow his top and commit the unthinkable. My guess was the father of Mona's baby was the most likely killer and that arrow still pointed to Hayes.

There was also the chance of Tabby's story having holes in it. She'd already said she had lost touch with Mona for the better part of a year. Who knew what could have happened in that time. If Mona had ended up working for Hayes in that other way there's no guarantee she would have told her friend about it. It's not the kind of career move you advertise to friends and family.

Whatever the case, I was reasonably positive that all roads led through Raddison Hayes' front yard. I just had to figure out where they crisscrossed. There was Jarvis Brown too but I had yet to find any connection between him and Mona. I wasn't ready to give up on the possibility, but it was looking more like a long shot and I didn't have much faith in linking the two.

Raddison Hayes was my best bet. Somehow I had to place Mona Cooper with Hayes on the night she died. When I met her she was in a hurry to go and take care of something, to meet someone. A dollar to a doughnut that person was Hayes. I had a hunch she was going to confront him about the baby and maybe try to extort some traveling cash out of him.

I began to wonder how that would have gone down. Would she have walked over to the Sea Shack or would they have met up somewhere else, probably in Atlantic Beach. If they had met up somewhere there was a good chance somebody saw the two of them together. Raddison Hayes was a big fish in a small pond and chances were someone would have noticed him. The small fish have a tendency to take notice when the big fish come swimming by. I figured it was time for me to pound the pavement for a while and see what I could come up with.

Nothing screams cop like a white guy walking through the streets of an all-black town, questioning the locals. You can imagine the response I was getting.

I'd found the most current picture of Mona I had and I was showing it to anyone who would take the time to look at it. There weren't many of them. Starting on the side Mack's was on, I'd worked my way down one side and half way up the other without much luck. I was almost directly across the street from the bar when I walked into a dingy looking shoe repair shop.

Behind the counter an older, heavyset black man with a gray beard and a bald spot was working on a pair of cracked leathers that looked long past repairable. He glanced up as I came in but went immediately back to what he was doing.

"Help you?" he asked, concentrating on the work at hand.

"I'm looking for some information."

"Don't deal much in information. Fix your shoes if you want, polish 'em up, patch the holes, even replace the soles if need be."

"My shoes are fine, thanks."

"Shoes are the most important part of the wardrobe. Can't feel like a man if you're walking around on busted up leathers with holes and such, soles flapping in the wind."

"Yeah, I'm OK in that department."

"I'll tell you what, a man never feels as tall as when he's walking about on solid tread, stomping around town on new leather."

I held up the picture where he could get a clean look at it. "Have you ever seen this girl before?"

He glanced up for about a half a second before returning his attention to his chore. "Mona Cooper. Pretty little gal. Very fond of two inch heels with ankle straps. Had a pair she wore forever. I must of fixed them up ten times for her. Wore 'em till there wasn't bout nothing left of 'em."

"When's the last time you saw her?"

"I reckon it wasn't but a few nights ago. I saw her the night she done got killed. Saw her come out of Mack's just across the street there."

He had my attention.

"It's a right shame bout that. She was a sweet kid. It just ain't decent what happened to her. They'll be burying her come Saturday."

"What time did you see her?"

"Wouldn't rightly know. Ain't got no clock. I was here working on a pair of loafers with a crack down the side for a fella in town. Had to bout replace half the shoe."

"Did you see where she went?"

"I reckon I did at that. She come walkin out a Mack's and stood out front there for a bit. Looked like she was waitin for a bus or something but there ain't no buses run through Atlantic Beach."

"How long did she wait?"

"Couldn't tell you, on account I ain't got no clock and all."

"Did you see where she went?"

"After a spell, she done got picked up in a car."

"Did you get a look at the car?"

"Yepper, I did at that."

"Do you know what kind of car it was?"

"Looked to me like a tan Plymouth, prewar, maybe forty or forty one."

"You're sure about that?"

"If there's two things I know its shoes and cars. If you think about it they both do bout the same thing, getting a person from one place to the next."

"Did you get a look at the driver?"

"No sir, can't say as I did. They was off on the other side, headin east, couldn't make 'em out. From the looks a the car I'd say they had a dollar or two to their name."

"Do you know Raddison Hayes?" I tried.

"I reckon I been fixin Raddison's shoes for near bout as long as he's been wearin 'em."

"Do you happen to know what kind of car he drives?"

"Raddison's been drivin the same car since before the war. Can't figure why a man like that don't go and get him a new one. I guess if it runs good that's bout all that matters."

"What kind of car is it?"

"It's a black Desota, round thirty-six or seven Airflow. Ain't much to look at but it runs like a dream."

It wasn't the answer I was looking for but I could tell the old geezer knew what he was talking about. Life would have been a lot easier if Hayes drove a tan Plymouth.

"Did you tell the police about what you saw?"

"Nope."

"Why not?"

"Can't say as anybody asked me, till you come in."

"When you saw her out front of Mack's, did she look bothered or nervous, anything out of the ordinary?"

"She looked bout like most folks a waitin."

I thought for a few moments, searching for another straw to grab at. "Do you know a guy named Jarvis Brown?"

"I reckon most folks around here know of Jarvis. He's hard to miss, about big as a house, he is."

"Did you happen to see Jarvis out by Mack's that night?"

The old man cocked his head to one side. "Now that you mention it, I do recall seeing Jarvis out and about that night."

"Did you see him with Mona? Did the two of them speak together?"

He shrugged. "I seen Jarvis. A little later I seen Mona. Coulda been they was there about the same time but I had my hands full with the shoes I was fixin. I couldn't rightly say for sure."

"Was Jarvis still there when the car picked her up?"

"I don't figure he was. Far as I recall, Jarvis had done gone by the time she got into the car."

"Was there anything else you noticed that night?"

He thought for a second, even taking the time to stop fidgeting with the old shoe in his hand. "As a matter of fact, I did notice something"

"What was it?"

"I noticed she had her a new pair a two inch heels with ankle straps. Figured I'd be fixin them too, fore long."

I spent the better part of the next hour working the streets and talking to anyone who would give me the time of day. Besides what I learned from the old shoe man, everything I gathered amounted to exactly zero. No one else in town had seen or heard anything about Mona Cooper on the night she was killed.

The things I learned from the old man were swirling around in my head with everything I already knew. The fact that she hadn't been picked up in Raddison Hayes' car didn't change anything, he certainly had the connections to get another car. The fact he was coming from the opposite direction of the Sea Shack didn't matter either, he could have been coming from anywhere. I was still reasonably certain that Raddison Hayes was the man I was looking for. I just had to figure out how it all pieced together.

There was also the Jarvis Brown angle. I had two witnesses placing him at the right place at approximately the right time. Other than that, I had nothing. I couldn't even be sure he'd even spoken with Mona that night. As far as I could tell, there was nothing I could find to link the two together.

Chapter Twenty-Nine

THE rest of my day was uneventful. The only other person I felt I needed to talk to was Mathew Baker, Rita's husband and Mona's former boss. He was the only principal I hadn't spoken with yet. I doubted he would be much help as he barely saw Mona except in the mornings and on weekends, what with him working late in Conway all the time.

Driving all the way to Conway wasn't very high on my priority list and I wasn't looking forward to it. There was the slight chance that he might be able to shed some light on where she got the flowers, if he happened to be home that day. I had serious reservations on that point and I knew it was a pretty flimsy clue at best. Once again, I was running into a dead end and grasping for anything I could get my hands on.

Back at the hotel, I went about my usual duties and killed some time. I had a big dinner at the Brookgreen Room, along with a couple of shots of whiskey. From there I went up to my room and waited around until it was time to meet the accountants in the lobby. It was getting to be party time.

There were sixteen of them gathered in the lobby and waiting for me when I got there. Every one of them was a wound ball of pent up sexual desire, skinny little bottles of nervous energy waiting to explode. I could see it in their eyes. They were like firecrackers begging to be lit.

We organized ourselves into car loads and spilled out into the parking lot where we formed a caravan of sedans and coupes. I led the way in the Ocean Forest's Studebaker with a ninety eight pound wild man by my side. He was jabbering on about booze and dames the whole ride.

I turned off at the Villa Roma with the others close on my tail, driving around the building and parking out in back. We got out of the cars and I led them up to the back door. They bunched up behind me, pushing and shoving at my back as I knocked.

The Italian opened the door and gave me one of his looks. He didn't seem impressed but opened it up wide and motioned us in. We filed through the kitchen and into the dining room where it was set up for a party.

Tables and chairs were scattered about with a makeshift bar set off to one side, covered with jugs of moonshine and a tub of iced down bootleg beer. Vincent and Harley were standing over toward the front door, smiling at the guys as they came in. A couple more of Vincent's cronies were sitting at one of the tables.

"Welcome boys," Vincent said in a friendly drawl. "You boys come on in and make yourselves at home. We're going to have us a good time tonight, Myrtle Beach style. We've got beer and shine and card playing and food. We're going to have some lovely ladies joining us tonight too."

With that, the CPAs began cheering and hollering, carrying on like a bunch of fifth graders.

"If there's anything else you boys need you just tell one of my guys and we'll see what we can do about getting it for you. The way this is going to work is it's going to cost y'all a measly ten bucks a piece. That gets you all the food and drink your bellies can hold. As far as the girls go, that's between you and them.

Again with the cheers and hollers. The accountants couldn't get the money out of their wallets fast enough. Vincent's men collected the cover charge from each. Once all the money was collected, Vincent clapped his hands together three times and said, "Ladies…"

From around the corner, where I knew the stairs to be, came a young redhead in a pink dress. The hooting and hollering grew deafening. Behind her was a blonde in a black lace evening gown, followed by a dark skinned brunette who might have been American Indian.

The girls filed out around the corner and were instantly surrounded by the horn dog paper pushers. There were six of them in all and the last was a petite brunette with sparkling blue eyes. She was wearing a green low cut dress and her hair was long and straight. The makeup on her face was thick, bright pinks and blues, crimson red on her lips. She didn't look much like the picture Eleanor had given me but there was no mistaking who it was.

"I want the brunette in green," one of the accountants beside me said.

"That one's mine," I shot back, a little more mean than I had meant it to be.

He gave me a nervous shrug of his shoulders. "OK, then I'll take the blonde with the black eye."

I turned back toward the doorway. A seventh girl had come down. This one was a skinny little kid with fluffy blonde hair. Her makeup was on as thick as Patty's but it couldn't hide the bruised eye and swelling in the side of her face.

Claire's eyes met mine for a moment but she looked away, down at her own feet, not wanting to meet my gaze. There was a lost sad look about her, the kind people get when life kicks them hard in the gut. She was too young for a look like that.

The festivities were in full swing. The booze was going down quick and it seemed everyone was partaking, everyone but me that is. I was nursing a beer and waiting for a chance to make my move.

Vincent had settled down at a table and was dealing cards to three of the CPAs. Patty was cornered at the far side of the room by four others. They were all talking at her at once and she looked confused and scared. Claire was over by the bar with a drink in her hand and one of the guys whispering in her ear. She was trying to force a smile but it didn't look very convincing.

I stepped into the pack of wolves that were surrounding Patty. She didn't look any happier to see me. Why would she?

"Sorry boys but as host of this shin dig I'm going to have to call first dibs on this one," I said to them. My announcement was greeted with a series of groans and boos.

"What do you say we go upstairs?" I asked Patty. She didn't respond one way or the other. I took her by the arm and guided her through the crowd, around the corner and up the stairs. Her hand was limp in my touch and she followed along like some obedient puppy, never uttering a word.

At the top of the stairs I stopped and turned to her. She was looking at me like I was lower than garbage.

"My name is McKeller. Your mother hired me to find you."

Patty's eyes got wide and she gave me a look like I was speaking some forgotten language. "Momma?"

"Look, we don't have much time. I have to get you out of here." I started to pull her down the hallway but she stood her ground, still not sure what was happening.

"What are you talking about?"

"I'm a private detective and your mother hired me to find out where you were. She's worried about you and she wants you to come home."

"Momma is here?"

"Yes, she's here in Myrtle Beach and she's worried sick. I'm going to take you to her now."

She still didn't budge. "I can't."

"Of course you can. Just come with me. Everything is going to be all right."

"You don't understand. I can't go. He'd never let me."

"You let me worry about Vincent."

"He'd never let me go. You don't know what he's like. You don't know what he's capable of."

"Look, I know you're a good kid who got herself in a bad position. These are bad people and you have to get away from them. Trust me. I'll get you out of here."

"I can't," she mumbled. "He'd kill me."

"We'll be gone before he knows what's what. I'll have you back with your mother in no time."

She paused and looked me over. I could smell the fear on her and I could see that she wanted to come with me but the hold Vincent had on her held her paralyzed.

"Patty, there's no time for this now. If you stay here these people are going to eat you up and spit you out. They're going to use you until there's nothing left to use and then they're going to toss you aside. If you're lucky you'll end up alone and destitute. If you're not so lucky you'll end up dead and buried in some hole in the woods.

"This is no life. You have a mother who loves you. She's gone to a lot of trouble and expense to find you. You've got a real life out there waiting for you, a whole future ahead of you. All you have to do is come with me now."

Tears misted over in her eyes. Her chin trembled slightly as if she were attempting to speak but couldn't. Instead, she gave me one quick nod.

I took her arm and yanked her down the hallway, to the window on the front side of the building. I opened it up and climbed out on the balcony, the top of the double front porches. Patty was right behind me.

We slipped down the staircase and over the side balcony, me first, catching Patty as she made her way over. We crept around the building and into the parking lot and I let her into the passenger seat, shutting the door as quietly as I could. I moved around to the driver's side and got in. The key was in the ignition and all I had to do was turn it. Patty would have been back in her mother's arms in ten minutes.

I looked over at the girl beside me. She was small and frail and she had that deer in the headlights look about her. The problem was when I looked at her all I could see was another young girl, a little blonde who could have been anybody's kid sister.

"I have to go back," I told her.

"What?" Her eyes went wide, full of terror.

"Five minutes."

"No, we have to get out of here."

"There's one more thing I have to do. I'll be back in five minutes."

"You can't leave me here."

"It's going to be OK. Get down on the floor and stay there. Don't move and I'll be right back."

I started to slip back out of the car but she grabbed hold of my arm and held me there for a second. "Promise me you're not going to leave me."

"I promise."

In order to avoid any suspicion I went back in the same way

I came out, up the stairs and in the window. Nobody paid me much attention as I rejoined the party.

The boys were pounding them pretty hard and the room had turned into a drunk-fest. Some of them grabbed at my arm and thanked me for the great party as I made my way through the room, looking for Claire. Vincent caught sight of me and lifted his glass at me, toasting me with a grin. I smiled back as best I could.

Claire was nowhere to be found but I figured there weren't too many other places she could be. I went back upstairs.

Listening at the first door, I surmised it was being used for exactly what those rooms were meant to be used for. I flung open the door and found myself staring at a drunken accountant, half naked, with a topless redhead straddling his chest, pouring moonshine down his throat.

"Sorry," I said, shutting the door and moving on to the next one.

In this one I found two people going at it in the more traditional method, no less disturbing to witness. I apologized again and moved on to the third.

The ninety eight pound weakling I had driven up with was sitting on the edge of the bed in his boxer shorts. Claire was standing in front of him, the front of her dress completely undone and she was just pulling it off her shoulders.

"Get dressed," I told her.

"What?" the guy gasped in shock.

"Not you, you're fine."

A smile burst onto her face, one that I'll never forget as long as I live. It was the first time in my life I felt like the knight in shining armor.

She pulled her dress together and buttoned enough buttons to keep it together before I took her by the hand and pulled her toward the door.

"What do you think you're doing?" the guy snarled at me.

"Trust me, you don't want this one. You'll catch stuff from this one the doctors don't even have names for yet."

We were out in the hallway and moving to the front window. As I eased it open, Claire gave me a slap on the arm.

"What's the idea saying that stuff about me? I ain't got nothing like that."

"Sorry, I had to come up with something. I didn't want him to come chasing after us or making a fuss. That ought to make him think for a minute or two."

As we were about to go through the window there was the slam of a car door and we both froze for a moment. We heard the car take off and it pulled into sight, out in front of the Villa Roma, making a left on Kings Highway and heading off north.

When it was far enough away, I slipped through the open window and helped Claire out behind me. I had her by the forearm and was guiding her across the upper balcony and down the stairs, moving as swiftly and quietly as we could.

"What are you doing here?" I whispered to her as we moved.

"I wanted to go to the pool. He had one of his men at the hotel."

I resisted the urge to throw her an "I told you so."

It was dark, with almost no light peeking out of the restaurant's blacked out windows. As we came to the front porch, I didn't notice anything out of the ordinary. Maybe I didn't take the time to check.

Timothy Vincent's voice sounded like ice, a lethal blend of Southern charm and pure evil, even and steady as any I'd ever heard. "Are you planning on taking all my girls, McKeller?"

Claire and I stopped dead in our tracks. I could make out his outline leaning back on the front railing, cleaning his finger nails with a long thin knife. Off behind him was the large silhouette of Harley and I could almost see the gun in his hand. For a moment I thought about going for mine but I figured he'd get three slugs in me before I could get it out of my holster.

"I knew there was something fishy about you from the start. I just couldn't put my finger on it."

I didn't respond as I wasn't sure what to say and I could feel Claire pressing herself up against my back.

"Patty told me the score. Her Momma sent you to fetch her, is that about it?"

"Something like that."

"Well, I'll tell you what. Patty don't want to go anywhere. She's happy right where she is."

"Where would that be?"

"She's not waiting in your car, I can tell you that."

"What did you do with her?"

"She wasn't feeling so well. I had one of my boys take her

home. She'll be fine."

"Kidnapping is a serious crime, a lot more serious than prostitution and moonshine running."

Vincent laughed. "There ain't nobody been kidnapped down here. She just reconsidered is all."

"Vincent, this can stop right here before things get too ugly, before you dig yourself too big a hole."

"You know, there was another fellow that came looking for her awhile back, a private eye out of Greenville. Of course, he didn't play silly games about it like you did. It didn't take him near as long to track me down either. He came right out and told me what he was here for."

"What happened to him?"

"Him and me, we sat down and had us a long talk. I got him about as drunk as I ever seen a man. I introduced him to some of my girls and we even smoked us some of that wacky tobacco. We had us a fine time.

"In the end, he went on home and told Momma Highsmith he couldn't find hide nor hair of her little girl."

"I don't work like that. What do you want for her?"

Vincent laughed again. "The thing is, McKeller, you ain't got nothing I want. I'll tell you what, you can keep that one there as a consolation prize. She ain't good for but one thing anyway. Isn't that right, Claire? Hell, I make more on booze in a week than I make on any of these girls in six months."

I felt Claire press in tighter against my back. Neither of us said anything.

"When I found her she was working the Pavilion, begging for change. I imagine that's where she'll end up again when you're through with her. Before long she'll be crawling back to me. Until then, you kids have fun.

"As far as those boys in there," he said, motioning with his head to the party inside. "We're going to let them finish up with their good time. That cut you were going to get, we'll call that an inconvenience tax. That ought to set us about even."

"I'm not going to quit coming after Patty."

"Well, that would be a mistake on your part. You're out of your element down here. You mess with the gators and there's a good chance you're going to end up getting something bit off. You go back to Momma Highsmith and you tell her Patty is very happy right where she's at. You tell her to go on back home and I'll see that her daughter starts writing her regular again like she used to."

"I can't do that."

"You're new down here. You don't know these parts like I do. There's lots of wide open land around here, places where a body can get buried where nobody will ever dig it up. There's the ocean too. Lots of folks end up out there, never to be heard from again."

"I'm not afraid of your threats, Vincent."

"Who says I was talking about you, McKeller? Maybe it ain't you that ends up missing. Maybe it's a little blonde-haired whore, maybe it's a nosey old lady. Maybe it's even some pretty little brunette with big blue eyes. I'm just saying people got a tendency to disappear around here in places they don't ever get found."

"It doesn't have to be like this. I'm not looking for trouble. I just want to get Patty back to her mother," I tried.

"That's very sweet, Mckeller, but trouble is exactly what you found. I'm feeling good-natured tonight because you brought me some business and things have been pretty slow as late.

"I'll tell you how this is going to go down. You're going to take that little whore and go back to that big fancy hotel of yours. You tell that old lady to go back home and mind her business. If I find you poking your nose in my affairs again you and me are going to have trouble like you ain't never imagined.

"Now, I'm going to go back inside and me and your friends are going to finish up our party. I got a feeling those boys ain't done spending their money just yet. I'll send them on back when we're done here."

It was like sparring with Satan and being on the losing end. He had me and there was nothing I could do.

Vincent stood up and put the knife he was picking his fingernails with away. He casually walked over to the front door. Harley went in first and Vincent hesitated for a moment, looking back in our direction.

"Oh, and Claire, when I want you back I'll come and get you like I always do. You be looking out for me, OK?" With that, he walked back inside.

Chapter Thirty

THE problem with juggling live hand grenades is that sooner or later they have a tendency to explode. It's kind of like juggling eggs except they can take your hands off. This one had gone off and there was flesh and fingers everywhere.

Everything had come apart at the seams. Not only had I been minutes from getting Patty out of harm's way, I had plunged her back in deeper than she was before. Now Patty's life was in serious danger, as well as Claire's, Eleanor's and my own. Vincent was a psychotic maniac and I had pushed enough buttons to send him off the deep end. None of us were safe.

I had shown my hand and called his bluff, all the time holding a pair of deuces. Vincent called with a full house and I was left holding the bag.

The drive back from the Villa Roma was a quiet one. Claire didn't have much to say. I got the feeling I was no longer her knight in shining armor.

There was no way I could take her back to the Ocean Forest. It would be the first place Vincent came looking for her, if he decided to. I needed somewhere she would be safe for a few days. Atlantic Beach seemed like a good idea.

Tabby gave me a weird look when I came walking into Mack's with the young painted-up girl at my side. Claire seemed just as confused.

"What are we doing here?" she asked me as we took seats at the bar.

"Soaking in some local color," I replied.

"I don't know about this place."

Tabby was on us before we could even order drinks from Russell.

"Date night?" she asked me.

"I need a favor."

"You do like the young ones, don't you?"

I introduced the two and both were more than a little stand-offish with each other. With Tabby I guessed it had something to with our brief and recent history and with the fact she'd never had to share my attentions before. With Claire I got the idea it was something else.

"What kind of favor?" Tabby asked, almost totally ignoring Claire.

"We're in kind of a bind. I need a place to stash Claire for a day or two."

"I don't need to be stashed anywhere," Claire interjected.

"She says she doesn't need to be stashed anywhere," Tabby reiterated.

"I can take care of myself."

"She says she can take care of herself."

"Is there an echo in here?" I asked.

"I'm just saying, your little friend doesn't want any help."

"Can I talk to you in private?" I asked Russell to bring Claire a Coke and I took Tabby off to the far side of the room. "What are you doing?"

"What are you doing bringing a girl like that in here?"

"A girl like what?"

"Please, McKeller, I didn't just fall off the turnip truck. You just need to look at her to see what she is."

"Wow, you're about the last person I expected that from."

"Why is that? Is it because I'm black or because I have a dead whore girlfriend?" she snapped at me sarcastically.

I paused about a beat before answering. "I was thinking more because you have a heart the size of Texas, and I've never seen you judge anyone on anything other than their soul."

I could tell that one stung a bit and she didn't respond, waiting for me dig in deeper. That was the last thing I wanted to do.

"Look, she's just a kid. She's made some bad decisions and she got herself in a bad way. She's mixed up with a rough crowd and she's looking to get away but it's not that easy. I tried to help her out but I screwed up. I might have put both of us, along with a few others, in danger."

"What people are we talking about?"

"Timothy Vincent."

"McKeller, I told you stay away from him, he's bad news."

"You know me. I never let a little thing like common sense get in my way."

Tabby gave me that look, the one I've been trying to describe this whole time but haven't come close. It was the look that turned me into a twelve-year-old school boy and made me want to pull her pigtails, or anything else I could to get her attention.

"What do you need me to do?" she finally asked.

"I just need a place she can lay low for a while until I figure this thing out."

"She can stay with me if you need."

"That would be great. Give me a minute to smooth it over with her."

When I got back to the bar, Claire was nursing a shot of moonshine.

"What are you doing bringing me to a place like this?" she asked as I sat down.

"What happened to the Coca Cola?" I responded, taking the shot glass from in front of her and chugging it back.

"I don't drink Coke. It makes my face break out."

"Trust me, honey, this swill do a lot worse to you." I ordered another. "I've got it worked out. You're going to stay with Tabby awhile."

"I am not."

"I need you tucked away somewhere Vincent won't look to find you. You got any better ideas?"

"I don't care. I ain't staying with no jig-a-boo."

The crowd around the bar went quiet. It wasn't the kind of term that got a lot of play in a place like Mack's, but I guessed it was the kind of term Claire had heard all her life. There were a few ways I could roll with this one but I didn't have a lot of time to pussy foot around so I picked my poison and went with it. I grabbed her hard by the arm and gave her a quick, violent jerk, hoping to shake some sense into her and pulling her in close to me.

She sat looking up at me in shock.

"Let me explain something to you. You're about neck deep in shit right now and you don't have a lot of options. That girl is my friend and I trust her completely. Look around, how many people can you say that about?

"If I were you I'd spend a little less time worrying about what color a person's skin is and a little more time figuring out how to pick out the good ones, something you don't seem too good at."

She still hadn't said a word and she was looking at me with those hurt puppy eyes. Tabby stepped in between us and gave me a glare.

"What do you think you're doing, putting your hands on a woman like that?" Tabby asked with fire in her voice and eyes.

"I just—" I started to explain but Tabby cut me off.

"I don't care why you did it. You don't lay your hands on no woman," she said, putting her arm around Claire and helping her off the stool. "You come with me, sweetie, we'll get you cleaned up and taken care of."

They walked off together across the room, Tabby with her arm around Claire's shoulders and the younger girl leaning in on her slightly. It was at that moment I knew Claire was going to be fine. She was in good hands.

From there I headed back to the Ocean Forest Hotel. There was one more person I'd hung out to dry and I needed to make sure she was taken care of as well.

Eleanor was still half asleep when she answered the door. Her gray hair was down long and haphazard and she was wearing a white cotton night gown.

"McKeller, what's wrong?"

"I need you to pack your stuff and get dressed."

"Why?"

"Something's happened. You could be in danger."

She opened the door and let me in.

"I don't understand."

"I screwed up royally, Ellen. I'm sorry. I saw Patty tonight. I talked to her. She was in my car."

"Where is she now?"

"She's with Vincent."

Eleanor let out a gasp. "What happened?"

The last thing in the world I wanted to do was lay it all out for Eleanor but I had sugar-coated it as long as I could. She needed to know what we were up against.

"You were right about Vincent. He isn't a nice man. He's into some really bad things and Patty has let herself get sucked into it too."

"What kinds of things?"

"Illegal things," I explained. "I found her tonight and I got a chance to talk to her. She agreed to come back with me and we were in my car…"

"And?"

"I made a mistake. I had to go back for something and I left her alone for a few minutes. Vincent took her."

"You left my baby alone with that monster on the loose?"

"I was only gone a few minutes."

"You had her safe and sound and you left her alone?"

"I know, I didn't think—"

"That's my little girl, Mr. McKeller. How could you just leave her like that?"

I didn't have an answer for her.

"Where is she now?"

"I don't know. Vincent has her."

"Well, what are you going to do about that?"

"I don't know that either."

"What exactly do you know, Mr. McKeller?"

"I know Vincent knows you're here. He knows what I'm after. He made threats. It's not safe for you here."

"I'm not afraid of Timothy Vincent. Let him come. I'll give him a piece of my mind."

I had no doubt she would, if given the chance. She was a tough old cookie and in a fair fight over her daughter I'd lay even odds on her getting Patty back. Unfortunately, I knew Vincent wasn't the type to fight fair.

"If he can get to you he can use it against Patty. You have to go somewhere safe."

"What about my daughter?"

I was fidgeting with my hat in my hands, my palms all sweaty. There was a knot in my chest the size of a Porterhouse. I wished I had something for her.

"We need time to regroup and think this out. I'll figure something."

"And in the meantime, what about Patty?"

"She's safe for now," I offered, only about half-believing it myself.

"Maybe we could make a deal? I have a little money and I have the house. I could borrow some from the people I work for."

"Maybe, I don't know. I'm not sure what he wants."

"Mr. McKeller, this is totally unacceptable. I trusted you with this. What are you telling me, we're going to turn tail and run?"

"I don't know what to do. He made threats against you and me and some poor kid that doesn't have anything to do with all this. He made threats against Patty. I need time to think, to sort this all out in my head."

She gave me a long hard look, the kind that feels like it's burning straight through you. I couldn't look her back in the eyes.

"I'll get dressed and gather my things. I'll meet you in the lobby in a few minutes."

All I could muster was a feeble nod. I started to leave but she stopped me.

"Mr. McKeller," she said. "You can't give up on this. My daughter and I are counting on you. You're all we have. I know you'll find a way to make all this right."

It sounded so simple when she put it like that. Maybe I could go ahead and find the cure for the common cold while I was at it.

I drove Eleanor into town and checked her into a place called the Chesterfield Inn. It wasn't the Ocean Forest but it was a clean and comfortable family-run establishment. It had been a staple in Myrtle Beach for about as long as the Big Digs, where

I worked. There was no guarantee that Vincent couldn't find her there but I figured it might buy me a little time before he did.

Things were all jumbled in my head and I needed some quiet time to figure things out. I ended up back at the Ocean Forest.

The lobby was dead, void of all people but the sleeping night clerk hunched over the front desk. There was none of the hustle and bustle of people checking in and out, groups congregating in the heart and soul of the hotel. Now it was still and quiet as death and I couldn't stand the loudness of it.

I pushed my way out the back door and trotted down the steps, limping my way out the back and across the lawn. I needed something in my ears to drown out the voices screaming in my head. I knew of one girl who was always good for that.

Tonight she was choppy and angry, foamy tips and rolls appearing and disappearing across her surface. Waves crashed across the shore haphazardly, with no set rhythm, and the wind was spitting grit and wet in my face. She looked about like I felt.

There was nothing soothing or calming about her and she reminded me of a spoiled child in the midst of a full blown hissy-fit. I stood and stared out at her just the same, unable to turn away.

Angry thoughts filled my brain and I stood cursing myself, trying to get a handle on just how bad I'd screwed things up. I was no better off than when I started, with either case. In fact, I was well below where I had begun. Things had turned against me and some good and innocent people were caught in the crossfire. My incompetence had landed me in a major pickle and I had no idea how to get out of it.

My first instinct was to admit defeat and walk away, turn it over to someone more qualified to handle it, someone who actually knew what he was doing. This seemed best for everyone concerned. I had done enough damage. Maybe it was time to call in the pros and let them clean up my mess.

I was pondering how to go about this when I caught a flash of something in the back of my brain. It was a memory I didn't allow myself to remember very often. On the rare occasions it poked up its ugly head I was usually able to push it back down with the help of booze and that brick wall I'd built in my brain to keep it locked away. There was no keeping it down this time.

It was a day a few years back on a beach not so different from this one. Visions of smoke and of explosions so loud they rattled my back teeth, the ping of bullets ricocheting off metal. The screams of my brothers echoed in my ears and I could smell the rot of burning skin and gunpowder. I could feel the mix of sweat, salt water and smoke burning in my eyes, my body vibrating every time one of those big guns were fired.

This was the memory I refused to let myself relive, but this time I was at its mercy, overcome by the force of it overtaking me, sending me back to that day. Men were shouting orders, too many of them, contradicting each other. Confusion ruled and I was trapped in a melee of sensations tugging at every nerve ending inside of me.

My eyes were fixed on the ramp in its upright position, a thick cold slab of steel at the front of the landing craft, olive drab, all that was between me and the hell breaking loose on the other side. I could barely breathe, my eyes fixed onto it, the water splashing over its top, running down the back side of it in streams.

I remembered when they dropped it and the horror of seeing the battle beyond it for the first time, men silhouetted against the dense smoke, some charging up the beach, others cowering in the sand, bodies floating face down in the water. This is where things get fuzzy. The confusion, bodies pressed against mine, seeing the back of the landing craft, somehow ending up facing the wrong way.

When the explosion went off I didn't hear a thing. Maybe that's normal, I don't know. Maybe I was deafened by it.

I remember the sensation of being tossed into the air like a rag doll and I remember the pain in my leg. I remember hitting the water and not being able to do anything about it. I remember sinking into the cold surf. I remember giving up and waiting to die.

My buddy came back for me. He grabbed me by the collar and lifted me out of the water. He dragged me to shore and tied up my wound. He saved my life that day. Ever since, I'd been wondering if he did me a favor.

The memories were coming back hard now, slapping me in

the face, pummeling at my gut. It wasn't the explosions or the bullets or the threat of dying that haunted me. The outside events I had no control over were what they were, they were the facts and what every one of us faced that day.

The things I was haunted by were deep inside of me, locked away in my own psyche. They were the ghosts of everything I'd had control over, the fear I felt when I looked at that ramp door in the upright position, the cowardice that ran through my body when it fell, the way I had given up and accepted my own demise without a fight, sinking away in the water. They were the flaws inside of me which came to the surface that day and made me come to terms with the fact I would never be the man I wanted to be. I just wasn't good enough.

Now it was happening again. There was no smoke or gunfire or 50mm canons going off in the background, but everything else was there. It was that same fear I'd had then. I'd it felt again when Timothy Vincent had spoken to me. I'd felt it in his threats of what he would do to me and Claire, Eleanor and Patty.

The cowardice was back too. I was over-matched and I knew in my heart I had nothing. I didn't have the cajones to stand up to Vincent and his men. I'd played it wrong from the start, in every way possible.

Worst of all was the feeling of complete surrender which was suffocating me. I was throwing in the towel again. I had taken this thing as far as my abilities could go and I'd ended up on the losing end. I was sinking back into her bosom and I didn't have the fight in me to stroke my arms or kick my feet.

The waves were a fitting soundtrack to my darkest memory and I stood watching them jut in and out, begging me to step into her and make it final. She was calling for me. I understood then what she had been trying to tell me all this time. Fate had allowed me to escape her grasp that day but she wasn't content with that. As far as she was concerned I belonged to her. I was a part of her now and she wasn't going to let up until she had me back in her clutches.

Faces began to drift in and out of my thoughts, men I had served with, Mona lying lifeless on a metal table, Tabby crying. I thought of Eleanor's words to me, telling me I was all she had, and of the smile on Claire's face when I barged into that bedroom. I thought about the cool cadence and nonchalance of Timothy Vincent's words as he told me how he was going to make me disappear. Most of all I thought about a promise I had made to a pretty brunette with sparkling blue eyes.

Promise me you're not going to leave me.

I promise.

A glimmer of an idea began to form itself on the outer layers of my thoughts, a point which hadn't occurred to me before. I was beaten and licked and ready to be thrown out with the garbage but I had one thing going for me. You can't make a man disappear if he's already gone.

I'd been living on borrowed time for years now. I was a worthless gimp who had screwed up everything I'd touched and my life was laid out in front of me in a puddle of muck. I was a fake and a drunk and I couldn't even be with the girl I loved. There was where my strength lay.

Maybe I didn't have the courage or skill or the moxy to go up against Vincent but I had one thing he didn't have. I had nothing to lose.

I spit into the waves, mocking her. "Not this time," I told her.

She answered back with a series of sputtering waves colliding over each other, spitting back in my face for good measure.

"The same to you," I said as I turned and made my way back into the hotel.

Chapter Thirty-One

I'D gone back to my room and tried to get forty winks. I managed about twenty before I made myself get up. I didn't see early morning often, but there were things to be done.

When you have an epiphany there's a certain peacefulness that comes over you. It's a sense that everything happens for a purpose. My purpose was clear now. Unfortunately the brass tacks were just as fuzzy as ever.

I kept replaying everything Vincent had said to me in my mind, hoping I could come up with something I could use but I was getting nowhere. Vincent was right when he said I had nothing he wanted, I had nothing to use against him.

Down at the front desk I found Buntemeyer in a state of near panic.

"What's wrong boss?"

"Did you know Eleanor Highsmith checked out last night?"

"Yes, I did. She had something she needed to take care of."

"She just up and left?"

"Is that a problem?"

"There's the little matter of her unpaid bill."

"I thought we were picking that up."

"Well, the stay of course, but there's also the charges she made to room service and to the restaurant."

182

"How much can it be?"

"That's not the point. This is a business. I am a business man and I'm here to make money. I offer goods and services in return for cash, that's how our free trade society works."

"I get that."

"If I don't get compensation for my wares, I might as well not have them. I might as well just open up the doors and tell everyone to just come on in and take what they want."

"It's one little old lady."

"That's where it starts. Where does it end?"

"OK, I get it."

"I don't think you do. You see I have suppliers and I buy their goods and turn around and sell them to my customers. I then take that money and use it to pay my suppliers, what's left is called profit. That is why we're in business. If I don't get the money from my customers, I can't pay my suppliers, I can't make any profit."

Something went off in my head. "Holy cow, you're right."

Buntemeyer looked around, a little confused. "I am?"

"You're a genius."

He gave me a suspicious leer. "Are you making a joke?"

I took his face on both hands and leaned in, giving him a big kiss on the cheek. "That's it, you're a regular Einstein."

"Have you been drinking?"

"I've got to go. I have some very pressing matters to see to. I'll tell you what, put whatever she owes on my tab, and take it out of my check." With that I was gone, half running out the door and leaving Buntemeyer wondering if I had lost my mind.

I jumped behind the wheel of the Ocean Forest Studebaker and took off for Atlantic Beach. It was still early when I began rapping on Tabby's door. It took her a few minutes to answer. When she did she was wearing a flannel night gown about three sizes too large and her hair was tussled about, her eyes red and sleepy. It made me sad to know I wouldn't be the one to see her wake up like this every day.

"McKeller, what are you doing here? What time is it?"

"Is Claire all right?"

"She's fine, she's sleeping."

"Good, I need to ask you about something. Vincent is the main guy in town for moonshine, right?"

"Yeah, I guess he supplies just about every bar that tries selling the stuff, before the sheriff and his men clamp down on it."

"But he has an in with the sheriff so things usually go pretty smooth."

"The sheriff don't mess with anybody about it unless they give him reason."

"How does he bring it in?"

"He's got him a driver, brings it in on a big flatbed truck."

"I'm trying to picture how this works. Vincent doesn't make the stuff, I know that, he's more of a middle man."

"Yeah, I guess so."

"So this driver I would think goes around to the people who make it and he loads up for his deliveries, then he takes it around and drops it off."

"I would think."

"You guys get yours from Vincent?"

"Most everybody does."

"Have you ever been there when they bring it in?"

"Sure, brings it right up to the back door."

"I would imagine it's loaded down pretty good, huh?"

"They come down from up north of here so we're one of the first stops before he goes into town and further south. It's usually loaded up about as much as it can be."

"You don't know when you're getting another delivery, do you?"

She crinkled her nose and frowned a little, trying to think. "Today is Friday, we ought to be getting one today, I would think."

"Today, right out in broad daylight?"

"It usually comes late morning. We open up for lunch on Fridays and they drop off before the place opens up."

I couldn't help myself. I leaned over and gave her a quick kiss on the forehead. If nothing else, I figured it would get the taste of Buntemeyer off my lips.

"What's this all about?" she asked.

"It's called Capitalism. It's what makes our country run."

"You're not making any sense."

"Last night, Eleanor was ready to sell everything she had to try and pay off Vincent. Before that, Vincent flat out told me I had nothing he wanted. It was staring me in the face the whole time. Vincent is a business man, pure and simple."

"I don't know what you're talking about and I haven't the foggiest notion who Eleanor is."

"It's OK. You've been a big help."

"You're not going to do anything crazy are you?"

"Don't be silly, you know me better than that. I'm just going to go out and get something Vincent wants."

"You better not go and get yourself killed." She sighed.

"Don't you worry about that, you just look after that girl in there."

"She'll be fine. It's you I'm worried about."

"I can take care of myself. If I don't see you later today I'll see you at the funeral tomorrow."

She looked up at me for what seemed like minutes. There was a mix of concern and sadness in her eyes and I suspected part of her wanted to talk me out of whatever I had planned.

Instead, she let out a soft breath and said, "Crazy white boy."

I always loved it when she called me that.

Chapter Thirty-Two

As far as plans and tactics go, mine wasn't exactly Operation Market Garden but I hoped it would be more successful. I was pretty much winging it, and if I hadn't come to the conclusions about my own life the night before I never would have been crazy enough to try it.

I sat in the front seat of the Studebaker, at the far end of the alley behind Mack's for most of the morning. Big time city cops have a word for that. They call it a stake-out and it's boring as hell. There was a point where I was wondering if the truck would even show, if maybe Tabby in her half-awake state had gotten the day wrong. She didn't.

Just about the time I was ready to make a food run, a big flatbed Ford came around the corner. It was packed tight with crates and it had old gray canvass tied across the cargo. The truck wound down to a slow crawl and came to a stop outside of Mack's back door.

I got out of my car and began walking toward it.

The driver was on the youngish side, tall and lean, wearing a baseball cap and denim pants. He had a wad of chewing tobacco in his jaw and he was untying some of the ropes holding down the canvas cover as I approached.

"Are you making a delivery?" I asked.

186

The kid spit a stream of brown juice on the ground and gave me a funny look. "Was it the truck that tipped you off or was it all those crates in the back?"

He got a nice chuckle out of his little joke. I even joined in. It was pretty funny.

"What are you delivering?"

He gave me that look again. "Rhinoceroses."

He got a kick out of that one too.

"I love Rhino's."

"Yeah, who doesn't? They're so cute and cuddly and all. If you'll excuse me I got to get back to work."

"I think you're done for the day," I told him.

"Are you some kind of cop?"

"No but I get that a lot." I pulled the .45 Automatic from the holster on my back and gave him a good look at the business end of the barrel. I think he swallowed his chewing tobacco.

"What do you want?"

"Tie that canvass back down." He did as he was told. "I'm going to take your truck and all that booze you've got there."

"Why you going to do that?"

"In case I get thirsty on the way home. I want you to give your boss a message for me."

The kid nodded, his eyes wide and scared.

"You tell him Frank McKeller took his truck and all the product on it."

He nodded again.

"Repeat that name," I ordered.

"Frank McKeller," he said.

"Very good. You tell Vincent to call me at the Ocean Forest if he wants it back. I'll be back there later today, maybe this evening."

"Yes sir."

"You tell him I'll be waiting on his call."

"Yes sir."

"What's that name again?"

"Frank McKeller."

"That's very, very good. You're not half as stupid as you look."

"Yes sir."

Chapter Thirty-Three

I⊤ felt a little strange driving a truckload of hooch down the road. The thing was packed up tight, loaded down to the hilt. I couldn't imagine what it was worth but I was hoping it was worth more to Vincent than hanging onto Patty Highsmith.

Alongside of the Ocean Forest sits a large outdoor amphitheater. Throughout the year it can feature anything from big bands, to touring Broadway plays, to magic shows. On the ocean side are the seats and dance floor, facing in to the main stage, a long wooden platform, partially enclosed. The stage itself is covered and built into the back of a barn-like building. This is where the stage props and musical equipment is housed and there are two large doors where the loading and unloading is done. It's big enough to drive a truck through, which is exactly what I did.

I pulled the entire flatbed into the structure and locked it away down below the empty stage. Then I went into the hotel and had the desk clerk call me a cab. Buntemeyer just happened to be standing there.

"Where's the Studebaker?" he asked.

"I'm heading up to get it now. I left it parked in Atlantic Beach."

"What were you doing in Atlantic Beach and why would you leave my car there?"

I thought about it for a second. "I high-jacked a truckload of bootleg liquor and moonshine at gunpoint so I could trade it back to the moonshine runner for a girl before she's thrown into a life of prostitution. I couldn't drive both vehicles at the same time."

Buntemeyer stood gawking at me. "You have been drinking, haven't you?"

"Not yet, but if you're thirsty I've got a whole truck full."

My boss began backing away, looking at me like I just stepped out of the cuckoo house. "OK, well, very funny, McKeller. I want that car back on property before nightfall."

The cabbie dropped me off in front of Mack's Dive and I decided to poke my head in for a quick one. I was in the driver's seat for now and I figured I'd let Vincent sweat it out awhile. It was still early afternoon and the lunch crowd was just dying off.

Tabby pulled me aside as soon as I set foot in the place, taking me off to a private corner. "We never got our liquor delivery today," she said in an anxious tone.

"That's a shame."

"Rumor is the truck was robbed at gunpoint by some white fellow. They say he took off with the whole load."

"Too bad it's all illegal booze or they could call the police."

"What are you up to, McKeller?"

"I've got to fix something."

"What's that girl going to do if you go and get your head shot off?"

"Hey, have a little faith."

"Frankie, you don't know what you're messing with here."

I gave a little chuckle. "You must be serious, you called me Frankie."

"This isn't a joke. You don't screw with a guy like Vincent."

"No, it's not a joke. Believe me, if there was any other way I'd be on it. I screwed up bad and I have to make things right. I made a promise to a girl out there and I intend on keeping it."

She reached over and took my hand in hers, giving it a little squeeze. Considering where we were, it was a pretty gutsy display of public affection.

"Be careful."

I squeezed back. "Don't worry, I will. If something does happen to me, I want you to go to the hotel and give them your name. I left a note saying you were to get whatever money and things I have. Use some of it to help Claire get out of town and start a new life. Do whatever you want with the rest of it. Buy yourself a new dress or something."

"Don't talk like that."

"Things are going to be all right but, just in case."

"Do you want to say goodbye to her?"

"Is she here?"

Tabby smiled. "I put her to work."

She guided me back through the bar and to a small kitchen in the back. It was a rusty, wet and peeling room with not much more than a small stove and sink. Claire was hunched over the sink scrubbing away at a plate. She was wearing baggy overalls and a tee shirt you could have put three of her in. Her hair was pulled up and there were miscellaneous strands hanging in her face.

"You missed a spot," I said when I saw her.

"Very funny. You see what they're making me do?"

"Ain't no free rides here," Tabby explained.

"A little hard work never hurt anybody. You'll be fine."

"I didn't sign on for this," Claire protested.

"You listen to her," I told Claire, referring to Tabby. "She'll take care of you. I have something I need to take care of. If anything happens, Tabby will know what to do."

Claire looked concerned. "What are you going to do?"

"I'm going to get Patty back."

Neither girl said anything. I turned back to Tabby. "I'll see you tomorrow at the funeral. Nothing's going to happen before then."

Chapter Thirty-Four

I WANTED to let Vincent stew in his own juices for a while so I figured I'd make myself scarce for the rest of the afternoon. It seemed like a good idea to let him know the power balance had shifted and I wasn't going to play the game by his rules. He knew what I wanted and I knew what he wanted. I was confident no harm would come to Patty until he spoke with me.

Mathew Baker was the only person I hadn't questioned about Mona and it sounded like a good diversion and a way to keep my nerves under control. I didn't have a lot of faith in getting anything from him but I was hoping there was an outside chance he could link Mona with Raddison Hayes. Those flowers on her dresser were still gnawing at me and in my pea brain I kept thinking if I could connect Hayes with the flowers it might be a starting point. It wasn't much but when you don't have anything a grain of salt can start to look like Mt Rushmore.

The drive to Conway was a grueling one. I found out first hand why so many people take the train. It took the better part of two hours and the business day was winding down by the time I got there.

Baker worked at the courthouse building which sat on the edge of a small park, directly across from the downtown district. It was a big old brick structure that looked like it had been picked out of a catalog of courthouses.

He worked as a prosecutor for the District Attorney,.and his office was on the third floor. His secretary took my information and went in to tell him I was there.

"You can go right in," she said as she came back into the outer office and I went on through where she had come from.

Mathew Baker was short in stature but well-built and athletic looking, in his early thirties. He had perfectly combed brown hair and boyish good looks which didn't look like they had faded much over the last decade or so. His jacket was off and he was wearing suspenders and a hand painted tie, leaning back in his desk chair and slicing an apple with a pocket knife. When he spoke, his voice was pure Southern charm, the kind juries in these parts would melt over.

"How do you do, Mr. McKeller?"

"I'm fine, thank you. I was wondering if I might have a few minutes of your time."

"Of course, whatever you need."

"I'm investigating the death of Mona Cooper."

"Yes, I know. My wife said you stopped by the house."

"Is there anything you can tell me about Mona right before she died? Was she acting funny, did she seem like anything was bothering her?"

"Not that I noticed," he said, popping a slice of apple into his mouth. "But then, I didn't spend a great deal of time with her. I saw her mostly on the weekends and in the mornings at breakfast. I work late quite a lot and she would sometimes cook me up some dinner when I got home."

"Were you two friends?"

He thought about it a second. "I don't know that friend is the right word. She did a good job, kept up the house, was good with the kids. She seemed nice enough, maybe a little quiet. Her and Rita got along well."

"You two didn't speak much?"

"Not about much more than the normal household goings on. I always found her to be very shy and introverted."

"Really? You're the first person to describe her like that."

"Like I said, I didn't spend a lot of time with her. That's the way she always came off to me."

"I get the impression Mona and your wife got to be very close."

"I don't know how close you can get with a live-in Negro maid but they spent a lot of time together and Rita counted on her a great deal. When our last child was born there were … complications. She's not able to do things for herself like she used to. Mona was a big help. We're actually in the process of trying to find someone else."

"I'm sorry to hear that," I offered.

"It's OK. Rita deals with it as best she can. As long as she doesn't over exert herself, stays on her medications and gets her rest she does fine."

"Your wife said that other than trips to see her father Mona didn't really go out."

"No, I don't suppose she did."

"Did she ever express a desire to move on, to travel?"

"No. As a matter of fact, a few weeks ago we had a discussion about her staying on for an extended period. She was very happy with our family and she flat out told me she'd be willing to stay and work for us as long as we'd have her. I, of course, assured her that she could stay on as long she wished."

"Do you know if she'd been seeing anyone recently?"

"It seems like I recall her mentioning a beau sometime back. I believe it was one of those boys up at Atlantic Beach. I got the impression she was very fond of him."

"Did she mention a name?"

"She may have but I don't recall. It was just something she said in passing one time. I'm afraid I'm a bit sketchy on the details."

"There was a vase of flowers on her dresser. They looked like they'd been there awhile. Do you remember when she got them?"

He thought hard about this one. "Yes, I believe I remember that. I saw her watering them at the kitchen sink one day, beaming like a schoolgirl with her first crush."

"Did she say who they were from?"

"No, I don't believe she did. I gathered it was from that beau in Atlantic Beach."

"Do you know if they were delivered to the house or if someone dropped them off, maybe she came home with them?"

"No sir, I wouldn't have any idea about that. I just saw her watering them one day."

"Did she ever mention a man by the name of Raddison Hayes?"

Mathew Baker bit into another slice of apple and shook his head. "The name doesn't sound familiar but I could be mistaken."

I sat back, thinking for a bit. There was something I couldn't get my head around and I needed to go back. "When would she have mentioned the boyfriend?"

"Excuse me?"

"You said that she mentioned a beau some time back. When exactly do you think she told you, like what time of day? I only ask because your wife said she hadn't mentioned one. Considering how much time she spent with her and how little you did, it seems a little odd."

Baker shrugged, tilting his head off in thought and tucking a thumb under his suspender strap. "I don't exactly know. I never paid much attention to such things. Maybe it was at night one time, when she cooked me a late supper. Rita takes her medications before she goes to bed and they put her out pretty good. If it was at night she told me, Rita wouldn't have been around."

"It just seems funny that she never told Rita."

"Maybe Mona and Rita weren't as close as my wife thought."

"Yeah, maybe."

I decided to bring the conversation back around to Raddison Hayes again, hoping I could spark something that might provide a link to my main suspect.

"Did Mona ever talk to you about her life before she came to work for you, what she did, who she worked for?"

"Not really, she provided references when we hired her but, truth be told, I never got around to checking them out. She seemed nice enough when we interviewed her and Rita took a liking to her…"

I tried again, from a few different angles, to bring up things that might bring Hayes back in the fold. Nothing worked. No matter how I went about it I couldn't find anything to link Hayes with Mona, not from Mathew Baker anyway. I asked him if he would be attending Mona's funeral in the morning. He assured me he and his wife would be there to pay their respects.

"Did Mona ever mention a man named Jarvis Brown?" I asked, desperate for anything.

"Mona? Why on earth would Mona mention Brown?"

"You know him?"

"Mr. McKeller, as an officer of the court, I believe it would be highly inappropriate and unprofessional for me to discuss the suspect in an upcoming trial. I'm sure you can understand."

"But Mona's relationship with Brown wouldn't have anything to do with his upcoming case," I pointed out.

"Mona's relationship? Why would you think she had some sort of a relationship with Brown?"

He had a point. "I don't know, actually. I'm trying to establish if she did."

"The idea of Mona having anything to do with the likes of Brown is preposterous. I can assure you that Mona had no such relationship with Jarvis Brown."

"It's just that—"

He cut me off. "Again, Mr. McKeller, my position prohibits me from discussing Jarvis Brown any further, I've probably already said too much."

We finished up our little talk and said our goodbyes, shaking hands, him promising to get in touch if he remembered anything else, me thanking him for his time. Baker had proved to be another dead end.

I walked out the front door of the courthouse building and out into the park it sat behind. It was a lush green field with regal looking oaks and elms scattered about, providing shade for the occasional bench. I parked myself on one of the benches to think.

The thing that struck me most was the picture Mathew Baker painted of Mona Cooper, unlike anything anyone else had told me. Every person I had talked to described her as a fun loving, out-going, free spirit. Baker said she was shy and introverted. She hadn't mentioned a boyfriend to anybody I had talked to, not Rita, not her father, not even the doctor who told her she was pregnant. Why would she choose to tell her boss, a man she wasn't particularly close to?

I sat back on the bench and looked around, mulling it over in my head. It was a pleasant enough day, a little cool but nothing unbearable. The park sat across from a little strip of businesses, the kind that catered to the courthouse crowd. The main business district in Conway was around the corner and up a few blocks but there seemed to be everything you needed within walking distance of the courthouse. There was a sandwich place on the corner, followed by a line of little shops, a drug store, a laundry, a florist and a bakery. I had just scanned down the fronts of them, half paying attention, when my eyes shot back up to the little green building in the middle. It was the florist shop and it was called Bartlett's.

My head whipped around, back to the courthouse, then back again to Bartlett's. It was directly across from where Mathew Baker worked.

Things were churning in my brain so hard I thought butter might start coming out my ears. My heart was pounding and a wave of panic swept through my body. Was it possible I'd just talked to Mona Cooper's murderer?

A scenario began running through my mind. It involved a viral young lawyer and his wife. After complications during child birth, things go bad and the wife develops problems, she becomes sickly. When the lawyer comes home from long days at the office his wife is passed out in bed on pain killers. A thing like that could put quite a damper on the romantic side of a marriage. If she were dealing with female problems brought on by a difficult child birth there would be a good chance she wouldn't be as willing and receptive to the lawyer's needs as she once was. A guy could get pretty frustrated with a situation like that, especially a successful, good-looking guy like Mathew Baker who's used to a lot of attention.

Enter a young pretty girl who signs on to help around the house. Maybe she's a girl who's always dreamed of something better, a girl with big plans of her own. Maybe a girl like that could get a little star-struck by a wealthy and worldly man like Baker.

It would be easy to see how it started. Baker was lonely and unhappy with his life. Mona was escaping a relationship with a man she couldn't be with, a man who dealt in a seedy world she wanted no part of. Baker would have seemed like the total opposite to a girl like that.

The whole thing would have started with Baker, the jokes, the teasing, the flirting, turning that Southern charm up full blast. Mona might have been flattered by the attention at first but she was good friends with Rita, she would have resisted. Mathew Baker had it all, everything Mona wanted. How long would it be before the gullible young kid fell for his line of crap? How many late night suppers with his wife passed out upstairs did it take before Mathew Baker was able to seduce the impressionable young girl living with him?

The lies he handed me began making sense. Mona was never shy or introverted and Baker knew it. He was trying to distance himself from his victim. That's where he screwed up. If she had been like that with him, why would she choose to tell him about the man in her life, something she had kept from everyone else around her?

There was no beau. It was an attempt to throw suspicion off himself and send me looking for a lost boyfriend in Atlantic Beach.

I had to find something more concrete and I had an idea where to look. It was a long shot but long shots and luck seemed to be my best weapons.

Bartlett's Florist Shop was a quaint little place that smelled like springtime. This time of year the inventory was down to a bare minimum but they had about enough selection to keep the doors open. There was a middle-aged man with spectacles and a receding hairline at the counter.

"We're just about to close up," he told me as I went in.

"I won't keep you. I just wanted to ask you a couple of questions."

"Sure thing, mister."

I reached into my pocket and pulled out the stack of photographs I'd taken from Mona's dresser. Thumbing through it, I pulled out the picture of the Baker family.

"Have you ever seen this man before?"

He barely glanced at it. "Sure, that's Mr. Baker. He's a lawyer here in town, works across the street."

My heart was racing but I tried not to show it. "Does he come in here?"

"He used to be one of my best regulars, dropping by and picking up flowers for the little lady all the time."

"What happened?"

"I don't know, just stopped is all. Long about seven or eight months ago he just quit coming in. I think they had them another baby and I guess the romance kind of faded some. That happens sometimes. I don't think I've seen him but once since then."

"He's been in here once in eight months?"

"Say, are you some kind of cop?"

"Yeah," I said, pulling out a twenty spot and laying it on the counter. "Here's my badge. You got any idea when it was he was in?"

The guy eyed up the twenty. I could tell he wanted it bad. "I don't remember exactly, a month or two ago I guess."

"Do you remember what he bought?"

"Mister, I sell a lot of flowers. I can't remember every one that passes through the door."

"Yeah, I guess not."

"I could find out though."

"How's that?"

"Mr. Baker has an account here from when he used to come in regular. I usually just bill his office at the end of the month."

He reached under the counter and pulled out a cardboard box packed full of index cards. It was a heck of a filing system but he knew it pretty well and had Baker's card out in seconds.

"Yeah, he came in here about seven weeks ago. He bought some carnations."

Chapter Thirty-Five

I was downright giddy driving back to Myrtle Beach. It seemed I had the whole thing figured out. In reality I had bunch of possibilities tied together in a pretty ribbon. My only real evidence was an index card at a flower shop and some wilted carnations in a vase on top of a dead girl's dresser. If Baker came pulling up at the funeral in a tan Plymouth I'd have another witness to connect Baker with Mona's death but I wasn't sure it would be enough.

I'd have liked to go digging for more but I was about out of time. If things didn't go my way in the Highsmith case I might be out of time for good, in the six feet under kind of way. It was time to get back on that horse.

When I walked into the lobby of the Ocean Forest the desk clerk was on me like white on rice. He had an annoyed look in his eye.

"I'm not your personal secretary, McKeller."

"I never said you were."

"You've been getting calls all day, one after another. You tell your friends this is a place of business. Personal phone calls are frowned on by management."

"Did they leave a name?"

"No, they said they'd call back and that's what they've been doing, every twenty minutes or so."

"By they, I take it you mean a guy."

"Yeah, he's a guy and not a very friendly one, I can tell you that. You might want to teach your pals some phone manners. The guy is flat out rude if you ask me."

"I'll be sure to mention it to him. This guy is going to call again. I'll be over there when he does."

I took one of the complimentary newspapers off the desk and headed over to the overstuffed chairs in the center of the lobby. I plopped myself down and opened up the paper, settling in for my wait. I had a feeling it wouldn't be a long one.

The clerk let out a huff and went back to his station. I could hear him mumbling about having better things to do and not having to answer to me.

Have you ever been reading something but the words weren't registering in your head like your mind was lost somewhere else? That was me. I was reading the words in the newspaper but none of them were fitting together, making any sense.

My mind was running scenarios, jumping back and forth between Patty Highsmith and Mona Cooper. One second I was picturing Mona collapsing in the sand, bleeding out through the throat, Mathew Baker standing over her. The next second it was Patty being brutalized by an evil bastard named Vincent.

I was still trying to decide if I was on the verge of saving Patty Highsmith and bringing in Mona's killer or if everything was about to crumble in my hands. Part of me was ecstatic about solving Mona's murder, which I was positive I had done. Another part wondered if I had enough to make it stick.

There was also the little matter of not knowing how I was going to go about making the swap for Patty. It was still very likely that both her and I would end up dead at Vincent's hands and he'd be back in business as usual. I was running possible plans through my mind when the call came.

"Hello?" I said into the receiver.

"You're a hard man to track down, McKeller," Vincent said.

"I had some errands to run."

"I hope one of those errands was getting your affairs in order."

"I take it you called for a reason."

"Have you lost your mind? Do you know what you're messing with here?"

"I've got a pretty good idea."

"I'd just as soon kill you as spit on you."

"Why don't we skip the lovey-dovey stuff and get down to business?"

"How about you give me back my property and I won't gut you like a pig?" He didn't say it as a joke.

"That doesn't really work for me."

"Give me one good reason not to kill you."

"I've got a whole truck load of reasons."

"You're a very stupid man."

"That may be but the way I see it you have something I want and now I have something you want. It's basic economics."

"What makes you think I'd make a deal with you?"

"You said it yourself, you make more money in a week on the booze than you make on the girls in six months. It's good business."

He paused for a moment. "Where do you want to do this?"

"The 2nd Avenue Pier, I'm guessing you can find it. It's right between 1st Avenue and 3rd Avenue. Meet me there tomorrow at one o'clock."

"Can't we take care of this tonight?"

"Sorry, my dance card is full for the moment. I've got something to do in the morning but one ought to be OK." Not only would it give me time to get from Mona's funeral but I needed the time to work out some details. I was still putting the plan together in my head.

"Why don't we meet somewhere a little more private, somewhere we can talk?"

"I'd say the fact you want to is reason enough."

"You're stirring up a hornets nest, McKeller."

"Oh, and by the way, if there's so much as a hair out of place on Patty Highsmith you can kiss your inventory goodbye, just in case you had any ideas about taking your anger out on her."

"You just have my property there," he snarled.

Next I put in a call to Deputy Dale. He was surprised to hear from me. I began the conversation by asking if he intended to attend Mona's funeral. When he began hemming and hawing I suggested he might want to. I told him something important might be going down.

Next I asked him about Mathew Baker, what he knew about the good counselor.

"I've known him for years, grew up with him. He's a good man from a good family."

"He comes from money?" I asked.

"No, not Matt. His family were hard-working locals. His father worked three jobs to send him through law school."

"And Rita's family?"

"Rita's family is a different story. She comes from one of the oldest, wealthier families in Myrtle Beach, conservative and old Southern money

"So Baker is rich now?"

"No, not at all. Rita's family isn't the kind to give anyone a free ride, not even a son-in-law. I imagine they're in line for a serious inheritance one day but, until then, I assume they live on Matt's salary."

I thought long for a few moments. "Do you happen to know what kind of car he drives?

Deputy Dale had to think about it as he didn't see Baker around town much these days but it eventually came to him. He knew exactly the kind of car Mathew Baker drove. He knew the color too.

Chapter Thirty-Six

My plan was to get to bed early and get a good night's sleep as I figured I needed to be sharp and alert the next day. It didn't work out like that.

I elected not to stay in my usual room and instead swapped the key to one I knew was empty. I lay tossing and turning for a while, trying to will myself to sleep but there was no doing.

Instead, I went down to the Brookgreen Room for a couple of swigs of the finest bourbon the Ocean Forest carried. What the hell? You only live once.

After, I went back up to my new room and tried again to grab some shut eye. I ended up lying awake and staring up at the ceiling fan for most of the night, fretting and worrying about what was going to happen in the morning.

By the time daylight began to break I was still awake and I stepped out onto the balcony with a cigarette just in time to watch the sun come up. I'm not the kind of guy who gets to watch a lot of sunrises.

It started out with the skyline turning a light shade of bluish green, contrasting the dark seam of the Atlantic, both stretching out forever. A purple cast began to overtake the air and the edge of the sun, now a deep burnt orange, began to peek out beyond the horizon like it was emerging from the water.

It rose up from her steady and slow, showering the area in a yellow tint and illuminating the clouds, sending golden shimmers of light reflecting off the surface of the water. The sky turned a thousand colors over the next few minutes as the sun climbed out from behind the cold-hearted bitch which continued to taunt me, winning the battle with her and taking its rightful place above her. By the time I was finished my smoke it was over and the world had turned back to normal.

Sleep was no longer an option and I had things to do. I threw on my suit, tucked my .45 in my holster and put on my fedora. I took a quick look in the mirror, not particularly impressed with what I saw, and headed out the door for what I hoped wouldn't be my last day on earth.

After taking care of all the things I needed to take care of I headed off to the funeral of Mona Cooper. She was being buried at a small cemetery just south of Atlantic Beach and a little inland. By the time I got there a small crowd had gathered and more were arriving by the minute. I parked my car in the line of vehicles off to the side of the graveyard and got out, leaning against it and waiting.

People were somber and quiet as they pulled up and parked, heading over to the grave site in pairs, wordless and expressionless. Raddison Hayes pulled in alone. He got out of his black Desoto and came walking past me, shooting me a glare as he did.

"Can I have a minute?" I asked him.

"Not now, McKeller. This isn't the place."

"I just wanted to apologize. I was wrong about you and I know you didn't have anything to do with Mona's death."

He didn't answer but stood looking at me, a blank expression on his face.

"I also know why you didn't want to talk about you and Mona. It must have been difficult."

He still didn't answer.

"It was nothing personal. I was just trying to do my job. No hard feelings?"

His expression never changed and he turned, walking away to join the others by the place Mona was about to be buried.

It was about that time a green Chevrolet came rolling to a stop behind me. My stomach did a somersault when I saw who was driving it. I told myself that it didn't change anything. Anyone can get their hands on another car.

Mathew Baker got out of the car before walking around and opening the passenger door for his wife. Rita was a wreck as he helped her up and out, her leaning on him as they walked. In her heels, she was a little taller than her husband. Both greeted me with polite but forced smiles as they walked past me. I imagined Rita was overcome with grief and Mathew had other demons filling his head.

I followed them over to stand with the others. Doc Pearson, the old shoe repairman and some of the others I had met were all there. One of the last to arrive was Deputy Dale. He came right over to me.

"What's this all about?" he asked me. "Why did you call and tell me to be here?"

I leaned in close to his ear so I could speak without being heard by the others. "I thought you might want to be on hand to arrest the murderer of Mona Cooper."

Dale looked around, glancing about the crowd. "Who?"

I shushed him and nudged my head in the direction we had all come. A black hearse was driving in toward us followed by a black sedan.

The hearse stopped and some of the men from the grave site went over to meet it. Out of the sedan stepped a tall lanky preacher, followed by Clarence Cooper, Tabby and Russell.

The men gathered at the back of the hearse and opened it up, slowly sliding out the plain oak casket and taking their positions at its sides. They hoisted it up and came around the vehicle, pausing for a moment before beginning the precession to Mona's final resting spot.

The pallbearers made their way toward us with the preacher and what was left of Mona Cooper's family close behind. They gently placed it on the ground in front of the open grave and stepped back into the crowd as the preacher took his spot in front. With Tabby on his arm and Russell beside him, Mr. Cooper took his place at the front of the crowd.

The preacher read from the Bible for a bit, a handful of passages he'd thought would best describe Mona Cooper and the life she had led. He talked about her for a while after, sharing stories he knew first hand and others people who knew her had related to him. From there it was hymns from the crowd, loud sorrowful songs which everyone but me knew the words to.

It was sad and powerful, even bringing a tear to a lunkhead like me. Tears flowed freely and more than one person cried out in a wail. The entire time Clarence Cooper stood rigid and tall, Tabby leaning into him and holding tight to his arm, weeping gently throughout.

The time came for Mona's body to be lowered into the ground. The pallbearers placed two ropes under the casket and took positions on either side of the grave. While the group of mourners sang Amazing Grace, they gently eased her down into her final resting place. Clarence then stepped up and took a handful of dirt and tossed it onto the casket. He was followed by Tabby, Russell and the rest of her friends.

When it was over people began to separate off into groups and clusters, some of them heading back to their cars. Rita Baker was standing in a group of people, waiting to pass on her condolences to Mona's father. Mathew headed toward the car.

I gave Deputy Dale a nudge and we went over to head him off. "Counselor, can I have a minute?"

He turned to greet us. "Sure. Hi, Dale."

"Matt," the deputy nodded back.

I wasn't in the mood to play nice. "Wouldn't it have been easier to just pay her off?" I asked. "Did you really have to kill her?"

I don't know which guy's jaw dropped farther.

"Look here, McKeller, Mathew Baker is one of our most respected citizens," the deputy offered.

"That's all well and good but it doesn't change the facts."

"You might want to be careful here," Baker jumped in. "You can't just go throwing wild accusations around like that."

"Who are we kidding, counselor? We both know you did it."

Deputy Dale gave me a hard look. "I take it you have some sort of proof?"

"Let me tell you how it went down. You can correct me if I get some of the details wrong, Matt, but I think I've got the gist of it. Mr. Mathew Baker Esquire was having an affair with Mona Cooper. As near as I can figure it started awhile back.

"Mrs. Baker had some health issues after the birth of their

latest child and romance was on the down swing at the Baker household."

"That's none of your business, McKeller."

"Mona was a pretty, young, impressionable girl and, even more than that, she was always there. Seeing her day in and day out, a guy starts thinking things. Who knows how you got the ball rolling. I'm guessing a kid like Mona was pretty impressed with a young hot shot lawyer like you.

"Maybe you told her what she wanted to hear. Maybe you made her some promises, like throwing her some money for the big trip she was planning. However you did it, you and Mona had your fling. I'm not even sure how long it lasted. Maybe it was a one-time deal. Maybe you were seeing her right up to the end.

"What you didn't count on was Mona getting pregnant. She didn't count on that either. It moved up her time table for moving away and threw a monkey wrench into her plans.

"She needed cash for her move and I'm guessing you were a willing mark. The last thing you wanted was for her to be around after she started showing. Your wife's family, the ones with all the money, wouldn't be too keen on you having a bastard child with a young black woman. That would have been a real deal breaker, not to mention a blemish on your blossoming career.

"I figure Mona Cooper for a good girl at heart. She probably didn't see it as blackmail. She wanted what was best for her baby and, if it provided her with a way out, so be it.

"I don't know what the plan was but I know you agreed to meet her. Maybe you were going to give her the money, maybe you weren't. Maybe you were having second thoughts and were afraid she'd come back looking for more. Maybe you figured the safest thing was to wipe the slate clean.

"Either way you took her out to a secluded stretch of beach. I think we all know how it played out from there. You're the lawyer. What does that sound like to you? I'm guessing most juries would take that as premeditated. That's murder one.

"I don't know exactly how the rape thing came into play. Maybe she didn't take it so well when you told her you weren't going to cough up the loot. Maybe you did it for effect. Maybe you just wanted one more roll in the hay with her but she put up a fight. When you were done with her you slit her throat and left her to die on the beach."

"That is the most insane thing I've ever heard," Baker said. His face had turned white as a ghost.

"What's going on here?" Rita Baker asked. She had wandered up in the middle of my rant and I hadn't seen her coming. I had no idea how much she'd heard. I glanced around. The crowd by the grave site had taken notice and they were all looking over, wondering what was going on.

"This lunatic accused me of killing Mona."

Rita was calm as a cucumber. Maybe she was in shock. She turned to me and asked, "Why would you think such a horrible thing?"

I paused for a moment, not sure if I should answer. I hadn't planned on doing this in front of the wife.

"Mr. McKeller, what would make you think something like that?" she asked again.

After another pause I decided to lay it out for her. She had as much at stake here as anyone.

"On the night Mona was killed your husband picked her up outside of a joint called Mack's. I have an eyewitness who saw her get into a tan Plymouth sedan."

Mathew Baker stepped toward me, taking up an aggressive stance. "Take a good look at my car, McKeller. Does that look like a tan Plymouth?"

I glanced over to Deputy Dale. He shrugged. "He used drive a tan Plymouth."

"I did. I traded it in on the Chevy two weeks before Mona was killed."

I could feel a cold sweat break out on the back of my neck and my knees went a little weak. Those familiar self-doubts were tugging at my insides but I decided to press on.

"When I met with you yesterday, something didn't jive with your statement. You told me she was shy and never much talked to you but she told you about this mysterious boyfriend of hers. Why is it she never mentioned the boyfriend to anyone else?"

Baker smiled. "I don't know. I guess Mona took that little secret to the grave with her."

"There's the little matter of those dead flowers on her dresser too. They came from a place across the street from where you work. You were smart enough not to sign the card but you charged them to your account, the bill was sent to your office."

Baker laughed. "That's it? That's what you've got, a bunch of dead flowers?"

I didn't respond. I didn't have much else to throw at him. It sounded like more in my head before I spilled it all out. Deputy Dale was looking as confused as anyone, like he was having trouble following what was happening.

"Do you really think a jury is going to convict me with that? I'm a successful and respected officer of the court, McKeller. I'm in line to be the next District Attorney. Besides that, I'm innocent. I didn't kill anyone."

"You and Mona?" Rita said in disbelief, looking down at her husband.

"He doesn't know what he's talking about," Baker assured her. "He's grasping at straws."

"You had an affair with her. She was carrying your child. You couldn't afford to let a thing like that go public," I said.

"Do you know who you're dealing with here? Do you have any idea who I am? Take a good look around you, McKeller. This is South Carolina and you're going to need a lot more than that to convict somebody of killing some nigger girl."

The slap across the face from his wife was hard enough to jar teeth loose. It caught him by surprise and he stood gawking back at her and holding the side of his face.

"She was my friend," Rita said with a tremor to her voice. "She was a part of our family. She was all I had. You were never home. When you were you didn't pay me hardly any attention. She was sweet and kind and as good a soul as I ever met.

"I knew things were bad between us. Do you think I couldn't tell something was wrong? Do you think I couldn't feel it every time we were in the same room together? I knew you were having an affair. I could sense it. I never dreamed it was with—"

"Rita, that's crazy. You know better than that," he tried.

"Why Mona? Why couldn't you have had the decency to run around behind my back with some secretary from work? Why did it have to be with my friend? You know how she was, Mathew. She was just a kid and she was so full of hopes and dreams."

"You don't know what you're saying, Rita. It's the medication."

Deputy Dale inserted himself between the two, trying to diffuse things. "OK, let's just calm down. Why don't we take a ride down to the station and sort this out, Matt?"

"What? I will do no such thing. I didn't kill anyone. There's a perfectly logical explanation for all this."

"I'm sure there is but I'm going to need you to come downtown and give a statement. The sheriff is going to want to ask you a few questions."

"I'm not going anywhere," Baker said with huff. "This entire thing is ridiculous."

"Matt, I don't know what's going on here," the deputy replied. "I'm not accusing you of anything but a young girl is dead and I'm going to need you to come down and answer some questions. You can either cooperate and come along, of your own free will, or we can do this the other way."

"Are you arresting me?"

"I would hope it wouldn't come to that," Dale offered.

"Dale, I'm going to be the District Attorney of this county one day. Is this really a battle you want to wage?"

"Yeah, well, I might end up being sheriff one day too. You might want to consider that."

"You can't do this. This is slander. I'll have your badge over this."

Deputy Dale stepped in close to the sweating counselor. "I'm going to ask you one more time politely. After that, I'm going to use force if necessary."

"I hope you know a good lawyer," I added.

It was like someone let the air out of Mathew Baker. His body went limp and he began to nod slowly. "All right, let's go talk to the sheriff. Anything I can do to help with your ... investigation." He took his wife by the arm and began guiding her away, back toward their car. Rita looked a little reticent to go along.

"I'll follow behind you," the deputy called after him before turning to me. "I hope you know what you're doing, McKeller."

"Me too," I answered before giving the deputy a long look. "Let me ask you; are you a fisherman by any chance?"

"As a matter of fact I am. Why do you ask?"

"I have something I need fished."

I met Deputy Dale and the Bakers back at the sheriff's office. The sheriff didn't seem very thrilled to see me. I went through everything I had on Mathew Baker and laid out for him the best I could.

"Uh-hu," he grunted after I was done. "And you have an eyewitness that saw Mona Cooper get into a car just like the one Mr. Baker used to own?"

"Yes."

"And you found proof that Mr. Baker bought flowers for a girl who worked for him?"

"He lied about it, Sheriff. He lied about a lot of things. I also know, for a fact, Baker got home late on the night Mona was killed."

"All right, McKeller, we appreciate all the help but we'll take it from here."

"He was having an affair with Mona Cooper. He got her pregnant."

"Yeah, I heard you the first time. My men and I will take over from here."

"Are you going to arrest him?"

"As a private citizen, I don't see where that's any of your concern, but I can assure you that we will look thoroughly into your allegations. Mathew Baker and I are going to have us a long talk."

"But, Sheriff—"

"That will be all, McKeller."

That was that. The sheriff made it very clear my assistance was neither needed nor wanted. I could only hope that I'd given him enough to implicate Baker in Mona's murder. I had a feeling I hadn't.

I couldn't worry about that right then. I had another pressing matter to attend to.

Chapter Thirty-Seven

My lack of sleep was getting to me some and I could feel it in my leg. I felt it every time I worked the clutch in the old flatbed. It was a constant ache for the most part but when I pressed down on the pedal it sent a burning sensation through the joints.

I still had plenty of time before I was going to meet with Vincent but it was imperative that I get there first. My entire plan depended on it.

It was before twelve when I pulled up at the 2nd Avenue Pier. It was a big rustic fishing pier that was built in 1936 and it was about wide enough to park a car and a half side by side. There was a thick wooden handrail that ran across its edges. The thing started off on dry land with a large ramp dipping down and stretching across the sand, to almost where the road and sand dunes met. The pier itself sat about twenty feet off the ground and continued out over the ocean for 906 feet, setting a good ten feet off the water at high tide.

I turned the truck around in front of the ramp so she was facing away from it and began backing it up the incline. The old gal sputtered and strained, barely mustering up the muscle to get up it but she finally managed and I came to a stop where it flattened out, the beginning of the pier. I had the high ground and I'd be looking down on anyone who approached.

Now there was nothing to do but wait. I opened both doors and rolled down the windows, giving me a little more cover on the sides and allowing me a couple of options to shoot from if it became necessary. I'd made a makeshift torch out of a broomstick and some old rags that I'd soaked in moonshine and I sat it on the ground with the handle leaning into the crook of the door. The smell was getting to me and I wanted to get it out of the cab.

I took my .45 and an extra magazine of ammo and sat it on the seat beside me along with my Zippo lighter. Then I lit up a smoke and leaned back in the seat, waiting for the show to start. Everything was in place and I had to hope for the best.

For the next hour I chain smoked cigarettes and tried to ignore the throbbing in my leg. There were a few times I thought I might doze off but I managed to stir myself awake. The closer it got to one o'clock the more jittery I got.

At ten of, I spotted two trucks and a white coupe coming down the road. They were going at it pretty fast for a road like Ocean Boulevard and I figured it might be my party.

The vehicles turned off the road and came skidding to a stop in a line out in front of me at the bottom of the ramp. I could see six men in all and a small brunette in the backseat of the car.

Vincent was the first to get out. He stepped right out in front of the line of vehicles and stood looking up at me in the truck.

"What now, McKeller? How we going to do this?"

I picked up the torch and lit it with my lighter, grabbed my pistol and slid out of the cab. I was crouched behind the car door, holding the fire above my head in my left hand and my .45 in my right.

The other men were scurrying out of the far car doors and taking positions behind the car and trucks. I caught glimpses of rifles and shot guns in their hands.

"Can you smell that?" I asked.

"Smell what?"

"I took the liberty of soaking the truck and its contents in some of your precious moonshine. One false move and this baby is going up like a Roman Candle."

"Don't do anything stupid, McKeller. That truck is the only thing standing between you and a slow painful death."

"Send the girl up."

Vincent laughed. "Is this your plan? Did you happen to give any thought to how you're getting out of here? Were you planning on swimming to Europe?"

"You let me worry about that. Just send up the girl."

"I'll tell you what, McKeller. You're not the brightest guy but I have to admit you have a set of balls on you. You give me the truck and let me keep the girl and I'll let you walk away from here, no hard feelings."

"It's too late for that. You already hurt my feelings when you said I wasn't that bright."

Vincent laughed again. There was nothing about him that said he was feeling the slightest bit of stress or worry at having a gun pointed at him. I, on the other hand, was a wreck.

"It's not too late, McKeller. We can still settle this like civilized adults. Nobody has to get hurt."

"That's all well and good but where are you going to find a civilized adult to pull your end?"

I heard some snickers coming from the other side of the barricade.

"That's funny. You're a regular Groucho Marx."

"Look, I'd love nothing better than to sit around here and shoot the breeze with you but I have a late lunch date I'm trying to make. Do you think we could quit with the clever banter and get down to business?"

"I'm just trying to give you a way out of this mess. If I were you I'd take a good look at where you're sitting."

"Thanks for your concern but just send Patty up here."

Vincent motioned to one of his boys and someone opened the car door. I saw Patty slide out of the back and come walking around. As she got to Vincent he grabbed her by the back of the hair and pulled her in close to him. He pulled a .38 caliber pistol out from behind him and shoved the barrel to the side of her head.

"How about if I just go ahead and blow her pretty little head off? I'm guessing that between me and my boys we could take care of you before you can do any damage."

I took the torch and raised it up so it was hovering over the canvas tied to the back of the truck. "That would be a bad guess on your part."

Vincent's demeanor had changed and his eyes were wild with rage. I could see that he wanted nothing more than to pull the trigger and snuff out Patty's life with me watching.

"It's your call, Vincent. How much do you figure this load is worth?"

I was standing awkward, pressed into the side of the truck with my gun hand through the window and the torch off behind me and over my head. Part of me wondered if I could get a clean shot off without hitting Patty. Even I wasn't quite that stupid.

"What do I care?" he said, giving her a shove toward me. "I'll have her back before supper time."

Patty came running up the ramp, half stumbling and off balance. She came around the truck door and pressed herself in behind me. She was about as scared as anyone I had ever seen, just about as scared as I was.

"Get in the truck," I told her.

Patty went in through my door, climbing across to the passenger side and I slid in beside her.

"Take this," I told her, handing her the end of the pole as I started up the truck and threw it into reverse.

The cab instantly filled with smoke. With a squawk she thrust the torch out the door and we backed down the pier coughing and hacking.

I didn't have to tell her to get down when the firing started. She was practically on the floor with the torch sticking out the still open door. I was down as low as I could get and still see the mirror.

The truck jolted backwards and began picking up steam and I was doing my best to keep it straight as we went barreling down the pier in reverse. I hadn't gone twenty feet when I veered off too far to Patty's side and the door caught on the wooden handrail and sheared off, tumbling across the wooden platform in our wake.

I managed to straighten her out and get back on track but with my adrenaline pumping like it was I was having a hard time of it. I kept swerving to the left and the right, alternately slamming against the rails, struggling to keep the truck in the middle of the pier.

When I glanced back up through the windshield I saw the pickup truck come up the ramp and onto the pier. The bed was loaded with Vincent and his cronies. They were leaning over the roof of the cab and firing toward us. They were also moving forward and having an easier go of it than me and they were gaining on us fast.

Bullets were ricocheting about the hood and roof, occasionally cracking into the glass in front of me. I gunned the throttle hard and the truck heaved backwards, rolling along and bouncing up and down with every plank we crossed.

My .45 was in my left hand and I stuck it out the window and fired off six rounds at the oncoming pick up. This slowed them down for a second but it also caused me to lose my concentration and I lost control of the flatbed. It swerved hard to the left slamming into the guard rail.

We came to a stop with a sudden jolt and I heard the sound of crunching metal and cracking wood. The force of the impact threw Patty out the side and onto the pier, almost sending me out with her.

I tried to throw it in first gear to straighten it out but it was no use. I'd wedged the truck in on an angle between the two railings and she wasn't going anywhere. We were about three quarters of the way down the pier.

My mind was racing and I scooped up my gun and extra magazine as I pulled myself out from where the passenger door once was. Patty was just getting up from the planks and the burning torch was lying a few feet away from her.

"What now?" she screamed.

"Run," I shot back as I picked up the torch and tossed it into the back of the truck. I grabbed hold of her arm and took off running, pulling her with me as I limped my way down the length of the pier, moving faster than I knew I could.

When we got to the end we stopped and looked back. The flatbed was ablaze and the pickup truck was visible on the far side of it, the men off it now and trying to maneuver around the fire. Shots were still coming in our direction and we both hit the ground, me peering off the edge of the platform and into the water below.

It was somewhere between low and high tide and I guessed the depth around twenty to thirty feet. The waves were crashing hard into the thick wooden beams that held the pier and I could see three feet of wet and barnacles above the water. It looked cold and angry and it was the last place in the world I wanted to end up.

I glanced back toward the truck. Two men were climbing over the hood, the only place not engulfed in flames. Two others were crawling under it and Vincent was maneuvering around the side, climbing across the split railing. Maybe the ocean was the second to last place I wanted to be.

I fired three more shots in their direction and they all paused, crouching low for cover. Crawling on my hands and face, I peeked back over the structure and back down to the ocean. This was not the way I had envisioned my plan playing out.

"What do we do now?" Patty yelled.

Ignoring her, I took another look down. "Come on, where in the hell are you?" I said.

"They're getting closer!" she yelled.

Patty and I were lying on the pier, trying to present the smallest targets possible. Vincent and his boys were crouching low too, moving up past the truck and closing in. If any of them had taken the time to stop and aim, we would have been goners for sure. I poked my head over the edge of the pier for one last desperate look before it was time to go to plan B. I was also wondering what plan B might be.

When Deputy Dale's boat came gliding out from under the pier it was the most beautiful thing I had ever seen. Little, dirty and rickety with a small outboard motor and not much room for anything other than the deputy, it was like beholding the Queen Mary on her maiden voyage. It was just like the movies and Deputy Dale was the Cavalry coming to save the day.

"Jump!" I yelled to Patty.

She looked at me like I was crazy. She hadn't seen the boat yet.

There was no time for explanations or arguments. I did what I had to. I took her by the shoulder and gave her a shove. She let out a yelp as she went rolling off the edge and down into the water. I didn't look to see but I heard the splash when she hit.

Vincent and his gang were past the flatbed and low crawling up the pier, trying to stay down but moving in. I looked back down over the edge as I switched out my magazine.

Patty was in the front of the boat and Dale was at the rear by the motor, looking up and waiting for me to follow. "Come on, let's go," he screamed.

I shot another look down the pier. They were moving in faster, gaining confidence with every second I didn't shoot back. I fired two rounds, which held them up briefly.

Back in the water, Dale was yelling for me to jump.

"They're too close. You'll never make it. They have rifles and they'll pick you off before you can get far enough away."

"There's no time," he screamed back. "We have to go now."

"Get her out of here! I'll hold them off until you get away."

"Don't be stupid, McKeller!"

"It's too late for that."

I rolled over and into a prone position, both hands extended in front of me and holding my pistol. There were seven shots left and I had to make every one of them count. In the background I heard the buzz of a motor putting down the shoreline and away from the danger.

They were still moving, none of them taking the time to aim and get off a good shot. This was my only advantage as I tried to keep as low as possible and set my sights on the closest one.

I fired off one shot at a bulky looking guy with a shotgun in front of him. He kept coming. I fired again.

This time he let out a wail and rolled over on his back clutching at his shoulder. That sent the rest of them scurrying for the sides and trying to get behind what little cover the railing could lend.

With the next shot I got a guy in the leg and he was screaming louder than the first one. Nobody was moving forward, I'd bought a little time. From there I tried to space out my shots as far as I could, picking my spots and not hitting anyone but placing my bullets in places that made them think twice about coming closer.

When my last shot was spent I maintained my position, hoping to bluff them into thinking I had more for them. They bought it for a while.

Eventually they began to move again, actually taking the time to aim their shots at me. It was a little unnerving lying there pointing my empty gun at them and holding my breath as the bullets came in closer and closer. When I got winged on the right arm I knew the jig was up and I began back crawling toward the edge of the pier.

This was akin to throwing up a flare and telling them I was out of ammo. They began to stand and came running at me, bullets blazing. I did the only thing I could do. I let myself fall off the edge of the pier.

The Atlantic felt like ice when I hit her and the cold sent a surge of pain through my entire body. It was all I could do to keep from gulping for air and taking in water. I'd like to say I'd never felt anything like it but the truth was I had. It wasn't the first time I had been in her belly.

My clothes felt like lead, weighing me down and sinking me deeper into her. I tried to kick and squirm but everything about me was sluggish like my mind no longer controlled the parts of my body. A cramp bit into my bad leg and I stretched it out with no relief. Everything about me was going numb.

A thought crept into my head, a memory from long ago.

Those familiar ghosts were gnawing at the base of my spine while the cold and wet tried to take me back to that day on a foreign beach. Flashes of things long ago zipped through my brain and forgotten sounds were ringing in my head. I could feel her pulling me back to that place and time; flexing her muscles, letting me know who was boss.

She had me right where she wanted me.

Not this time, bitch.

The fight was on. I kicked and punched, trying to break free from her hold. I cupped my hands and grabbed up at the water above me, pulling and slapping at her, pushing her away from me. She fought back too.

I could feel her at my ankles and suppressing my wrists. I could feel the weight of her on my chest and shoulders. She was in my ears, seeping her way into my brain. She was all around me, holding me down, swallowing me up.

This wasn't my first rodeo. I'd been here before and that last time she'd had me where she wanted too. That last time it took my friend to save me after I had given up. This time I wasn't giving up. I wasn't giving her anything.

Pain surged through my bum leg, begging for relief but I kept kicking, refusing to give in to her. My mind was swirling with anger and pain and fear. The world was upside down and my lungs were aching but I continued to fight.

When I broke the surface I was disoriented and panicked. I caught a glimpse of dry land through burning eyes and began to paddle toward it, kicking my feet for all I was worth. It seemed to take forever and, somewhere in the back of my mind, I wondered if I was gaining any ground. Eventually I felt my hands and knees hitting the bottom and I realized I had made it to the surf and I began crawling through the waves pounding at my back.

My breathing was labored, my body spent. I had just enough strength to pull myself up onto my knees, trying to catch my breath. That was when Timothy Vincent kicked me square in the chest.

I fell back, unable to pull any oxygen into my lungs. My arms were behind me pushing down on the sand and trying to keep my head above the waves.

Vincent cracked me upside the cheek bone with the butt of his pistol. I nearly blacked out from the force of it and I thought I felt bone sheer off. He hit me again, this time catching the corner of my eye socket with his gun. Stars flashed in front of me as hit me again and again.

I didn't have the energy to breathe much less fight back. I lost track of how many times he pummeled me about the head and face. My mind receded, barely aware of the beating I was taking.

I felt him pull me up out of the water, bringing me back to my knees. My face was stinging, wet with saltwater and blood. The cold hard barrel of his pistol was pressed into my temple.

"Do you have any idea what you cost me? Who do you think you are, you Damnyankee, coming down her and interfering with my business? I'm going to make you pay, you son of a bitch. I'm going to make you pay like you never imagined."

His words were barely registering in my groggy head.

"When I get done with you you're going to wish you were dead. Then I'm going to make you pay more. When I finally put the bullet in your brain it's going to feel like Christmas after what I've done to you."

"Let him go, Vincent," a voice said.

Both of us looked up to see Sheriff Talbert standing on the

beach, his service revolver pointed in our direction.

"This here's between me and him, Sheriff. You go about your business and I'll take care of this."

"You let him go right now, Vincent. This fight is done."

"Ain't nothing done till I say it is. This Yankee bastard cost me dearly and he's going to pay."

"It's over, Vincent. You put down that gun and go on home."

"Did you see what he done to my truck? That's my money burning up there. That's your brother's money burning up there."

"What's done is done. There ain't going to be nobody getting killed here today."

"Whose side are you on?" Vincent yelled.

"I'm the sheriff and this is my town. I'm on the side of the law."

"Ain't that convenient, all this time of you looking the other way and now you're going to be the law?"

"Don't kid yourself, Vincent. I've always been the law down here. I tried to look the other way as long as you boys weren't doing anybody no harm but this has gone too far. This stops right here."

"He done all this over some whore, Sheriff. He's going to pay for what he done."

"You put that gun down right now. It's over."

"I'll tell you when it's over!" Vincent screamed, turning as he did and bringing the gun up and around, turning it toward Sheriff Talbert.

I don't know if he meant to point the pistol at the sheriff or if he was just motioning with it by reflex. The sheriff didn't take the time to find out. He fired two rounds, catching Vincent both times in the chest.

Vincent stood stunned for a moment, looking down at the wounds in disbelief. Then he dropped to his knees before falling over face first into the surf.

I was still punch drunk from the pistol whipping he had laid on me. I had nothing to offer as Talbert walked into the surf, grabbed Vincent by the back of the shirt, and dragged him out of the water and onto the beach. He came back and took me by the arm and helped me up, leading me out and away. Somehow I managed to spit out a thanks. The sheriff didn't acknowledge it.

Chapter Thirty-Eight

My wits had just about come back to me by the time the sheriff dumped me into the back of his cruiser and drove me to his office. Another deputy stayed behind to oversee the clean-up.

Patty Highsmith and Deputy Dale were already there. She was wrapped in a blanket and sipping a cup of coffee. He was parked at a desk.

After the funeral I had given Dale a brief rundown on what was going down. I'd explained how what I was up to wasn't exactly legal and how it was probably not a good idea for him to be directly involved. He agreed to bring his boat out to the end of the pier to give us an easy escape route. Too bad it didn't quite go down like that.

Dale had stopped by the office and filled the sheriff in on what was going on. I guess the sheriff was perfectly willing to let us settle our dispute between ourselves until things got out of hand. He'd taken his sweet old time getting to the scene.

Patty cringed when she saw my face. "Are you all right, mister?"

"Sure, just another day at the office." I turned to Dale. "I owe you one," I told him. "A big one."

"Don't mention it."

The sheriff interrupted. "Dale, get out there and help those boys out. We got a hell of a mess on the beach."

"Yes, Sheriff."

After the deputy left he turned his attention to me. "What in God's name were you thinking?"

"It seemed like a good idea at the time."

He sighed. "Well, you certainly did it up right. Do you have any idea how many laws you broke out there?"

"A few, I'm guessing."

"Vincent's been a thorn in my side for about as long as I can remember. There wasn't much good about him and I don't imagine he's going to be missed by many so here's what we're going to do.

"I'm going to make out my report and it's going to be about a bootlegger and a truckload of moonshine. Me and my men spotted him in town and we proceeded to give chase. It ended up in a gunfight at the pier and the bootlegger was shot and killed by yours truly. There ain't going to be any mention of a missing girl or a private citizen getting involved. You got that?"

"It suits me fine."

"You blurred some serious lines here, McKeller." He paused and took a deep breath. "I suppose there's lines on both sides that have been blurred a while. I mean to fix that but good."

It was as close to an admission of guilt I was going to get out of the sheriff. That was all right by me. I was just happy to be on the other side of the good ole boy system for a change.

"As far as I'm concerned this case is closed," I told him. "All I ever cared about was the girl,"

"That works for me."

"What about Baker? Did you arrest him?"

The sheriff let out a sigh. "We didn't feel we had enough evidence to hold Mr. Baker."

"What about all the stuff I gave you?"

"What, some dead flowers and hearsay?"

"He lied, Sheriff."

"About what? About talking to his housekeeper about her boyfriend? About sending some flowers to a girl who worked for him?

"What about the car? What about his coming home late that

night? It might not be a lot but it all starts adding up when you start putting the pieces together."

"Do you know how many tan Plymouth sedans there are in this county? Besides, he traded that car in a week and a half before Mona Cooper was murdered. I called over to Louden Motors and verified it myself.

"It also turns out that Mathew Baker has an alibi for the night in question. He was a little leery about mentioning in front of his wife but he has an alibi just the same."

"What kind of alibi? He's got to be lying."

"It turns out that Mathew Baker took a little trip down to Georgetown the night Mona Cooper was murdered. He and a friend were at the Sunset Lodge."

"What does that mean?"

The sheriff cleared his throat. "For a big time city slicker detective, you're pretty dense, aren't you? The Sunset Lodge is about the most famous Cat House in these parts. That would explain his hesitance in coming forward with the information."

"He's lying, Sheriff. He has to be."

"McKeller, he was there with a very prominent district court judge. I talked to the judge personally. He was more than a little embarrassed by the situation but he confirmed that he was there with Mathew Baker till well after two in the morning. When you figure in the drive back, there is no way he had time to get up to Atlantic Beach and murder Mona Cooper."

The wind had been sucked out of my sails but good. All my careful deductions had turned out to be a big pile of zip. My detective skills had fallen short once again.

The sheriff called over to the doctor's office and he came over and patched me up as best he could. He figured I had a fracture to the left eye socket and another to the cheekbone, not to mention an array of cuts and bruises. There wasn't much he could do, short of placing my entire head in a cast. I told him I'd be fine.

After that, the good sheriff volunteered to give Patty and me a ride. I told him we needed to go to the Chesterfield Inn.

Patty was distant and quiet during the short ride over, us in the back seat and the sheriff driving. I could tell she was nervous.

"Your mother is really excited to see you," I tried.

Patty nodded.

"She's been worried about you."

She nodded again.

"Everything is going to be OK, Patty."

"I know," she replied in a soft voice. "It's just kind of weird and all. I'm a little scared. I'm afraid about seeing her again. I ... I did some stuff."

I looked into those big innocent blues and saw a confused and scared kid.

"We've all done stuff," I said. "I, personally, have a list of regrets longer than my arm, but I'll let you in on something. The mistakes we've made and the things we've done don't define who we are. It's what we do from here on that matters.

"You start out slow, one step at a time, and you keep plugging away, doing things the way you know you should. Before long the things you're doing become the things you've done as well. After a while, the things you're doing will outnumber all those other things you did and they'll keep pushing them farther and farther back. Before you know it those things you're doing become who you are and those other things are just bumps in the road."

Patty sat back in her seat and closed her eyes. I didn't get the impression she put much stock in what I'd told her. Why would she? How many kids heed the advice of grownups? That's the way kids are, the way they always have been. Down the road, she'd figure it all out.

The mother and daughter reunion was just like you might imagine, just like out of the movies with a lot of hugs and tears. I knew then and there they were going to be fine. Aside from the fuss Ellen made over my face, I might not even have been in the room.

Ellen kept thanking me for what I had done and offering to pay me back in some way. She even offered to send me monthly installments but I told her to keep her money.

"Please, Mr. McKeller, you have to let me pay you somehow. Isn't there anything I could do for you?"

I thought about it for a second or so. "There is one thing."

"You name it, anything you need."

"I know this girl. She's a little younger than Patty. She doesn't have any family or anywhere to go and she got herself in a fix. She's a good kid."

Ellen smiled.

Later that evening, when I got back to the Ocean Forest, Buntemeyer was waiting by the front desk. He had that look in his eye like there was an ass chewing he was saving for someone. My guess was it had my name on it.

"What happened to your face?"

"I slipped in the tub."

"Where's my car? Did anything happen to the Studebaker?"

"Thanks for your concern, Boss. The car is fine."

"Look here, McKeller, I'm beginning to question your methods. I'm wondering if you're the kind of man we need here at the Ocean Forest Hotel."

It was just then a pack of the accountant types came walking up. They began slapping me on the back and thanking me, inquiring about my face. It was a genuine love fest and each of them to a man took the time to tell me how I had been personally responsible for the best convention they had ever attended. They made sure to mention how they planned to come back to the Ocean Forest the following year.

Once they had all gone I turned back to Buntemeyer. "Were you saying something, Boss?"

He hesitated, weighing his options. "No, not at all. Keep up the good work, McKeller, and make sure you have that face looked at."

Chapter Thirty-Nine

My face was throbbing, my leg was aching and the graze I'd taken to the arm hurt like a bee sting. On top of that, I was dead tired. Every part of me wanted to go up to my room and sleep for three days but I knew that wasn't an option.

I'd screwed things up royally in the Mona Cooper case and I was left holding nothing. I felt like I needed to get back out there and try to put the pieces back together and make some sense out of everything I knew.

The problem was I didn't have a clue as to where to begin. I got behind the wheel of the Ocean Forest's Studebaker and started driving. It was late afternoon by the time I turned into the lot of Louden Motors. I had no idea what I was looking for or what I might find there but it was the only starting point I could come up with.

Louden Motors wasn't anything more than a sand and dirt lot on the south end of town, sitting on the corner of Kings Highway and Third Avenue. There were less than a dozen used cars on display and a small wooden shack at the far end. For decoration and advertising purposes, they featured a hand painted wooden sign with a string of Christmas lights draped over the top of it.

The tan Plymouth sedan was parked prominently at the front of the lot. The doors were locked and the windows were up and

I took a few moments to peer inside before heading into the wooden shack that served as an office.

Bill Louden was a likable old timer, short and stocky, with a rugged and weathered face and a pair of thick spectacles sitting low on a wide nose. He was dressed in black slacks and white button up shirt and was wearing a dirty baseball cap crooked on his head.

"Howdy," he greeted me with.

"Hi,"

"What happened to your face?"

"My cat scratched me."

"Must be some cat," he snickered. "Nice Studebaker."

"Thanks, it's not mine. I was wondering about the tan Plymouth."

His eyes lit up with the prospect of a sale. "She's a dandy. Haven't had her but a couple of weeks and she runs like a charm."

"What can you tell me about it?"

The old man rummaged through some papers scattered across the top of his desk until he found the one he was looking for. He was half reading from it as he gave me the lowdown.

"She's a thirty-nine, prewar. One owner, immaculate condition and only thirty-two thousand miles on her."

"Only thirty-two thousand, huh?"

"Thirty-two thousand, three hundred and twenty-three, to be exact. I could let her go for around six hundred dollars."

"Do you mind if I take a look?"

Louden was quick with the keys and we were out the door. I opened her up and climbed inside, settling into the driver's seat and soaking her in. Immaculate wasn't a clean enough word for her. She looked brand new and unused.

The seat was pushed back into the farthest setting and I had more than enough room for my legs. In fact, my feet barely reached the pedals and I had to lean forward slightly to get my hands around the steering wheel. I'm not a small guy but it made me feel like a little kid.

"Have you had much interest in her?"

Louden chuckled. "This time of year, there ain't much car buying in Myrtle Beach. Nobody's got any money for luxuries till the season swings back around. You're the first customer I've had on the lot since I took her in. That's why I can let her go so cheap. Come spring she'll cost you another two hundred."

"You haven't had a single customer since you got her?"

"The Missus keeps telling me I ought to shut down for the off season, says I'm just wasting my time out here. I keep sayin, 'you never know.' Truth is, what the heck else am I going to do, sit home and listen to her yacking away all day?"

I sat back in the seat, stretching my legs toward the pedals, my eyes scanning the dashboard. "So, nobody has even had her out for a test drive?"

"I haven't even started her up since the fella I got her from pulled her up into that there spot. She runs like a dream, though."

"How about you? Do you ever take her out, running errands and what not?"

"You hard of hearing, son? I told you, she ain't been moved since I got her."

I climbed out of the car and leaned back in, reaching my fingers down in her nooks and crannies, searching into the seats, hoping to find something, anything. "What did you tell me the mileage was on her?"

He paused behind me like he was looking it up on his piece of paper. "Thirty-two thousand, three hundred and twenty-three miles."

"That's what I thought you said. Only thing is, this car has thirty-two thousand, three hundred and fifty-seven miles on it."

"That's impossible," I heard him say as I reached under the driver's seat and groped around, still not sure what I was looking for. I stood up and went around to the passenger side, the old man following. I opened the door and lay across the seat, reaching under as far as I could.

"You really check a car out before you buy it, don't you?" the old man asked.

"You can never be too careful," I answered. Way back, my fingers happened on something small and solid. I pulled it out and sat up in the seat, staring down at my find.

It was two inches in length and an inch-and-a-half wide and it was made of wood. Flat on the top and bottom, it was rounded at the back and cut straight in the front. It showed wear on the bottom and was scuffed along its surface. You didn't have to be a cobbler to know it was the heel of a woman's shoe.

"What you got there?"

I took a deep breath and let it out slow. "In my business we call it a smoking gun. You got a phone in that office of yours, Bill?"

After a few phone calls I was able to track down my old buddy, Deputy Dale. He came alone as he wanted to see what I had first, before we took it to the sheriff.

Dale stood watching me with his hands on his hips, showing nothing as I ran through what I'd found. When I was done he scratched his head and gave me a funny look. "But, Baker had already got rid of the car when Mona was killed."

"Look around, Dale. There's no fence or anything. Anybody could come by in the middle of the night and take the car. Nobody would ever know it was gone as long as you had it back before they opened in the morning. All you would need is a spare key."

Dale looked more confused than ever. "But Mathew Baker has an alibi."

"Have a seat in the car, Dale."

He reluctantly climbed in. Like me, he had to lean forward some to reach the steering wheel and his feet barely reached the pedals.

"How tall do you think Mathew Baker is?"

Dale shrugged. "I don't know, a couple inches shorter than me."

"This car, supposedly, hasn't budged since Baker pulled it into this spot, yet there are twenty-four extra miles on the odometer and the seat is pushed back as far as it will go. Like it was set for a big man."

"I don't get what you're saying."

"Don't you think it's a coincidence that Mathew Baker was in the company of a well-respected judge on the night Mona was killed?"

Dale shrugged again.

"It's almost like he wanted to make sure he had an air-tight alibi."

"You're confusing me, McKeller. I thought you were convinced Baker killed Mona?"

"The problem was, I was trying to connect the wrong dots. Let me ask you this, say you have a guy in town, a guy that's always been bad news. Suppose this guy has been a thorn in the side of this community for years, fighting and starting trouble. One day this guy crosses the line but good and half kills his boss in an angry rage. You have multiple witnesses to the crime. It took three deputies to subdue the big man. Why would you drop the charges from attempted murder to assault and battery?"

Dale didn't answer.

"What do you figure the difference in sentence would be in the two charges?"

"I don't know. Attempted murder might get you ten years, maybe twelve or thirteen. With assault you're looking at a year or two, maybe six months with good behavior."

"And who would be the guy to make that deal? Who is the guy with the power to have those charges dropped down?"

"The prosecutor," he gasped in shock.

"It fits. Baker had his fling with Mona and she ended up pregnant. Baker couldn't risk her going public. Between his rising career and his wife's conservative big money family it would ruin him. Even if he could lay his hands on the money she wanted, there was no guarantee she wouldn't show back up later.

"Around this same time, a case comes across his desk. It's a no brainer, slam dunk. He's going to put this trouble maker away once and for all, but he gets an idea. He sees a way out, a way to eliminate his problem without getting his hands dirty. In return, he gives Jarvis Brown ten years back of his life. What do you figure a guy like Brown would do to stay out of prison for an extra ten years?"

"So, you're saying Baker didn't kill Mona after all."

"Oh, he killed her all right. Maybe he didn't drive her out to that secluded beach and maybe he wasn't the one who sliced her throat, but he killed her just the same."

Dale got out of the car and stood up. "I think maybe it's time we brought the sheriff in on this."

Sheriff Talbert didn't seem too happy to see me. "I would have thought you would have had enough trouble for one day," he told me as he came walking up.

"What can I say, Sheriff? I just can't get enough of your smiling face."

I let Dale take the lead. He walked the sheriff through everything I'd found and he pieced it together with everything we already knew. He presented the case with clarity and logic, making sure to fit every detail in where it belonged. I couldn't have done better myself.

Afterward, Sheriff Talbert cocked his hat back on his head and stood staring at the tan Plymouth sedan. "McKeller, did anyone ever tell you you're a real pain in the ass?"

"Actually, I get that a lot."

He gave an exasperated sigh and turned to his deputy. "I reckon you ought to get a few fellas together and take a ride out to the old Brown place. I want Jarvis brought in for questioning."

"Yes, sir," Dale answered.

Chapter Forty

I DROVE with Dale back into town and we collected a couple of deputies to take with us. I was kind of shocked that the sheriff allowed me to tag along, but I guess he figured I couldn't cause any more trouble than I already had.

It was dark by the time we go to the Brown place. It was outside of town, inland and set on an old dirt road. There was a single light coming from the front window and it flickered like it might be a lantern or candle.

The four of us walked up on the front porch. We looked each other over once before Dale reached out and rapped on the door like he was all business.

"What you want?" a deep voice said from the other side.

"Jarvis, it's Deputy Dale and I need you to come out here."

"What you want?" the voice asked again.

"Me and the fellows need to have a word with you."

"I didn't do nothing. I been home all night."

"Jarvis, I need you to get out here right now."

"What's this all about?"

"Jarvis, you best open this door or me and my boys are fixing to break it on down. You get yourself out here before you make even more trouble for yourself."

"I didn't do nothing. What you want with me?"

233

"We need you to come out and come downtown with us. We need to ask you some questions about Mona Cooper."

There was a long silence but it didn't last. The first shot came through the door and caught Dale in the gut. He doubled over and fell. The other two deputies took cover at the edge of the porch and began firing back. I had dropped down to the floor and was lying beside Dale.

He was cringing and moaning, the bullets flying over our heads, deafening shots exploding in the night air. I took him by the arm and pulled him away, dragging him across the porch and down the steps, keeping both of us as low to the ground as possible. I propped him up so he was tucked in under the overhang.

Both of his hands were holding his stomach and covered in blood and he was grunting in pain. The other deputies were hollering and yelling, firing off shots random and erratic. It was total and utter chaos and it reminded me of a day on a beach a half a world away.

When the shooting stopped I glanced up to see the two deputies off to the sides, struggling to reload their handguns as quick as they could. They wouldn't be quick enough.

The front door flew open and the doorway was filled with the silhouette of a giant. I couldn't make out his features but I could see the mammoth girth of his frame and two thick arms held out in front of him. There were pistols in each hand.

Without thinking, I reached over and pulled the service revolver from Dale's holster. I didn't hesitate and I didn't take time to aim. I simply pointed it at the large frame blocking the light in the doorway and fired off three rounds.

The big man stumbled backward two steps but caught his momentum and stepped forward one. His arms dropped to his sides and he stood wobbly, unsteady on his feet, before falling forward, all of him toppling over like a tree in a forest. He hit with a thud that echoed across the old wooden porch and lay motionless.

It was over.

Chapter Forty-One

About two weeks later, just before Christmas, I was sitting in Mack's Dive, listening to the musical stylings of Blind Eye Regis. Tabby was off work and sitting beside me, paying me a lot of attention.

Since the whole Mona thing was wrapped up she'd thanked me about a thousand times. It got to where it was difficult for me to pay for a drink at Mack's, between Tabby, Russell and all of Mona's friends. Tabby and I were back like we had always been and neither of us ever mentioned what could have been between us or what almost happened.

The crowd at Mack's made a big deal about the job I'd done and treated me like I was some kind of hero. The whole thing didn't sit too well with me.

The man who had taken Mona out to that secluded stretch of beach and snuffed out her life didn't recover from three gunshots to the chest. It was fitting justice for what he'd done.

It would be years before I could get that image of a raped and mutilated Mona Cooper out of my head, or at least push it back to where it didn't haunt me on a daily basis. I still can't help wondering why Jarvis felt it necessary to rape her before he killed her. Maybe it was the way Baker wanted it done, another diversion to point the crime away from himself. Maybe it was part of the process for Jarvis, working himself into a frenzy until he was capable of committing the horrendous act against an innocent young girl. I don't suppose we'll ever get the answer to that one.

Mathew Baker was never arrested. The feds might have a law against what they called "conspiracy," but they'd never heard of such in South Carolina, especially where a white man just might be involved in the death of a colored girl. Maybe it wouldn't have mattered. Without the testimony of Jarvis Brown, the evidence I had gathered against him was circumstantial at best.

It mattered to Rita and her family, however. She filed for divorce, and Baker was let go from his position with the District Attorney's office. He would never realize his dream of becoming DA. I hear she took the kids and moved to Charlotte, North Carolina, where she met a nice guy and started a new life.

Baker ended up staying in Myrtle Beach. Stripped of his prestigious position, he hung a shingle out in the downtown district and began a modest firm specializing in legal defense. These days he represents every two bit dirt bag and low rent hustler who can come up with the few bucks he charges for a retainer. It seems somehow fitting.

I see him around town, every so often, but we make it a point never to acknowledge each other.

I got a nice thank you note from Clarence Cooper after I'd forwarded the things I'd had of Mona's to him, the letter and pictures and such. It was sweet of him to take the time.

Raddison Hayes and I got to where we could almost stand to be in the same room together. We even conducted a little business deal between ourselves. It seems I was in the possession of a large quantity of moonshine and I wasn't sure what to do with it. I ended up selling it Raddison at a discounted price and he brokered it from there.

You didn't think I would really burn up that much booze did you? In my defense, it was actually my back-up plan. If things hadn't gone well on the pier, I'd stashed the majority of the liquor to use as a last ditch bargaining chip.

The whole Vincent incident was covered up pretty good. As far as anybody knew some local bootlegger got himself killed trying to outrun the law. Nobody seemed too concerned one way or the other.

The two guys I had wounded decided not to press charges. I never heard another word about it. The sheriff thought it would be a good idea if I didn't press the issue on my end either. I agreed.

Deputy Dale and I got to be pretty decent friends. The gunshot wound kept him down for a while but he recovered just fine. He offers to take me fishing with him every time I see him but I've yet to take him up on the offer. I'm not really the fishing type.

Things with the sheriff are still as dicey as ever but he puts up with me and doesn't give me too hard a time. He still runs the town with an iron fist but it could be worse. I understand his brother is out of the moonshine racket for good.

Ellen Highsmith took the girls back to Greenville with her and set up house, taking in Claire and giving her a new life. It was meant to be a temporary thing but, from what I understand, they're getting along splendidly. I get letters from Ellen and Claire on a regular basis. Patty even drops me a line every once in a while but I'm guessing it's at her mother's insistence. When I get one from Claire, she never fails to ask how Tabby is doing or to tell me to say hi for her. Maybe she's starting to get it.

I think about the girls from time to time, wondering how they're getting along, if they're staying out of trouble. I'd be lying if I said I didn't feel a certain amount of pride and satisfaction when they come to mind, like I realize what part I played in getting them to where they are now. Sometimes I think about that drive I took with Patty in the back of the sheriff's car and about what I said to her that day, wondering if she's figured it out yet.

When I do it makes me think about the things I've done and the things I've been through. Part of me wonders if that stuff I told Patty Highsmith doesn't apply to me as well, if maybe I was never the non-entity I thought I was. If maybe there's more to me than what happened on a beach half a world away and a lifetime ago.

A guy can hope. In the meantime, I keep doing things the best I can, making my share of mistakes along the way, prodding and pushing ahead. Those ghosts still haunt me but time has a way of making them a little easier to live with. I try my best to keep them pushed aside, concentrating on the things I do rather than the things I did. Eventually, maybe the things I'm doing now will become who I am.

My volatile relationship with the Atlantic has cooled some over time. I find that if I don't bother her she leaves me alone for the most part. I figure we'll never be friends but we're learning to live with each other.

Blind Eye Regis was playing one of his slower tunes, a catchy little pounding number that made you want to tap your toes. I had just shot back a swig of shine and was taking it all in when a guy approached from the side. It was Tyler Wilkins. He had been out of jail since Mona's funeral and he had a big smile on his face. Part of me thought he was coming over to thank me, as I was getting used to the attention I was getting from just about everyone in Mack's.

I was wrong. He leaned right past me and got up close to Tabby's ear. "Do you want to dance?" he asked her.

Tabby gave me a weird look, like she was worried I might get upset. I smiled at her as best as I could.

The young couple got up and went over to the makeshift dance floor at the foot of the stage. They wrapped their arms around each other and began to sway gently to the beat of the music. They were a good looking couple. While they danced, I caught her shooting me a look from time to time.

Myrtle Beach is growing on me and I'm feeling more at ease in my adopted home as time goes on. There's something about her that's starting to feel like home and, on good days, I almost feel like I belong. That said; the thing I hate most about her is the way she keeps breaking my heart.

The End

Made in the USA
Columbia, SC
02 July 2019